NYC 1970

Pairing Off

Novels by Julian Moynahan

PAIRING OFF

SISTERS AND BROTHERS

Pairing Off

Julian Moynahan

NEW YORK 1969 | WILLIAM MORROW & COMPANY, INC.

For Catherine, Brigid and Molly

• •

I ◯

It had been agreed between Miss Roberta Colley, Chief of Cat. & Class., and Dr Georghi Petkov, Director of Rare Books and Honorary Curator of the Chester A. Arthur Collection, that Mr Myles McCormick, although officially transferred as of February 1 to an Assistantship in Rare Books, should continue to spend a portion of time each day downstairs at his old job of cataloguing books in odd alphabets.

The date is a Friday in late January 1959, and the IBM wall clock behind Miss Colley's desk shows 3 : 58 : 34. Her desk is placed just halfway along the long narrow Book Processing Room, where she commands views of the Classifiers on her left, the Cataloguers on her right and, through an arcade directly opposite her, of the high school girls who come in the afternoon, some of them wearing tight pants and pony tails, to file Library of Congress printed cards into the new hardwood cases which have been set up in an area only recently harbouring a stack of outsized atlases. Miss Colley, who has been reading a memorandum from the Director's Room, drops it into an overflowing waste basket and says in her flat voice, 'Well, Mr McCormick, so we lose you. About four-fifths of you anyway. I guess we should exchange nice words for the occasion.'

McCormick pulled forward the hard straight interviewee's chair next to her desk. 'Four-fifths parting is such four-fifths sweet four-fifths sorrow,' he volunteered.

'How about an unqualified "To part is to die a little"?'

'Good. If youth could only, if only age knew how. Chief, have you considered how false most traditional sayings and proverbs are? There is *some* use in locking the barn door after the horse has bolted. It may prevent thieves from sneaking off with the horseless carriage. A stitch in time saves an indeterminate number, not nine necessarily. The earth shall disinherit the meek.'

'That last one is blasphemous. . . . Now that we've had our nice words, I'll see you Monday. What hours can you spend down here anyway? What does Dr Petkov say?'

'He doesn't give a Bulgarian hoot. How about 4 to 5:30?'

She looked doubtful. 'You're forgetting that psychiatrist you go to two afternoons a week. Now that you're out of the department I wouldn't want you making up any more time on Saturday mornings. I'd never know how your work for me was going.'

McCormick smiled luxuriantly. 'My dear Chief, not any more. Many exciting changes are coming into my life. Young Dr Beispiel is giving me my last session this very day. Either he thinks he's cured me or he's cutting his losses.'

She inspected her department, first the left side, then the right. 'You might ask him for me to hold your hours open. I've got a dozen people in here for him to work on. Just the same, I'm glad you're over whatever was ailing you. Not that I'll ever understand why a person with your education and travel experience should have nervous troubles. Actually, I've always thought they were only experimenting on you at that hospital. I understand the Hospital for Psychopathology is very interested in experimenting.'

The implied compliment in the trend of her remarks

2

was gratifying. Yet it was chastening to recall what he had thought of her during his first weeks in the Free Library nearly two years before. Roberta Colley, A.B. Emmanuel College, A.M. in Lib. Sci. Simmons, was five foot ten or so with thick strongly muscled legs, flat wide hips, an undeclared bottom, and a Brunhilde bosom which she kept severely restrained beneath the close buttonings of her dark, heroine-of-soviet-labour suits. Her face was broad and pallid. Her bleak hazel eyes evoked burned out coal fires and the craters of volcanoes that had seen their last bright days about 1,000,000 B.C. When he had first been learning his trade out of the A.L.A. *Rules for Cataloguers*, she had spent a lot of time leaning over his desk patiently indicating his errors, and her body odour, stealing through the scent of musty serge, had seemed offensively non-carnal, even for an iron-haired spinster of forty-five. In those days he had disliked her and had taken vicious satisfaction in imagining she made homosexual advances to Betty Costello, the graceful redhead from the typists' pool who sometimes stayed late to receive Miss Colley's forceful dictation.

He had even dreamed of her once in those early days: of finding himself cradled in Miss Colley's powerful arms. She rocked him strongly to and fro as she whistled the *Marseillaise* at the base of a disused guillotine the blades of which were rusted together. She was wearing faded blue culottes, was naked to the waist, and her dream name was Mistress Pretty Kitty Kelly. Before he could struggle awake Uncs. had jazzed up the manifest content by forcing him to trace the contours of her alpine breasts and to palpate her nipples, which were inverted. In session, after associating briskly to 'mounds bars' and 'sans-culottes', he had gone on to suggest a subtle relationship between his anti-social tendencies, an old interest in the history of non-totalitarian socialism from Fourier to the Fabians, a weaning trauma, a castration fantasy, and certain infantile ideas about the feminine pudenda. After

3

the obligatory period of knuckle cracking and lip biting on Beispiel's part, the psychiatrist had seen fit to greet the construction derisively and had warned him to stop reading *American Imago* and the *Psychoanalytic Quarterly*, 'at least until the current fashion for over-literary and wholly superficial interpretations has run its course'.

Miss Colley wanted to know whether they had any business to talk over before he went off : 'Do I need to order any new Vari-type founts?'

'I still haven't worn any out. I'm trying to save you money to make up for my slow rate. I do the Bulgarian books with the Russian fount and I put all the Yugoslavian books into Roman because the Croats at least never did knuckle under to the Cyrillac alphabet. The Celtic and Greek stuff is ninety per cent available on LC cards, and most of the Hebrew books have been coming through with a second title-page in English or German tipped in.'

She interrupted rather abstractedly. 'How many languages do you know anyway?'

'I don't really know any languages any more. Only alphabets and how to use dictionaries and basic grammars. . . . Now the Armenian and Amharic books are very few, and furthermore I just haven't got time to figure out those alphabets. You probably wouldn't want me to spend a month reading up on two new elementary grammars for the sake of a dozen dog-eared volumes of unknown value. Let's suppose one of the Amharic books is a lost masterpiece of Coptic literature. Suppose, on the other hand, it turned out to be a translation of *Black Beauty* for the Addis Abbaban juvenile market? With my time here cut down so drastically I think I should get on with the cataloguing I'm doing now.'

'Yes. You should be getting on with whatever you're doing. We can always present those odd books to the Boston Public. What are you working on?'

4

'Pardon me for yawning,' McCormick said. 'Gorokhov, Ivan T. ed. Bracket. *Collection of Russian Music Including Liturgical and Secular.* Close Bracket. Petrograd, 1887—. Ivan T. was very big on something called neumic canons and Kievan chants, and among the secular name composers he had a soft spot for Grechaninov. He seems to have been the unselective sort of compiler. Thirty-five main cards so far and it may run to a hundred by the time I transcribe the last "Kafizma—Blazhen Muzh".'

She was not paying close attention. Twisting the nylon watch band on her large wrist, she asked, 'Are you in a hurry? There's something of a personal nature I'd like your advice on.'

He was startled. Although always frank to an extent which many people in the department found brutal—for instance she had once told him he was not entitled to take off the two days of paid up sick leave per month because he didn't menstruate—she had never been in the habit of honouring him with confidences. He said, 'I'm not due at the clinic until five. What's up?'

'Keep your voice down,' she warned. 'Tell me what you think of Alice Dwyer and Mr Coakley.' They both looked, covertly, towards one end of the room, where Alice Dwyer, the Deputy Chief, and Jerry Coakley, the new Classifier, sat at facing desks. Miss Dwyer was wearing her big crystal beads, a ruffled white blouse, best tan gabardine suit and too much eye makeup and rouge. Her hand trembled as she turned pages of a printed catalogue and her face and neck became deeply flushed whenever she glanced across the little space separating her from Mr Coakley's bald and shapely lowered head.

McCormick groaned softly. 'You should hear the ribaldry from those wicked old women on my side of the room. Miss Tallby's the worst—"And how are our own Eloise and Abelard today?" It looks bad, doesn't it? I understood last night was going to be the big night. It looks like he didn't show.'

5

'He showed up all right. Alice sent her mother to the movies and set the table for two and then he arrived with *his* mother. Just as she got the dishes done his mother complained of severe heartburn and he had to take her home.'

He grimaced from shock. 'My God! But he's not that sort of jerk at all. I suppose he isn't as much of an *ex*-monk as we thought he was, so he had to stop poor Alice right in her tracks. Look at his bald spot, it's a natural tonsure. One of these days he's going straight back to the Passionists. What a waste!'

'We obviously disagree about the value of monasticism, but I want your views on Alice. What do you think's the matter with her?'

'How disingenuous can you get, Miss Colley? She wants Jerry Coakley. She is burning up with passion for him. So what if she is forty-two or forty-three years old. He's handsome, he's not queer or married, and he obviously isn't a boozer, and he's been living under her eye eight hours a day, five days a week, for the past two months. Why, every time he looks up with those melting golden eyes she has to bite her heart back down her throat. She's going to make herself really sick and go off in a galloping consumption if something isn't done. Look at her suit. It's merely hanging off her!'

'Shh. Keep your voice down. She hasn't lost all that much weight. I was with her last month when she bought a new foundation garment that has very unusual properties. If you ask me, I think it's the Change.'

'The Change?!' McCormick waxed indignant. 'Miss Colley, how can you talk like an ignorant washerwoman? A person of your intelligence. Shame! Of course it's not the Change. It's love. What kind of woman are you anyway?'

She grinned widely, showing her big dingy teeth. 'You should know the kind of woman I am by now, Myles. I'm a librarian and apart from that I'm an aunt. If it's love, it's out of my line. You're the psychologist. Give me some advice.'

He took another sidelong look at the situation. Miss Dwyer had closed the volume and was looking down at her clenched hands. Under the scalloping of her new French wave her neck showed fiery red. 'I'm not the psychologist, I'm the patient, remember?' He clawed savagely at his left forearm where a ravening itch had suddenly embedded its fangs. 'I think she's gathering her forces for some sort of outburst. If it happens here in the Room she'll feel terribly ashamed. Send her home, or at least call her outside and talk to her. And I wouldn't delay very long either.'

'No, *you* ought to talk to her,' Miss Colley amended. 'She likes you, and she thinks you have an unusual knowledge of people. You can talk to her like—an uncle.'

'Me!' he exclaimed. 'I don't understand people at all. Ask Beispiel. Besides she's your friend. You go on pilgrimages together to the Saint Anne de Beaupré shrine.'

'That doesn't qualify me as an expert on her love life. Do me this favour, Myles. It would shame her to tell me anything more than she told me this morning. She needs a man's shoulder to lean on, and if it can't be Mr Coakley's it might as well be yours.'

'I'm flattered, Miss Colley. Any filthy, silted-up, by-passed old port in a storm, hey? Maybe I'll ask you for a peculiar favour sometime. So how do we work this?'

There was a glint of friendliness in Miss Colley's bleak eyes. 'Call me Roberta, Myles. Some of us will miss you around here. Do watch out for that man Petkov upstairs. I don't think he's vicious, but I know he hasn't got any sense. Anyway, if the worst happens you can always transfer back to working full-time for me . . . Now, go back to your desk for about five minutes. I'll get Alice to look up some slips for me in the LC catalogue. She'll be in the RST tier. That's secluded enough. Stand up and I'll

7

give you a congratulatory handshake just in case she's seen us staring at her.'

A few minutes later, while threading his way among the catalogue tiers, McCormick found himself feeling rather intimidated by the Chief's request. The problem was to think of something to say that at best wouldn't make Alice feel humiliated and at worst wouldn't send her off into fits. It was largely a matter of tone. Avoid at all costs the purring, canaries-in-sour-cream tone of the fat cat, Bay State Road sort of wigpicker: *The Art of Loving and Losing*, a course in six lectures by Myles McCormick, M.D., D.Phil. (Oxon.), D.D. (Cantab.), A.P.A. On loan from the Boston Psychoanalytic Institute to the Temple Obai Shalom Adult School. Enrolment restricted to the twice divorced of all three sexes. Ladies under forty may substitute a fifty minute *viva voce* on the couch for the written exam. . . . It was not at all a matter of tone but of other things. Life and death for example. If only she wouldn't have hysterics.

He found Miss Dwyer crying quietly into an open catalogue drawer which rested on a sliding shelf she had pulled out from the middle of a tier. 'Good old LC cards, what would we do without them?' he hazarded.

She blew her nose on a crumpled tissue before greeting him with a smile of ghastly brightness. 'O hello there, Myles. I hear you've gotten the transfer to Rare Books. I've been meaning to congratulate you. It should be a great opportunity to take over Doctor Petkov's job when he retires next fall.'

The smudging of her eye shadow made her more interesting looking. With less of an overbite, firmer facial contours, and a fighting chance at Mr Coakley, she would have been almost pretty considering her years. He muttered, 'I'm sorry for your trouble, Alice.'

She answered on a high interrogative note which climbed higher as she went along. 'What trouble? What is your meaning, Mr McCormick? What kind of non-
8

sense has Roberta been handing you about me? There's nothing between me and Mr Coakley. Nothing at all! Nothing!'

'Hush Alice.'

She whimpered and tried to put her face into the drawer. Then she turned and leaned against his shoulder stiffly. Her beads pulled where they had snarled on the top of the ball-point pen in his breast pocket. It was extraordinary how thin her shoulders were for a woman who had spread so spectacularly around the seat, until love, unhappiness, or a new kind of girdle had gathered her in a little there. Of course it all belonged to a type: the slender, slightly hunched shoulders, the exquisitely kept hands and hair, the fundament flowing and fusing into the oaken desk chair as the years and books-for-processing droned by. Only Alice, poised slenderly and fastidiously above the grossness of her own lower self, had been fated to look up from her catalogues and classifications and meet the strangely luminous eyes of a Coakley.

'How low can you sink?' she muttered from somewhere under his chin. Her hand came up to free the beads and she began to pull herself back.

'What do you mean low?' he countered, holding her. 'You fell in love. That is marvellous. You might have missed it. Don't you know how jealous of you all those old bags in the department are?'

She ducked under his arms and stood away, looking at him with new composure. 'Really, Mr McCormick, we don't know each other well enough to be found embracing among the LC cards. You, and Roberta, and the rest of the department are making a great mistake in thinking I'm in love with Jeremiah. I gave up on the single men in this town a long time ago. Spoiled priests and drunken bums and perverts for the most part. All the really nice men in my age group came back from the War married.'

Her formula was about ninety per cent valid. But

9

there wasn't any point in taking it personally. He wasn't quite in her age group. 'But Miss Dwyer . . . what were we to think, after all . . .' he gestured vaguely, 'when we saw you obviously so upset—'

'I'm very fond of that man,' she said calmly. 'He's had to leave a place where he was happy, all things considered, and come back here to look after his mother. But he's a fish out of water in the secular life. I was only trying to make him feel more at home—until he's able to go back.'

Her explanation had the ring of half-truth. 'I thought something happened last night.' This said casually, yet with an undercurrent of relentlessness. The proper Beispiel note.

'Of course you've heard about last night. Naturally. I suppose there'll be a full account in the *Boston Evening Traveller*.'

'The Chief only wanted to help.'

'I know. The library's an awfully friendly place, quite a love nest, don't you think, Mr McCormick?' She had plunged her hand into an alligator purse which lay open on the sliding shelf. Manipulating lipstick, compact, and paper tissues, she restored her face with a steady hand. Miss Colley's rescue ship seemed to be foundering in subarctic waters. First Mate McCormick cudgelled his brain vainly for a useable exit line while the salt spray froze on his eyebrows and ear tips. Miss Dwyer closed her purse, smiled briefly, as if running a test pattern on the new complexion, and lightly placed a fine white hand on his jacket sleeve. 'I'm obliged to you and to Roberta for caring, so I'll let you in on the true facts of this pitiful case. Years ago, I fell for a man and became engaged to him. He was of Italian descent and his business position required him to go live in Mexico City. These two things made my mother sick to death, but just as soon as she persuaded me to break the engagement she got well and has stayed well ever since. After poor Jerry and his mother left last night I started thinking about this man, and I also thought about my own life, past, present and future, with loathing. But now I seem to have come to the end of it.' She added archly, 'Isn't it interesting that the present Governor of this Commonwealth is of Italian descent?'

'Fascinating,' he said dryly. 'Mothers—who needs them?'

'Oh no, Myles, the mothers aren't to blame. After all, she thought I had a certain position to maintain. As a Dwyer. One of the Dover Street Dwyers, the under-the-Elevated Dwyers. Ha! ha!' Without being exactly hysterical the laugh was a brutal explosion.

McCormick brooded, then brightened. 'Look Alice, you're not so old. Why don't you look this man up?'

'I did. A few summer vacations ago I looked him up in Mexico City. It was very nice—I mean he was very polite about it. We had tea in his beautiful apartment on Calle Liverpool. He, his German wife and I, while the youngest of his five sons ran in and out prattling in Spanish. Imagine that. A German wife with a good figure after five kids and she even knew how to make a good cup of tea.'

She was smiling blandly and had picked up her bag, no doubt to demonstrate that the conversation had reached its terminal phase. *The terminal phase.* No he would not think about that just now. If time were infinitely divisible, which it wasn't, and if the right sort of quarter hour could outlast sextillions of boring years, which it couldn't . . . Then? He was not grateful for the confidence Miss Colley had reposed in him. Surely there would be fewer, preferably there would be none, of these human complications in Rare Books.

'Well anyway, the best of luck, Alice.'

'Thanks, Myles. I like your not suggesting we have a drink together sometime. You know, so I could talk some more. Because I'm not going to talk any more. The hell with it.' With which, and after conferring a wink from an eye still swollen from grief over lost opportunities, she slipped around the side of the tier and back into Book Processing.

The hell with it indeed. There would just be time to look in on Angelina before setting out for the Pilchard Clinic of the Boston Hospital for Psychopathology. Would she be there? He walked quickly behind the card catalogue and into an alcove surrounded on three sides by empty steel stacks, on the fourth by the rear of the new catalogue. She was there all right and alone, bending over her shoe boxes of unalphabetized cards under the egg-crate neon lights. Angelina Stratis. *Mens sana in corpore bellissimo*. Girls' Latin School Salutatorian and vice-president of the Athenian Club, 1958. A small brunette with cleanly separated breasts under her tight red jersey, with race-horse legs and big sooty eyes. I.Q. 145, age 17. There were thirty-one doric pleats in her swinging white skirt. He had counted them a few weeks before when she stood up in the same outfit reciting Pushkin's 'To A. P. Kern' kak mimolëtnoye viden'ye!—with closed eyes, while her work gang of high school girls giggled and gaggled in a circle around her. Now she was continuing her Russian language studies in a Lowell Institute evening class and would soon outstrip her old teacher, Gaspodin McCormick. *Of course* she should be in college, but the helot father, John Stratis, had offered her upon graduation merely the bitter choice between work at the family spa in Coolidge Corner and the sort of crummy clerical job the Free Library had found for her. It was sad. She would marry a coffee salesman and grow fat. On the other hand, she might be no happier with a Radcliffe Ph.D.

'Hello, Angel Ivanovna. Are you happy?'

She looked up squinting. 'Hi, Mealss Ossipovich. This work sometimes makes my head numb. I'm glad it's Friday.'

'Where are your gaggle?'

'Miss Colley caught them jiving to a portable radio when I was out so she sent them home early for punishment. Some punishment!'

'What do you do with your weekends, Angelina?'

'Oh, if I can keep out of the family store, various things,' she said evasively.

'For instance.'

'Well, for instance, one of the stack boys is after me to go dancing.'

'Which one?' What did he care which one? They were a scruffy bunch, except for the occasional mute inglorious Milton who could be found sneaking reads in out-of-the-way corners of sub-basement D. Milton would not have gotten around to learning how to dance though.

'The one with the duck cut and the little moustache.'

'Oh that's very bad. Leave the kid alone or you'll ruin him.'

'I'll ruin *him*, Mr McCormick! I like that.'

'You wouldn't want to. Listen. You go out with him once, twice, and then steady, and he calls you his little hoodess. You put your hair in a pony tail and wear toreador pants and lots of eye glop. Then you get bored. You tire of his jargon of rumbles and hotrods. Soon you meet a Harvard freshman who takes you to a harpsichord recital after a dinner at Locke-Ober's. So you drop the hot-rodder and start going in for straight hair, black tights, baggy tweed skirts and no makeup. But the first boy keeps trying to get hold of you again. He sulks in the stacks and makes scenes in the Reading Room. He broods and suffers until one night he gets drunk on Pickwick Ale and sets his gang on a bunch of Harvard boys coming back on the subway from a jazz session at Storyville. He is arrested and put in custody of the juvenile court. We fire him. The judge says, "Reform school or the Marines, take your choice, sonny". He volunteers for a six-year hitch. You see, I'm just trying to save him from having to go in the Marines.'

'How you do go on, Mr M.,' she said, opening her eyes very wide and looking him up and down. 'I like the part about his calling me his little hoodess though. That and the toreador pants. After all, as you like to say, "All creatures are experiments—G. B. Shaw".'

'All *living* creatures are experiments.'

'Well, what other kind is there?' She got up, stretched, and walked around the alcove before sitting down again at her work table. Her face went moody. A heaviness came into her features that made her look twice seventeen. 'My father only wants me to go with Greek boys anyway,' she said.

'You should keep at your father to send you to college, Angelina,' he said seriously. 'Even if he can't afford it, which I imagine he can, you could get a scholarship.'

She leaned her chin on the heel of her hand. 'My father won't stop me from getting to college. Maybe I'll go next year. But that isn't it. I'm very ambitious. I want to be something and go somewhere. Sixteen was too young to start college after Latin School. This is my year for figuring things out and getting ready to go somewhere. It's amazing how much thinking I get done while I'm alphabetizing.'

An impulse to play a part in the fulfilment of Angelina's ambitious dreams, whatever their content, awakened in him. He said, 'Let's run away together. I'll show you the world and devote myself to your future. You can discard me when you hit the big time, but I'll always be there, hiding among the adoring crowds, gloating while they cheer you.'

She frowned and shook her head. 'Don't talk to me like that, Mr McCormick. I'm too old to play Lolita. And don't make fun of me. Maybe I could make fun of you too—necking with that old cow, Miss Dwyer, behind the catalogue.'

'I wasn't necking with her,' he said indignantly. 'At Miss Colley's suggestion I was trying to calm her down

14

because she's gotten herself upset over something you're too young to know about. You shouldn't talk that way yourself, Angelina.'

Stretching her arms towards the low ceiling she laughed, yawned, and said, 'Tit for tat. Why don't you run away all by yourself, Mealss Ossipovich? You don't have a father to keep you down, and you've already been to college, so you're free to go anywhere.'

'I've been there—on a bicycle mostly. It always turned out to be cold and crowded or cold and empty. Or too hot. And so the library. Infinite reaches in a little room.'

'You mean infinite file cards in a shoe box,' Angelina said, laying her Antigone head beside her work and closing her eyes. Had she been his child. And had they been travelling together across the Atlantic on an opulent liner, the suave, rich and powerful father, and the beautiful talented daughter. To London, where she would enroll in some Royal Academy or other. He would? Have raised himself quietly from his deck chair. And before tiptoeing away to work on uranium stock option deals in their splendid cabin suite. He would? Have drawn up around her shoulders the thick fringe of the monogrammed steamer rug. And? Have kissed her forehead between the jetty black brows. How? Tenderly.

Descending in the cage-like staff elevator to the side exit on Grant Street, he studied the fly-specked placard above the control panel. THERE IS ROOM AT THE TOP. Quite a joke on the two hunch-backed octogenarian elevator boys who divided the work when they weren't having simultaneous strokes. He hoped they appreciated it. Or was it their hope of heaven? Rare Books, on the fifth floor, was the top stop. And the room there was for Myles McCormick, Harvard A.B. in Classics, '48. *Cum grano sali*. A TCD man too by God. Many alphalangs and langabets. Hasn't he done something with Amharic, Alf? Ah bet mah brown betty he haf. Goodbye and bon voyage, Dr Petkov. Have you thought of settling in St Petersburg? One hears that it is pleasant and cheap. Something in a trailer might suit you. Wednesday night there is shuffleboard. Beano on the weekends. Never fear. I shall carry forward your splendid work to its termination. Stop! Brute. Wallowing swine. Sorry for your trouble, Millicent. Sorry.

An enemy, Edgar Rooney, was standing near the swinging doors to the street. Mad eyes, the livid, crazy quilt complexion of a confirmed wino, a brandished Public Catalogue rod key glinting dull bronze. Snarling.

'You in an open department, McCormick! They must be crazy. A communist, an atheist, and a whore master! *Domine! Quare via impiorum prosperatur?*'

'Out of my way, card puller, before I push that key down your throat.'

Rooney jumped aside, dancing his rage. 'Off early again to the balmy house, hey haahvid man? I'm onta you and I'm gonna get your job! Tell that to your masters in the Cambridge Kremlin.'

O Red Massas, Sheriff Rooney he makum posse fo' to ketchum dis po' Apache chile. 'Rooney, the sneak Feeneyite! Blessed Edgar Rooney, the fighting monk of Thunderbird Abbey!' he said ringingly over his shoulder, biting off each syllable as he went out.

But McCormick was not to have the last word. Bursting between the still-moving doors and into the street came a strident bellow:

'*Extra Ecclesiam nullus salvus*, shit-ass!'

2 ◡

'Hello—Pilchard Clinic. May we help you?'

. . .

'Yes. This is the out-patient part of the Hospital for Psychopathology.'

. . .

'No. Not for psychopaths, for psychopathology.'

. . .

'Certainly there is a difference. What is your business please?'

. . .

'Both insulin *and* electricity. Other things as well, I imagine. But what did you want?'

. . .

'What?! Now just hold on. Who is this speaking?'

. . .

'Yes I got that. Sure it's O.K. to be from Methuen. Our patients come from all over the state and even from abroad. Were you referred by your doctor in Methuen?'

. . .

'For pity's sake—No! You can't just walk in and have electric shock treatment and walk out again. I mean it's not like having a corn or a wart removed.'

. . .

'It's none of your business whether I've had one!'

. . .

'No. Our staff physicians have to prescribe the treatments. Afterwards it would take several days to get over the effects.'

. . .

'The effects of the shock—what else?'

. . .

'Well really! I don't care how many shock treatments your family doctor in Methuen used to give you during your lunch hour. And I don't believe it either.'

. . .

'You have to be interviewed and tested and diagnosed. You would need to be admitted as a bed patient before—'

. . .

'I understand that.'

. . .

'I understand that your bus is leaving Park Square at 6.30. There's nothing I can do about it.'

. . .

'No. I'm sorry.'

. . .

'Goodbye then.'

As McCormick put a half-dollar on the counter the henna-haired middle-aged receptionist yanked the connection out of the switchboard and muttered 'Some people.'

'You seem upset, Miss Barber,' he said smiling sympathetically. 'I suppose you must get a bit fed up with us zanies.'

She prodded a receipt across the counter. 'Brother, you don't know the half of it.' Wasn't she giving herself airs for a former live-in patient rumoured to have first arrived there foaming at the mouth? Still, hers must be a maddening job.

Early. The waiting room was very crowded. He crossed glances with half a dozen of the regulars. Who in Greater Boston was not in Treatment? Honkus Welch the barfly mayor of Inman Square, Cambridge, Joseph Specs O'

Keefe and Cardinal Cushing. *Das kleine Wien* Anna Freud had said on her recent visit. It was not that Bostonians were crazier; merely that they defined sanity more rigorously than, say, in L.A., and they thought about their minds more than anybody. Something to do with the Puritans. And of course the Concord crowd. In this bumpy century the oversoul had shaken loose and fallen down into the id. Raised all kinds of hell down there. From Bronson Alcott to the Bebrings, from Fruitlands to McLean. C'est toute la meme chose. He had been bug-eyed nervous coming to his first appointment and had crept down the drab street between the staring, Johns-Manvilled two and three deckers as if heading towards a tryst with a faggot under a bridge.

The only vacant seats were at a low, circular kiddies' table in the middle of the waiting-room. He went to it and sat down with his kneecaps up around his ears and began flicking through a tattered scrapbook on Canada. As was evident from these cutouts, Canada was a conspiracy of boredom, from the little lost churches of the Gaspé to the grimacing totem poles of Puget Sound. And what about Lake Louise? Blowsy old Lake Louise, the stale bait of ten thousand C.P.R. publicity campaigns. The only lake worth thinking of was blue-est Baikal, doubtless brimming over with Khirgiz undines. A sheet of the scrapbook, come loose, fluttered to the floor. It was not a sheet of the scrapbook. Someone had hidden the front page of a recent *Midtown Journal* among the Calgary Rodeo pictures. Evil fellow. Peter Quint! You shall not corrupt these innocent if autistic children.

There were two feature stories meandering down the page between assorted bum & bust photos: BALL BOUND GIRL GRABS DICK and HUBBY RAPED WHILE WIFE TEAS. The first was straightforward *double entendre*, about a girl on her way to a dance who stumbled on ice and clutched at a passing plainclothesman. The second, owing to the unusual sequence of verb tenses, the oddity of

19

'teas' used as a verb in the present tense, indicative mood, and the consequent grammatical ambiguity of 'raped', was more artful. Hubby Charles Houlihan had screwed a marginally unwilling Polish waitress in the bathroom of Houlihan's cold water flat in Roxbury while wife Irma drank (drinks) tea in the kitchen. Entry effected approximately 5 a.m. Judge Adlow, gulping amphi-jel pills the while, remands to a higher court.

It was just after five. The *angst* level in the waiting-room began to climb sharply. Some powerful senders today. Not me not me. On a bench near the corridor leading to the consultation room sat a fat woman holding across her thick thighs a thin, depressed child. The boy lay face down, his arms wrapped awkwardly around his head to shut out the light and sound. The mother, if it was the mother, looked bewildered and worried. He wanted to go over and shout, 'Get up, little boy, and go play. It's easy. Don't let things get you down.' Yet it wasn't easy when one came to consider particular cases, although why not was always an intricate puzzle. For instance, take his own case, which would cease to be a case within the hour. Had it ever been? No—if to be a case required that you were depressed, or hallucinated, or enraged, or too horny, or not horny enough. He had never been over-whelmed by compulsions to conceal scandal sheets in children's reading matter, take things from stores without paying, turn doorknobs with a trouser pocket pulled inside out and used as a glove because of all the syphilis germs going about. He had never heard a voice commanding him to pray—eat—fart incessantly. And so forth.

How about a brief wallow in reminiscence? Certainly.

. . . Certainly the oedipal business had been splendidly eased by the old man's disappearance. He had had all the speaking parts at the Russell Grammar School Commencement except the Mayor's, plus gluey kisses from hyper-nubile Helen Kearns after the gymnasium dance; and if the year at Trade studying electricity was a waste of time, the following three at High & Latin doing the pre-college course with sneak Greek on the side from saintly Martinsgale, Ph.D., were not. Then Harvard on the Doyle Scholarship: 'Full tuition plus twenty-five dollars a semester for ex-newsboys, orphaned or with but one surviving parent, residing in a rental-unit of a multiple dwelling situated no more than two thousands yards from the roadbed of the Boston and Maine Railroad, who meet the admission requirements with distinction. Preference will be given to candidates offering Greek or Hebrew.' The category was so exquisitely restricted that his had been the first award in nearly two decades, and the admissions office had had to jettison the requirement of distinction altogether. Thank you F. X. Doyle. The poignant intellectual idealism of that 19th century Hiberno-American autodidact! Brakeman Doyle, surrounded by patristic texts and handbooks of popular science, penning his unregarded refutations of Darwin and Tyndall under a jiggling caboose lantern as the flatcars slid beyond Augusta into the northern jungle, came alive in the mind's eye. What had later persuaded him to abandon polemics and make a fortune in Maine lumber and power? A woman in the case? By Gar, dat Evangelina Dubois she mak' mon bateau ivre! La reine du bois de charpente raising her buckskin skirted nutbrown knees on a bed of heaped spruce boughs while the sickle moon came up over Katahdin.

Doors were opening along the corridor. The four o'clock patients began to drift out, a few knuckling at their eyes, and the weary young training psychiatrists in their rumpled white clinicians' coats came out after them to beckon the next wave of psychos. Today's consultation room was the tiny sit-up one at the very end of the corridor, furnished with a carved desk of the Clyde Fitch era, two upholstered iron-legged chairs in early Reilly-Wolfe modern, and a distinctly irrelevant birdcage holding an ancient stuffed goldfinch wired to its perch. The window overlooked the live-in patients' softball diamond where the annual game between schizophrenics and paranoids always ended with the latter mobbing the umpire (a sufferer from chronic aboulia) while the schizophrenics lay down and curled up at their fielding positions like hedgehogs.

Dr Beispiel settled himself, dodging his head into the bad light behind the desk lamp. Challenge. 'How's it been going?' he said neutrally. Formula.

'I was just remembering how sore you got when I had that fantasy about the patients' softball game,' McCormick said. Challenge.

'I didn't get sore. If you recall, the problem was you just weren't paying attention to your actual feelings. I like your jokes but as defence they make for difficulties.' Aspersion of negative counter-transference refuted, a warmly positive counter-transference cunningly suggested. Beispiel had already passed Go and collected two hundred dollars. 'How's it going?' he said neutrally. Formula reinstated.

'The past is over, all I care about is the future,' McCormick lied. 'As Ford said, "Case histories are bunk".'

'The past *is* the future,' Beispiel said evenly.

Sidney was sharp today. Maybe he was feeling good thinking about his new research job in Topeka. Just wait until that blow-torch prairie sun had fingered his bald spot, or a winter breeze out of the Dakotas blew him off his feet and rolled him across two thousand acres of frozen stubble. 'Don't I get a certificate or something today, Doctor?' McCormick asked disingenuously.

'What do you mean don't you get a certificate or something today?' Beispiel droned disingenuously.

'You know. For remission of symptoms. For passing the course. No more conversion hysteria psychosomatic kidney pains; markedly increased ability to relate success-

22

fully at work and at play; significant reduction of anti-social manifestations like sneering, knocking and white-sheeting. Or do they give *you* the certificate? For making a bum out of a—shit!—I mean for making a steady-eddy out of a bum,' he finished despairingly. A double Freudian. Sidney's showy Morris Lapidus apartment hotels, unmortgaged and with No Vacancy signs in every one of them, controlled the board from Park Place to Boardwalk.

Dr Beispiel came on point. He leaned forward, simultaneously lowering his full face until the tilted Soapy Williams bow tie almost disappeared under his chin. 'Jargon and whimsy!' he said with feigned disgust. 'What's the matter with you, Myles? You haven't talked shit like this in months. What's eating you?'

Blocking. The old snow on the diamond was dirty, and the sycamores beyond the Fenway runway bore no leaves, as was to be expected. Then when say was Ash Wednesday and Saint Blaze's day anyway and whoever starched Beispiel's white shirts could not prevent them riding staunchly up his paunch. The goldfinch was not going anywhere in particular so that whoever had wired him down and padlocked the heavy cage was unusually cautious. On the other hand, he may have thought he was dealing with a bullfinch, when any fool could plainly see *es war eine Kuhfinch.*

'Come on now,' Beispiel wheedled. Cupping his third ear with his ninth hand. A martian. I'm onto you, space pirate, I'll get your job!

'I don't like this room at all. In fact I can't stand it. What maniac stuck the cage in here? Is that somebody's idea of human relief?' McCormick raged.

'We haven't needed a couch since before Thanksgiving.'

'What do you mean *"We"*?'

'Come on Myles, what can't you stand and what's this relief you're talking about? Something's happened and you'd better tell me. No more putting things off till next time.'

'I will not have my words taken out of context and thrown back at me!' he howled, pounding the edge of the desk with clenched fist. He was immediately sorry. It was intolerable that Dr Beispiel, a highly trained and brutally hard working man, should have to put up with this non-sense, and with the patients getting out of it for fifty cents a session. Grief filled him. He wished he was asleep. Lowering his head and resting his forehead on his fist he said, 'I'm very sorry, Doctor. I'm afraid it's Millicent Rogers.'

'What's happened?' His voice was full of foreknow-ledge of disaster.

'Her cancer came back.'

'That's too bad,' the psychiatrist said. With all the sympathy a reasonable man can muster for the trouble of someone he has never met, and now would never meet. 'In the lymph nodes of the chest cavity I suppose. It could be worse. They may be able to get at it again with the Cobalt machine.'

'Not just there—everywhere. Old Doc Warren at N.E.G. took out her ovaries yesterday—as a therapeutic measure—and it's in that area too.'

'I'm sorry to hear that. Of course they've got a great team of radiologists at New England General. And cancer's a funny sort of disease. Each case establishes its own pattern and you can never tell when you're going to get a break.'

'Sure. I know that line. They wouldn't waste all those million volt charges if there wasn't a chance. So they stick her down in the cellar and blast her with those fucking rays from behind lead shields, only they make a small error and burn her like they did once before. That way she gets to die with the pain and nastiness of a sloughing ulcer added to the cancer pain.'

Dr Beispiel got up from his chair and went to fiddle

24

with the cage, as if in a thousand sittings he had never really seen it. Still standing, he turned and looked down at McCormick, who sprawled back in his seat with his fingers locked behind his head. 'Professionally speaking, I'm sorry this has to come up just as we're launching you on your own. But not very sorry. Personally I'm much sorrier for her than I am for you.'

McCormick stiffened. He said primly, 'Sorry sorry. The hell you ever cared about Milly. You always made it clear with the arching of an eyebrow or a well-timed grunt— that you thought she was an odd-ball. A crazy nurse who used to go out with coloured market research executives. Just another one of patient McCormick's symptoms of near-psychopathy.'

The psychiatrist flushed and, bending down with his hands on the back of his hips, said, with a quiet emphasis which was quite menacing, 'You're wrong. So wrong! When you first came in here we had absolutely no reason to assume that therapy would do you any good at all— that you wouldn't treat it as just another episode in McCormick's sentimental education. At the case reviews in the monthly staff meetings, when decisions were taken about continuation of treatment, you used to squeak by on a split vote.'

'You don't have to tell me how *you* voted.'

'Let me continue. Then you met Millicent and lo and behold you held firm on *something*. You began to pay attention in here and then the library job steadied down. Maybe I did think the girl was an odd-ball. But just where the hell do you think you'd be now if you hadn't run into her?'

He said sullenly, 'Who knows where I'd be? Maybe back in Europe living it up. Maybe rich and famous and beloved— You certainly can't deny you disapproved of my marrying her.'

'I disapproved of what? You didn't want to marry her and she didn't want to marry you. A society of two for

25

mutual aid, sex and laughs, that's what you called it. Maybe you were pulling my leg. How should I know? Maybe there isn't any Millicent Rogers. All I can know is what you tell me in here.'

'She exists all right—for another six weeks at the outside.'

Dr Beispiel went back behind his desk and sat down. 'So get busy and see that she goes easy. There'll be expenses. If you want me to co-sign a small bank loan I'll do it. But quit grousing. All along you've known this could happen. You must have thought about what it would be like.'

McCormick sat up, kneading his fingers nervously. 'Of course I've thought about it. But she was all right for three years, Doctor. And she says she was never careless about the scheduled check-ups. Money isn't a problem. She trained at N.E.G. and they take care of their own. Warren got her into an endowed ward and for a few dollars extra I traded it for a private room. She never makes demands but she wanted the private room when she realized how things stood.'

Beispiel sighed heavily. 'Can you blame her?'

McCormick bit dry skin off his lower lip and twisted in his chair. 'Look, Doctor, you won't get sore but I read a paper.'

'You read a paper. I asked you not to read any more clinical papers and you read one and it's not my function to get sore,' Dr Beispiel affirmed with a note of cosmic weariness.

'This man at Beth Israel examined a lot of statistics on cancer way back into the nineteenth century. He points out that it was usually regarded as a kind of psychosomatic disease in the Oliver Wendell Holmes era. Especially female cancer. Women would get the disease because of a sudden emotional shock, like seeing their own kid killed by a runaway horse. Or they got it because they were stuck in an intolerable situation—maybe they were

26

married to a wife beater—or because they had a deep secret sorrow they couldn't shake or tell anyone about, and they kept fretting about it.'

'I know the paper,' Dr Beispiel said sourly. 'Suggestive but sketchy. Read any other good papers lately? Isn't that the *Midtown Journal* sticking out of your pocket?'

'Dr Beispiel! You aren't paying attention. Please. I haven't been good for Milly—not really. She wanted something from me I didn't, or couldn't give her, and I think she fretted about it.'

'Do me a favour and shut up a minute,' Beispiel barked. 'So Mr McCormick gave his girl friend a deep secret sorrow and it brought her cancer back. Christ! I've got a sorrow only it's not so secret. A patient who after nearly two years in treatment is unable to recognize a simple, lousy, upstaging fantasy of omnipotence when he indulges in one. If this gets around I'll have my reputation to fret about.'

McCormick started, then gasped. 'Fantasy of omnipotence? No.' A sickening, abashed sense of relief welled up in him, then funnelled itself into his throat. 'Fantasy of omnipotence,' he gargled. 'Say I was lousy for her, only I don't think I've been lousy for her. Say she knew I was lousy for her, or thought I was when I wasn't. Even so, I couldn't have brought her cancer back. What a disgusting person I am,' he finished, deeply ashamed.

Dr Beispiel did not deny he was a disgusting person. 'Who has a claim on secret sorrow in this situation?' he asked. 'The radiologist, of course. He has to inflict further discomfort and sometimes pain and new sickness on a patient who's just been carved up by some witty sympathetic surgeon. He can't even assure the patient that the radiation treatments will work because if just a few cancerous cells survive the rays, there may be a recurrence. The body contains billions of cells. Those few cells can hide and hold out for years. That is the secret sorrow of all good radiologists and of every cancer sufferer. And it does not fall under your control!'

'Call me anything, Doctor,' said McCormick with conviction. 'Christ what a relief. She may even recover.'

Dr Beispiel put one foot up on the desk and sat back with his thumbs hooked into the slits of his trouser pockets. McCormick inspected him, sensing a difference. 'The treatment's over, isn't it? I could just get up now and walk out. Except maybe you want to give me the old Now Voyager routine.'

The psychiatrist grinned wickedly. 'You'll have to inflict that routine on yourself. Sure the treatment's over. You always could get up and walk out. Now I can too. We're just having a conversation.'

He wished that Beispiel would ask him what it felt like to be through with the treatment so he could try to decide what it felt like. 'How does it feel to be through treating a patient?' he asked cunningly.

'I never discuss my feelings with former patients.'

'But you might answer some kinds of direct question from a former patient? Especially since you were never any good at answering questions during the treatment?'

'I might,' Beispiel said. 'Maybe I'd answer just one question.'

'You might even interpret a dream?'

'Sure. Why not?'

The opportunity was unparalleled. Sidney had always refused to interpret any of his dreams, saying that because it was his dream and not Freud's, Fromm's or Beispiel's it must be interpreted by McCormick or else left uninterpreted altogether. If now he could be brought to explain, for one first and last time, a McCormick dream, the psychiatrist would be forced to show a hand and a set of cards which he had always held close to his chest for the whole previous twenty months of twice-weekly sessions at Pilchard. A dream came instantly to mind. It was a

28

nasty, brutish and short one, but he had dreamed it and it would have to do.

Scene. A rustic tavern with a muddy dooryard and thick ivy growing up around the open entry. The interior badly lighted and featureless except for a crowding of dark sneering faces. *Action.* McCormick Dreamer is being ejected from the tavern against his will, and that is why he screams a thin wordless scream. Two short powerful dwarves, one on either side of the Dreamer, are squeezing his arms down against his sides and shouldering him out into the yard, where he pitches headfirst into the mud. He wants to get up and re-enter the tavern but the doorway is now filled solidly with the sneering dark men— Dorset rustics borrowed from a Hardy novel? fisher-folk from Dingle? Kulaks from the Mtsensk district?—who gaze sardonically over the tops of their tankards. *Feeling.* Not angry but extraordinarily energetic, as if the Dreamer could, if he wished, bound over the tavern roof and swarm in a rear window; not distressed but nonplussed, because he wishes to be inside and it is all a mistake. End of dream.

Beispiel listened with apparent attentiveness, then laughed immoderately. McCormick was shocked. This was the first dream the psychiatrist had ever laughed at out loud.

'What's so funny?' he asked peevishly. 'And what's it mean?'

Beispiel wiped his eyes. 'Why can't a dream be funny? As for the meaning, it's perfectly obvious. The man getting thrown out of the tavern is the penis, and the two men shouldering him are the testicles. You can certainly work out the rest of it for yourself. But why bother? You have more important things to do now.'

Beispiel went off in sibylline chuckles again and after a bit McCormick, banishing an impulse to beat him, joined him. Like a certain character in a fable he had asked for a wish to be granted and been handed a standard

29

issue black pudding for his pains. Here was a truth not at all too deep for tears, except that his crying days were supposed to be over. If he hurried he could make New England General in time to get a report from the surgical resident, Dr Walski, before he went off duty for the day.

3 ∾

From the direction of the cellar the good fairy landlord, Prentiss Beal, lean to the point of emaciation, limber beyond the respectable, in filthy white ducks, slashed sneakers and grey cotton shirt, with white locks flying erupted, as the librarian, whey-faced through weariness, holding the day's mail—a bulky dispatch from his mother—entered the dim hallway from the draughty vestibule. Two reached the foot of the steep stairway at once. P. B., braking, McCormick, sagging, manoeuvred to avoid collision. Groaningbeal clutched the struts of his ribs. Quizzically, McCormick stared.

He said like a sigh, 'You have to stop taking stairs three at a time, Prentiss. Except maybe going down. Try to remember that your Davis Cup days are over.'

'You're right, Myles. If people only knew the condition of my poor heart. But I want to hear about Millicent and I've got a complaint.'

'What sort of complaint? Tell me on the way up. I'm beat.' As he put foot to the first tread, the landlord darted past and reached the second landing in four enormous strides. With elbows on the landing rail and long bony face glistening dully, he downgazed at the plodding librarian.

'It's that man, Frank Meat. He was around here again this evening looking for you. This time in a kilt! And there were three huge young black men with him—also in kilts. Now Myles, you know I can't have *that* element on the premises—and I'm not talking about colour either. And you shouldn't be associating with that type. Not with Milly in the hospital.'

McCormick came to the second landing and paused. It was all a mistake. 'It's not what you think, P. B. They weren't in drag. Probably not a queer in the bunch. Once a month Meat conducts the local chapter meeting of the veterans of his old Canadian Army regiment. The Canadian Inverness Highlanders or something like that. He was an officer and those Negroes used to be his enlisted men. The kilts are the regimental dress uniform.'

Beal fingered a withered stretch of skin below a jutting cheekbone and grimaced. 'How odd. Were you in the regiment too? To my knowledge, you've never descended in a kilt as long as you've been living here.'

'No. I was a medic in the A.U.S.'

'Do you like him?'

'So-so. He's a bit of an idiot.'

'Why do you let him come around here then?'

What was the point of telling Prentiss it was none of his business? It was as much his as anybody's. 'Mainly I guess because he amused Milly.' McCormick sighed. 'Frank's been trying to persuade me to let him enter my name for election to a local Irish snob society—HOBOH —the Honourable Order of Boston Hibernians.'

'But he isn't Irish, is he? He sounds demented. Also British from his accent—fake British that is.'

'Actually, he's from East Boston. I suppose he is demented. He seemed that way when I knew him at Trinity. Now he's turned up here in Boston and wants to put me up for HOBOH. Furthermore, he's become an agitator for the New Conservatism. You know, that *National Patriotic Examiner* cu-kah. He sells them articles. It doesn't make much sense, does it?'

Prentiss clicked his dentures and giggled. 'Everything

makes sense, after a fashion, but there's no money in it unless one gets in ahead of the fashion,' he said, and fled upwards, an ancient kitten, to the next landing. 'You understand, Myles, why I was suspicious,' he called down plaintively. 'Ever since that little bitch of an iceman's boy landed me in Deer Island for a year and a day—after rewarding my devotion by punching my eyes out and fingering me to the Vice Squad—I've had to be careful. This building is under police surveillance. I'm sure of it. If men wearing dresses start prancing in and out, they'll be down on me in a minute. Tell them to wear their trews next time.'

Poor disinherited Prentiss and his little bitch of an ice-boy, McCormick reflected, resuming his ascent. How the officers in Joy Street Precinct House would have capered, enjoying joyfully, had they known that a burnt out old faggot on Phillips, whose indiscretion with a six foot, 190-pound, twenty-four-year-old male prostitute and police informer back in 1939 had scarcely made one edition of the most salacious evening newspaper in town, imagined they still had their eye on him.

'Of course I understand. But what I don't get is why you're so straitlaced about keeping your homo and hetero acquaintances segregated.' He was on the landing by now and went to his own door. 'Why shouldn't I have homosexual callers as well as a homosexual landlord?' He stood leering, key in hand, as Prentiss retreated towards the stair head. 'Haven't you heard of bi-sexuality? Don't you know Freud says it takes four persons—a boy-boy, a girl-girl, a boy-girl and a girl-boy to bake a wedding cake?'

Prentiss worked his eyes, flared his nostrils and said disgustedly, 'I think bi-sexuality is disgusting. People ought to stick to their own line. Of course you're kidding. You just aren't the queer type.'

'Nonsense!' he snapped. 'I'm tired of the heterosexual struggle. Get me a boy, Prentiss. At once!'

The landlord backed slowly down the stairs. 'You can

33

joke about it,' he said sombrely. 'But lucky for you you don't care for them. They're such a rotten bunch—silly and vain and foul-mouthed. Little crooks who'd rob you blind as quick as look at you. And not a nice looking one in a car load. All acne and black-heads.'

'I bet you didn't talk that way twenty years ago. And we've all heard elderly girl-chasers talk that way about women too. What's the difference?'

'Plenty of difference. We're discussing queer boys, not folks in general. Now you'd certainly have to hunt a long time to find a queer boy who was as nice as Millicent. I won't insist there aren't *any* but—' Prentiss suddenly boxed himself on the ear with open palm. 'Why haven't you said anything about Millicent?'

McCormick said carefully, 'Everything's about the way they expected. I was told the doctors won't have much to report until the laboratory tests have been evaluated. We'll know more tomorrow or Sunday.' The truth could wait.

The landlord made as profound an oriental bow as his position halfway down a flight of stairs permitted. 'Poor child, poor child,' he keened against a tread, then straightened up. 'I can nurse her when she's convalescing, while you're at the library. This place runs itself, and I *do* mean into the ground.'

'Maybe it won't be necessary. But thanks.'

'I don't even want to know what you mean by that last remark,' Prentiss said loudly, and retreated into dimness below.

He was used to finding the sparsely furnished L-shaped flat empty and therefore full of subliminal whispers and stirrings, because so often she would be gone out of town in the crumpled grey Rambler on one of her agency cases. So perhaps the menace was there in the Piranesi engraving of Il Vaticano hanging against the rough white wall opposite the whitewashed bricks of the Beacon Hill kitsch fireplace. Yes it was. Bernini's colonnade, in so theatrical

34

a perspective, resembled a great claw reaching forward and downward to entrap and dismember—what? A scattering of pilgrims and mendicants, a line of moving coaches, two gushing fountains and an obelisk. The problem of living, McCormick enjoined himself, was to see and use life—a gift terrible, unmerited, unlooked for, dear—without hiding behind tropes and symbologies. The sessions with Zum-Zum Beispiel ought to have yielded that much truth at least. For instance, there was her closet. Behind the closed door, on a shelf above the hanger rod suspending her three dresses and six uniforms, lay neatly folded a green dressing gown which she would probably be wanting soon. It was a species of fetishism to feel that sadness clung about the garments of an absent person, or lay coiled in the toe of a walking shoe—as though one were the sort who would ever put Baby's first booties into a bronze dip!—or was exhaled in the faint scent of perfume on a sofa pillow . . . Fatigue and morbidity obviously shared some circuits in the central nervous system. Time enough to look into Milly's closet after a night's sleep, when the sight of a lot of feminine gear would be less apt to send sentimental shudders through him.

An elevated train moving out of Charles Street Station shrieked and whined on the curve before plunging underground through the very guts of a tall brick tenement on lower Grove Street. It was a good sound, he told himself bleakly, because it kept the neighbourhood rents down.

Seven weeks at the outside, Doctor Walski had estimated, his hands sorting and resorting a sheaf of reports from Pathology. Unless a miracle. No, it was not better to take these things lying down. Miracles didn't happen in bed. Not under God's eye, to put it bluntly, but under the cobalt beam. 'She's a pretty strong girl and she knows the score and she'll want to try,' he had maintained. And of course her knowing what was going on made it simpler for everyone. As for accidental burning, he would stake his reputation, as a matter of fact he would stake the jobs of the machine technicians, on it's not happening this time.

No doubt she did know what was going on, but she had been in no position to show it this evening, lying on her back under a single sheet with the head of the bed cranked up a few inches. Unknown hands had brushed her brown hair glossy and lipsticked her mouth. The intravenous feeding apparatus had been taken away and her cronies on the nursing staff had filled the room with half a dozen rococo floral offerings probably heisted from the bedsides of senile Commonwealth Avenue dowagers or machine-gunned South End mobsters. She slept heavily, a trace of blue visible between the dark lids of her eyes, her bare arms lying out upon the sheet palms upward, as if her physical self were confessing in the absence of its keeper, 'I am nonplussed.' For a while he merely held her arm above the elbow and listened to her deep slow breathing. When her eyes began to move without opening, he said quietly, 'Milly dear, old Myles here. Are you awake?' She woke up then, or half-waked, and turned her head. He had smiled stupidly while she creased her brow, perhaps in an effort to remember who he was. Then her left hand came up, reached across the bed, and in one sweeping movement plucked aside the sheet, exposing her bandages and the pink stain from an antiseptic solution with which they had painted her from her breast to her knees.

'First class. I couldn't have done a better job myself,' he had said shakily, readjusting the sheet and squeezing her right hand in his hand. Her eyes had held his while she moved her mouth and cleared her throat, trying to speak. 'Ruin . . . ruined me, Myles?' she asked hoarsely, bringing her free hand slowly down upon her wounded torso.

But he did not love her, and she didn't love him. They

36

suited each other in other ways entirely, and had agreed from the beginning that the whole thing was temporary. But not this way! He shuddered and went quickly to the plywood-door-table standing on black-painted saw horses between the casement windows overlooking Phillips Street, dropped his mother's letter on the table, and lighted the clamp-on Dazor lamp. From a half-gallon jug of California Zinfandel sitting on a shelf of the cupboard-kitchen he poured himself a tumbler of wine and brought it back to the table.

Mamashka's letter, indited on a dozen pages of onion skin in huge Palmer Penmanship cursive, came to the point at once:

Dear Myles,
    You say you want to know more about your father's side of the family. Why now and not ten or twenty years ago? I hope you're not getting morbid. You must know I don't believe in looking backwards and that's why I never sat around talking about Joseph after he cleared out.
    However, I might as well answer you because tonight's square dance in the Rec. Hall was called off, owing to the sudden death of our regular Caller. I thought of going up to the Boulevard to practise my shuffleboard strokes under the flood lights but my arms are sore from waxing the linoleum this afternoon.
    (I know you sneer at us 'senior citizens' in St Pete's going in for dancing and shuffleboarding, but you'd feel and look much better yourself if you took some regular exercise.)
    You get your muscles—UNUSED, FLABBY!—and the early grey in your hair from your father's side. Your looks, such as they are, come from my father. He was a handsome man, and came from Glencar by Caragh Lake in Kerry. By the time he died he'd built up a very tidy business, rendering carcasses for fat in

37

our yard in Somerville. The smell was vile but there was money in it!

Your father's father, the first Myles McCormick, was born in West Cork. Maybe you remember him. When you were about four, he came to live with us for a short time before he died. He used to sit up in the attic drinking immoderately, playing the harmonica, and writing a long poem about Nantasket Beach, which was pretty foolish because he'd been a teamster for Adam's Express and had very little education.

Now I will tell you something even odder which I learned from him. *His father,* Bartholomew McCormick, was also born in West Cork, and yet *he had been to America and gone back* before any of his children were born. It seems that about 1850 Bartholomew landed in Boston off one of the famine ships. He must have been green as grass, maybe twenty years old, and he drifted up to the Newburyport area and became a grave digger. I suppose he'd had a lot of practice, poor kid, burying people during the potato blight. But he didn't have any push, so after digging graves in Newburyport for about ten years he returned to Ireland, married, had children, and died. So it took *two* generations of McCormicks to get some sort of grip on the U.S.

Is this what you want to know about? It isn't interesting. Life's much more vivid nowadays. I'm not inclined to tell you about your father and me—if that's what you want. I met Joe in 1915—he was in United Fruit and talked as though he was going to take over the company and Central America as well in a few years. I had many 'gentlemen callers' including two who were famous Harvard football players—one a drop kicker I recall—and I was making a good wage for those days in the Somerville schools. So I certainly didn't throw myself at your father when he started to come around.

The weather here this morning was 67°, wind SSE 8 mph, partly overcast. You didn't mention the Boston weather in your last brief letter. I am interested in weather. Maggy Dunne, who used to teach with me in the Cambridge WPA nursery was here for two weeks over the Holidays. Her arthritis was so bad I had to cancel driving down to Cape Canaveral to watch the static firing of the new Aegena rockets. That man Von Braun has a nice smile, don't you think? But of course you don't watch Television.

Happy New Year and to Millicent Rogers too. I'm of two minds about that nice girl sharing an apartment with you, Mortal Sin apart. Of course you like living with a woman out of wedlock because you and your Harvard friends think it's the proper Bohemian thing to do. You should be married.

On the other hand, a smart, hard-working professional woman like Millicent should take a good long look before marrying anyone as vague as my son. I'm saying nothing about the future, or even the past year or so, just going on past performance as we like to say at the shuffleboard tournaments.

My arm is broken.

> Your loving Mother JWM
> (Mrs Julia Ward McCormick
> 11477 Gulf Park, Lot #119
> St. Petersburg 12, Florida)

Vaguemyles slid from his chair to the floor, where he attempted push-ups, subsiding after the sixth straightarm lift. She would be upset when she heard of Milly's misfortune. They had met twice and, for obscure reasons, had got along rather well. The horse knacker's daughter reported a tradition *chez* McCormick barren indeed. But the whole story was scarcely in hand yet. Now that she had begun to sing he would keep her at it until the missing central portrait in the family gallery had been relimned. So the daffy old gent in the attic, with his black bottle and glittering harmonica, was neither spook nor hallucination. Now he remembered him, perhaps only fantasied that he remembered him, hobbling between the window and the door and chanting. Was it something like 'From Allerton to Pemberton//From Kenburma to Black Rock'? Clearly there would be unexpected dividends along the long way back to 1915 and beyond. And what sheer unadulterated cow flap!, he told himself savagely, to pretend that the disaster of Dublin University, the futility of the lycée posts in Autun and Toulouse, the pseudo-exile in the London bed-sitters ('From Camden Town to Baron's Court//From World's End to West Ken') had anything to do with the fact that blood of a failed Irish grave digger ran in his veins. Besides, the whole point of trying to garner the historic Joseph from Julia Ward Mack's energetic silence was so that the poor man might, once and for all, be dismissed into history. Rest! much-too-quiet spirit.

McCormick shuffled wearily into the bedroom and undressed by the light issuing from the living-room. He did not want to sleep in full dark this night. Twelve tintinnabulated in the steeple of the Asher Benjamin church on Charles Street. He took a pillow from the unmade double bed, pushed open the window, placed the pillow on the sill and knelt down for a comfortable spy into a street containing nothing but parked cars and the filthy remnants of last week's heavy snows.

In this room they had woken on Sunday mornings, mildly hung over, and had made love to the piercing sweet melodies of the Bowdoin Square Salvation Army Silver Cornet Band performing for Jesus in the street below. No more of that, brother, no more.

At this window they had watched one night, part of an audience of three or four dozen Phillips Street rubberneckers gazing from windows up and down the block, as the tiny local druggist, who lived at number 12½, stood off with a revolver two brutishly intoxicated naval ensigns who kept circling like timber wolves. After the paddy wagon arrived from Joy Street and took away all three, and the windows were slammed down, and the street went back to sleep, Milly had tossed two light bulbs down onto the brick sidewalk, and they had lain in bed listening and laughing while the windows from Grove to West Cedar were opened again and people shouted back and forth about what the hell was going on anyway. No more of that then.

Sub-arctic air struck against his face and neck. He closed his eyes, trying to remember why, only a week before, he had been convinced that the golden age was dawning for Myles McCormick, A.B., flautist, former Harvard commuter, army medic, G.I. Bill foreign exchange scholar, traveller and lycée usher in post-war France, French teacher in London, traveller in the college textbook line from Duluth to Carlsbad, now librarian and Rare Books Assistant—he with the psyche freshly sandblasted, postulant, if he chose, to HOBOH, kind father, in the conceivable future, to rosy-faced and elfin-limbed children, the doting husband of a clever, passionate, beautiful woman as yet unmet but not undreamed of, who would take him, not for what he was, but for what he had in him to become, after he and the estimable, antimatrimonial Miss Oddball Rogers, R.N., had amicably parted.

And that, thank you, was all balls McCarty not-so-haleand-hearty. Milly and Myles Mumblecrust, barkeep and barmaid in the Last Chance Saloon, was much more like it. Only she had slumped suddenly behind the stained and bullet-marked bar counter, and he could do nothing for her now but carry her on the last ride to Boot Hill. It was in the blood all right. Famine-stricken Bartblood.

In bed he said aloud through clenched teeth, 'You are morbid. Turn your thoughts, Dick Whittington.' He turned his thoughts. To Penelope Dicey, the thin-legged, gap-toothed shop girl from Looe who had occupied the room opposite his in the rooming house behind Gamages in Holborn during the darkest months of the winter of 1951-52. She had been engaged to a hometown yob who threw her over after putting the blocks to her a few times, and she had come to London to forget him. This Cornish Sade would write Penelope a long letter every few weeks describing in graceless detail what he and his new girl friend did in bed together. She would sit in her room reading the letters and brooding. Sometimes, when things got too much for her, she would creep across the landing wearing a shaggy woollen sweater which nearly reached to her knees. He would wake up and find her lying in the circle of his arm, the peroxide wash she used giving her hair the smell of clean fleece.

Penelope would say sadly, 'And then he did such and such, and that dirty bitch did such and such, and do you suppose we could try that, Myles?'

He would answer sleepily, 'I don't see why not, Penelope.'

And after a while she would say, 'Then she and that bloody oick did —— and —— and —— ——. Do you suppose we should try that, Myles?'

And he would say judiciously, 'I think that's a bit much, don't you, Penelope? I don't care to try that at all.'

She would whisper, 'You're so right, Myles. It's a bit much. I wish they'd put the filthy bastard back in Borstal. And now do you suppose we could have another go at the other thing, Myles?'

4 ⌒

'My actual given name is Panayot,' said Dr Petkov. 'I discarded it when I fled Bulgaria in 1925. It is just as well. It would have been unrecognizable *as* a name to anyone in this dull town. You, of course, cannot be expected to understand why a brilliant young art historian at the University of Sofia, who had already published monographs on idealizations of the nude female in classical art, should foresake a great European cultural centre like Sofia, which means wisdom, for this god-forsaken home of the bean and the scrod. And that is because you do not know Balkan History.'

'I know a little,' McCormick said cautiously. 'Let me see. The Macedonian Brotherhood killed Stamboliski around 1923. The campaign of terror was stepped up and they went after King Boris but failed. Then General Kosta Gheorgiev was killed. Somebody exploded a bomb at his funeral in the Cathedral of Sveta Nedelia, killing over one hundred persons. I believe that was in the spring of 1925.'

'But you do know Balkan History!' Dr Petkov exclaimed, straining the lids of his great poached-egg eyes in an attempt to draw them together. 'Why is that? Maybe you are the last V.M.R.O. agent come to gather old Petkov to his tragic ancestors?'

'Not at all,' McCormick murmured deferentially.

'Macedonian terrorism was the stock-in-trade of several English thriller writers of my youth. The Eric Ambler set. What, by the way, are bashi-bazouks?'

'They don't come into the period we are discussing,' the old man said rather peevishly. 'So the English have written stories about the Sveta Nedelia holocaust. Interesting. One of these days you must give me the references.'

They were sitting at ease in Petkov's comfortable glassed-in study at the rear of the public area of the Rare Books Room, both facing a large photograph of the twenty-first President of the United States. Petkov, an ex-fat man in intricately rumpled, oversized tweeds, waved disparagingly at the picture, then wrinkled his long voluptuary's nose as an expression of extreme distaste struggled to rearrange the lines of moody boredom in which his large, pouchy face was habitually set. 'I had devoted myself to the feminine physique in art—from an ideal *standpunkt*, you understand. A few maniacs in stinking sheepskin jackets conceal a bomb under a pew, and by the time the smoke has cleared I am chained to a desk in Boston editing the state papers of Chester A. Arthur. This is not a career, this is nonsense!'

'Just the same, your Boston career has hardly lacked distinction. I gather that *Young Arthur*, the first volume of the biography, is already a standard work in its field.' Nothing ventured nothing gained, you old Vlach bandit, you.

Dr Petkov smiled unpleasantly. 'It has sold less than three hundred copies. Don't flatter me, Mr McCormick. The last man began that way. He ended by bursting in here smelling of whisky and screaming that I was an *Encyclopedia Britannica* scholar, whatever that is supposed to mean. You've started out well. In two weeks not a single question. Keep it up and we'll get along. No one is going to ask you to overwork, and there is always the chance that you may succeed to my chair next winter.

Perhaps your post-graduate studies have been somewhat irregular, but what of that? I despise the gardening variety American pesh-dee.'

A subdued fawning seemed in order. 'I like it up here,' said McCormick suavely.

'Good enough.' Dr Petkov yawned. 'Of course we're not the Boston Public. Their man has devoted his life to the Adams Collection, and I have worn my life away on Chester Arthur—that time server, that apologist for U.S. Grant, that son of an ignorant Irish peasant, if you will excuse me. It is the difference in an egg shell.'

'However, *we* have the journal.'

'So we do. We are certainly the class of this library. In a month or two Miss Kearsarge will ask you to contribute bibliographical notes on one of the manuscript collections. I am told the Assistants feel a certain thrill when they first see their names in the *Bulletin*.' He yawned again. 'I can't remember that anything I have ever done in this institution has given me the slightest tremor of emotion,' he concluded rather grandly and stood up.

What about the famous incident back in the 'thirties? He was supposed to have made sexual advances to a pretty young stack girl in one of the sub-basements and to have faked a heart attack when she ran to Personnel to complain. Had he carried that off without a tremor? Or was it merely a malicious rumour without substance?

While Dr Petkov made a dash through the Room, pausing momentarily to say something to Miss Kearsarge at the front desk, and to glare at a middle-aged lady reading a rare Christian Science tract of the Mary Baker Eddy era at a public table, before disappearing through the swinging doors, McCormick returned to his own desk at a more leisurely pace. Indeed he did, he liked it up here.

Like Cat. & Class., this department was several times as long as it was wide. That was the price the founder had paid in choosing to house a large library in a Renaissance revival palazzo (more Rucellai than Farnese, more Vidoni Caffarelli than Pitti). Nearly everything lay in a gallery—either North, South, East or West. And those unfortunate enough to work in departments on a lower floor, where the granite walls had been dimensioned according to early sixteenth-century specifications, found themselves poking long wooden pointers into five-foot horizontal tunnels whenever they wanted to open or close a window. In Cat. & Class., for example, the windows were as tiny and remote as D-deck portholes on a ship; and it would have surprised, would have disheartened, no one to see that department's fresh-air-fiend, Miss Lester, knocked down by a sudden inrush of sea water just as she was withdrawing her head and her pole from the tunnel next to her desk. The Renaissance revival style was even harder on the stack boys and girls, who spent their working lives circling a quarter-mile square like marathon cyclists in slow motion.

Rare Books lay in the eastern gallery of the fifth floor, where the inner walls broke out into tall, wide and frequent windows overlooking the cloistered central court, with its handsome fountain and, in season, dense lawn and herbaceous-gracious borders. The high ceilings, the quiet, the rich bindings of the first editions and incunabula which lay strewn on the mahogany desks and oaken work tables struck a note of baronial elegance, especially in late afternoon when the rays of the westering winter sun might slip under the Boston overcast and pour mellow light into the room.

Whatever Panayot may have left behind in Bulgaria—Snidemyles suspected it was a tangle-haired gypsy trull in a patched caravan on the outskirts of muddy Slivnitsa —he controlled an urbane petty princedom here. Rare Books had always stood outside the library's administrative divisions and was only accountable to the Director's Room. It possessed its own endowed funds, these being used to subsidize the *Bulletin*, to make acquisitions in

46

excess of the amounts allotted to it from the general fund for book and manuscript purchasing, and to fatten substantially the salaries of the Rare Books Chief and his First Assistant, Miss Dorothy Kearsarge. Up here the Rare Books Assistants did their own cataloguing, thus avoiding the rigours of Roberta Colley's supervision. And up here possession of a degree from a library school was not required, whereas everywhere else in the library it was essential to advancement in rank and salary.

It should have been a paradise of scholarship and gracious living but in fact was not. Petkov, on the whole, had made a mess of it. For years he had neglected even the decent minimum of cataloguing, so that more than half the material acquired since 1940 was inaccessible and unrecorded, much of it actually lost in certain crammed book alcoves at the rear of the room. Under his Editorship the quarterly *Bulletin*, excellent in its typographical design, continued to stupefy the scholarly world by its massive and inconsequential pedantry. And Petkov was also very bad at keeping an adequate staff together. He had never been able to endure another man in the department for more than a year at a time, and Miss Kearsarge, who was chastely but also jealously in love with her Chief, had a way of turning tigerishly upon every young female Assistant who took his fancy.

The pattern was always the same. Dr Petkov would ask that Miss X be detached from her other duties for a few hours a day to aid him with the Arthur papers. Miss Kearsarge never made any objections initially. After all, the monumental biography came first, and Dr Petkov never accomplished anything without an amanuensis, preferably a recent graduate of Radcliffe or Wellesley with a physique not wholly unrelated to classical idealizations of the nude. But then Miss Kearsarge would have a drastic change of heart and proceed to do the girl in, reporting her to Personnel for neglect of her ordinary work and holding her up to savage ridicule within the department.

If the girl ran to Petkov with counter-complaints, he would stare at the Arthur portrait with an air of morose detachment and say, 'It is not my business to settle women's quarrels.' Personnel always offered Miss X reassignment to another department and Miss Kearsarge made sure that she accepted the offer.

Petkov's worst blunder had been his falling out with the BFL's Director, Pillsbury Pinkham, a smooth spoken, Brooks-Brothers-suited reject from the world of Middle Management, with hair of Stetinnius silver and features resembling those of the late Paul V. McNutt. Pinkham concerned himself not at all with the day-to-day working efficiency of the library. He was away a good deal, pursuing ego-imperialistic adventures at the conventions of various regional and national library associations, or else consulting for one hundred dollars *per diem* in hinterland cities like Casper, Joplin and Boulder. When he was in town he spent most of his time on two grand projects; the first, and more recent, was a scheme for remodelling the Director's Room on the fourth floor into an authentic teak and bokhara executive suite of the kind described in the works of his favourite author, Cameron Hawley; the second, and more long-range, was a plan for revising the library's administrative organization according to 'blueprints' drawn from the current practices of the fifteen top United States business corporations. He had persuaded the Trustees to engage a local management consultant firm which kept busy running multi-coloured charts, brochures and technicolor film strips in and out of his offices. At first there had been a problem of vocabulary until Pinkham himself cut the Gordian knot by pointing out that Book Processing was obviously the same thing as Production, the Circulation Division equalled Marketing, and the Reference Service was a form of Advertising and Publicity. A young, self-starting Administrative Assistant for each side of the three-sided administrative pyramid had already been hired, and the complete plan of reorgani-

48

zation was scheduled for presentation to the Trustees at their June meeting.

Pinkham, sometimes designated by library employees as 'Pink', 'Pee-Pee', 'Lydia', or 'The Bitter Pill', looked forward to adoption of the Plan as a major triumph of his executive career, and there was a time when Dr Petkov could have expected a large share of the spoils of victory. For several years after accepting a call to the directorship of the B.F.L. in 1952, Pinkham had been quite impressed by Petkov's scholarly aura and had treated him as a favourite, even to the extent of fixing him up with frequent 'research leave' at full pay to visit the great sister-libraries of Europe. Unfortunately, the doctor had violated the Director's confidence in a particularly vicious way. He had had calling cards printed upon which he represented himself as supreme director of the B.F.L., and had passed them out everywhere in the civilized world outside the United States—from the first-class dining-room of the S.S. *Isle de France* to the sanctum sanctorum of the Vatican Library. Soon enough, one of these cards made its way to Boston and Petkov was exposed.

Pinkham prided himself on his wise tolerance and his worldliness. He could brook much in the way of laxity, laziness and pretentiousness from individual members of his management team. But Petkov had undermined the Chain of Command itself and this could not be tolerated. His manner with the Rare Books Chief, after an initial, bellowing confrontation, became icy and distant. He saw to it that Petkov's request to stay on beyond the regular retirement age of sixty-five was refused. Some said that the Director was also in cahoots with the Head of Maintenance to deny the Rare Books Room certain essential services such as replacement of burned out light bulbs, repair of the ancient, wheezy humidifiers and regular dusting and sweeping of the public areas. Certainly, neither the Rare Books Chief, nor his department were in

49

the Director's good books. But all that could be changed. It was nearly eleven. Unless he changed his habits, Petkov would not return from lunching at the Ritz much before 2 : 30 p.m. McCormick stretched, carefully closed B. Wormald's *Clarendon* on a book mark and contemplated the future. The pedantic and deceitful Bulgar had made a mess of this exquisite little department all right, and that was going to work out for McCormick's best. What fun to take over the glassed-in office and heave the Arthur photograph and the several dozen 'presentation' copies of *Young Arthur* which Petkov kept on a special shelf into the nearest swill bucket. He particularly itched to get his hooks into the magazine. Out would go all the crappy bio-bibliographical notes on abjectly minor eighteenth-century Rhode Island authoresses and in would go —what? A good deal of discussion of democratic socialism certainly and maybe some sparkling reviews of new books, plays and musical performances. When it came to peddling social doctrines a lot of circumspection would be required, not that anyone paid any attention to the contents of the B.F.L. *Bulletin*. But attention *should* be paid by an ever-growing circle of subscribers whom he intended to enlighten by subtle degrees. For instance? For instance, an exhibit of Shaviana in the Treasure Room with accompanying *Bulletin* article on GBS's vindication of Jevons against the Marxian theory of labour value. Maybe Gaitskell could be prevailed upon to contribute a reminiscence of the Coles or of Tawney. Much might be done with a Henry George number, or in an article on Boston medical practice of the nineteenth century containing a concealed plug for a National Health Scheme. He would buy up Orwell manuscripts if there were any on the market and would find the right sort of Englishman—perhaps a younger staff member of the *New Statesman*—to contribute a regular London Letter. In fact, from behind the stalking Loamshire plough horse of an appeal to traditional Boston anglophilia he would sow the seeds of Social-Democracy in the thin and flinty soil of old New England.

As for the present disarray and inefficiency of the Rare Books department, he had never been the sort of person to lose sleep because a bed was tumbled about or had dirty sheets on it. And what in comparison with Roberta Colley's fun farm did it actually amount to? There was no one up here as nutty as Roberta's old Miss Hope, who regularly stationed herself in front of the Chief's desk and made faces at her, and refused to get out catalogue slips on any book she hadn't read and liked from cover to cover; or Mrs Jacobs, who had stopped classifying for a whole month while she designed the headstone for her father's grave; or Mr Mantina, who went around with an enormous piece of unfinished felt on his head complaining of draughts; or Miss Tallby, who insisted on answering the phone in Sacred Heart Convent schoolgirl French and chattered constantly about losing her virginity in a canoe on the Charles at Norumbega during the Spanish-American War—or was it the War of the Spanish Succession?

It was true that in Rare Books Miss Meachum, a tallow-faced Philadelphian with hirsute nostrils, who had taken up library work after having been rusticated from an Anglican secluded Order on a finding of marginal schizophrenia, was a weak link. But she was certainly very good at covering the front desk, where her long blind stares, her disappearing voice, and the extraordinary positions assumed by her preternaturally inflexible limbs struck terror into the Old Howard types turning up from time to time to consult the pornography collection in locked Alcove A. Old Miss Humperdinck, who looked after the Treasure Room at the other end of the East Gallery, was perfectly decent, even though Miss Kearsarge hated her for dozing off at her desk with her foot on the alarm buzzer, which made Miss Kearsarge go racing down the corridor waving the lead-filled wooden truncheon issued to her father during the Boston Police Strike of

1919. The First Assistant was not only brave to the point of fierceness; she was also intelligent, learned and a workhorse who had held the Room together during the greater part of Panayot's negligent administration. She might snarl at the public and act the bitch with the doctor's Girl Guides, but she liked having a youngish man working in the department again and was perfectly ready to say so.

This left Helen White. They had become acquainted during Miss Colley's in-service course in advanced cataloguing and classifying for employees lacking a Library School degree. To fight off suffocating boredom they had all passed notes in Dewey's simplified spelling—OW R U? I M BORD!—while Roberta droned from behind her hand or covered the blackboard (blakbord) with the Library of Congress's cryptic system of letter-number combinations: 'What then, Helen, would you expect to find under HX758.36.T22?' 'I'm not too sure, Miss Colley. It wouldn't be some kind of comic strip, would it?' Helen covered the rare Romance Languages stuff and knew her way around in Provençal, ur-Tuscan, and primitive Spanish. But she carried her learning, like her physical person, pretty gracefully. She had an amazing voice—an unlikely combination of a South Carolina drawl and a fastidious selection of English vowels picked up at Girton College —which touched the ear caressingly. Of course she was married now, to a tall drink of water who taught Metallurgy at M.I.T. and often waited for her on Grant Street in the most non-carnal of the small European cars. So what? Marriage didn't stop her from being easy on the eyes, fun to talk to, and something better than fun to listen to.

As for the Room's daily working routines, there wasn't much actual work to them. Everybody except Petkov and Miss Humperdinck took turns at the front desk, where the idea was to discourage rather than to entice the couple of dozen tourists and perpetual scholars dropping in on

52

an average day. Everyone except Petkov took turns closing up at five o'clock. The *Bulletin* came out in January,
April, August and October. Everybody in Rare Books had
to do something for it, whether writing, copyreading,
footnote checking, or merely going back and forth to the
printer in Dedham. Beyond that, each Assistant had a
major project which was, theoretically, tailored to the
person's area of scholarly competence. Once a year you
had to tell Dr Petkov how your project was going so that
he could put this information into his Annual Report to
the Trustees, but, at least according to Helen, no one
would ever ask you to prove that you had accomplished
anything at all. The Rare Books Assistants traditionally
spent a lot of their time wandering throughout the library
on mysterious scholarly errands, and a full set of keys,
which unlocked just about every door in the building
except the door to Pinkham's wash room, had come to
McCormick with his new job.

The locus of McCormick's major project was the Augean
Stable of Alcove H. Here had lain, since its acquisition in
1920, a collection of about five thousand pamphlets, broad-
sheets and manifestoes from the period of the religious
wars of the English seventeenth century. A Professor Coxe
of Bowdoin College, Maine, had spent a lifetime collecting
this sad stuff and had willed it to the B.F.L. in the mistaken
belief that someone would soon whip it into shape for the
many historians and literature specialists who professed
an interest in the subject. A possibly accurate rumour
abroad in the learned world held that it was the outstanding collection of its kind. A second rumour, to the effect
that the Coxe Collection was resting and could not be
disturbed much before 1975, which had begun to circulate
about the time that Dr Petkov arrived at the B.F.L., had
cooled the ardour of the scholars very substantially.

Although fully expecting to shift to Management before a fraction of the time had elapsed, McCormick
guessed that it would take three years to whip the collec-

tion into shape. The crown of the undertaking would be a printed bibliography issued at the library's expense in a fine edition of three or four hundred copies, but first an enormous amount of Mexican stoop labour had to be performed.

In a word—he had to cleanse the collection from several decades of accumulated dust. He had to stand the stuff up on several rods of empty shelves so that he could begin to look at it. Next the signed material must be segregated from the contributions of ANON, an infamous sneak who had been peculiarly active in seventeenth-century England. After ordering the first group alphabetically by author he must order the second group alphabetically by the first significant word of the title; or, if a title was lacking, by the first significant word of the opening paragraph. Next he had to make an accurate list of every item in the two groups and spend some months dredging in the great bibliographical compilations for the period—the Wing Catalogue, chiefly—in order to find out which items were unique, which rare, and which as common as house flies. The next step was to collate several hundred presumed duplicates to discover whether they were indeed identical—McCormick would have liked to meet that man who, when faced with apparently identical copies of a work of no literary or human value whatsoever, demanded to know whether they were *really* identical down to the last semi-colon, so that he could hit this man in the stomach and rip down the panels of his sleazy double-breasted suit lapels. Next he had to make out catalogue slips on the entire collection, descending to such niceties as 'signatures', 'foxing', 'colophons', 'water marks', and 'chain lines' where unavoidable. Next he had to enter into correspondence with several dozen university pedants on bibliographical fine points. Finally he, or rather the unfortunate person who would take the job over in a few months, if all went well, had to compose the printed bibliography, climb up on the roof, and leap five floors down, head first, into the courtyard fountain.

He was beginning with little knowledge of seventeenth-century English history other than that which he had picked up from listening to measured denunciations of Cromwell, the butcher of Drogheda, in the Dublin pubs during the late 1940s. This ignorance dictated what proved to be a pleasing division of his working hours. Mornings, he sat at his desk, or at the front desk, reading the standard seventeenth-century histories and biographies. Afternoons, when he had grown tired of sitting, and just as Petkov returned in a liverish mood from over-indulging himself at lunch, he sauntered down to Alcove H, donned an old shirt and a pair of chinos he had secreted there and began moving cart loads of the Coxe Collection into a small empty stack located just behind the Rare Books Room proper. Here he had all the empty shelf space he required for sorting, several book carts on which the items could be tumbled about and dusted, a hand vacuum cleaner for the more sordid cases, two plumber's lamps with long cords and outsized bulbs for deciphering the more ill-printed of the Anabaptistical and Levelling effusions, and a small basin in the corner for washing.

At this stage the work was more akin to coal mining or bushwhacking than to ordinary librarianship. Once the heavy door between Rare Books and the empty stack was closed he enjoyed full privacy and could shout, whistle, sing, moan and caper with little risk of being spied upon or overheard. When he became restless, and yet did not want to return to the main room, he went to the far end of the stack and let himself into the South Gallery, locking the door behind him. Here lay a Deep Stack, its length half that of a football field, its shelves lined with nineteenth-century Massachusetts legislative reports and volumes of old municipal statutes which no one ever requested, its air desert dry and impregnated with the acidic dust of decaying books. The light was a mere half-glimmer leaking through from infrequent window slits in the outer wall, and one could stroll there in a profound silence only occasionally broken by the pistol crack of a leather binding rupturing in the parched air. At the far end a spiral steel staircase rose between the concrete floor and the high ceiling, but the openings above and below had been cemented in so that, strictly speaking, the stairs were a transition between nowhere and nothingness.

This Deep Stack in the South Gallery seemed to McCormick to stand beyond life itself and to provide, therefore, an ideal setting in which to brood up a storm on life's well worn enigmas. A Chicago nightclub metaphysician had recently demonstrated that one could, after all, step into the same river twice, so long as it was tidal and one caught it on the slack between rising and ebbing. But there were lots of other paradoxes still to be unravelled. A beginning must be made and if not here, where? He wanted to learn the byways of the Deep Stack so thoroughly that he would be able to run about in it at top speed with his eyes closed. It had an extraordinary set of resonances. Perhaps if he were to bring in his flute and bounce a little Gluck off the walls, certain veils would fall. Meanwhile, it fascinated him that very often when he went into the South Gallery to escape his work for a few minutes he would be assaulted there by devouring pangs of sexual desire. Maybe the place was haunted by the ghost of a by-gone nymphomaniac who sprawled invisibly on the spiral staircase casting her aura about. More likely it was the dryness. As nature abhorred a vacuum, so all those little homunculi swimming about in the vas deferens abhorred the desiccated, King-Tut's-Tomb atmosphere of the Stack and proceeded to register violent protest.

On the other hand, it struck him late on the afternoon of the day of his little conference with Dr Petkov, just as he was running the baby Hoover over a tattered and

56

grimy huddle of Puritan propaganda flyers, this work would be abhorrent without a vacuum cleaner. When the whine of the motor died away, he realized that someone was rattling a key in the door leading back into Rare Books. It opened and Helen White came through, first peering about near-sightedly in the dimness, then coming forward and raising her hand against the glare of the plumber's lights. She hopped up on one of the empty dollies and sat swinging her short legs and watching him work.

'Myles McCormick at the mill without slaves,' she said lazily.

'I guess the Pinkham-Petkov feud is to blame for our not getting any stack boys to handle the filthy work, isn't it?' McCormick said. 'But if you're going to loaf while I sweat, you'll have to entertain me. Say something in one of your lovely languages.'

'O.K. How's this?

> Quant'è bella giovinezza
> Che si fugge tuttavia.
> Chi vuol esser lieto sia;
> Di doman' non c'è certezza.

That's all I remember.'

'Say it again, would you?'

She carolled it again.

He turned around and examined her face and neck with some care. Her skin was very white and of a velvety texture, with a fine nap of blond hairs on it. Perhaps voices, like hair and finger nails, were a specially adapted form of skin. Freckled, sandy-haired people usually had freckled sandy voices, and Helen's voice seemed decidedly blond, velvety and with a fine nap on it. 'I love your voice,' McCormick said.

She leaned back on her little hands and accepted the remark with a smile. 'Don't you want to know what it means?' she asked.

'Not particularly. My days of giovinezza-ing are mostly behind me.'

'It means

How lovely is youth,
But it flies from us.
If you want to be happy, be happy now;
There is no certainty of tomorrow.'

He went to the sink and ran water into the bowl. 'How sad,' he said over his shoulder.

Helen got off the dolly and trailed over to the sink. 'Tell me about your girl friend, Myles,' she said softly. 'How is she?'

Her sympathy suddenly threatened to unhinge him because he was entitled to no sympathy whatsoever. 'Not much to tell,' he said drily. 'She's sinking fast. I believe that's the appropriate cliché. So tell me about how you like being married.'

'Married? There's even less to tell. After six months he still doesn't want me to come in the bathroom when he's washing up—like you're doing now.'

At that he stared at her. A tiny rounded girl in her late twenties, with a bright intelligent face and crisp blond hair, she had the good sense to wear straight skirts that moulded her hips, a plain white blouse open at the collar so that a certain amount of glossy neck was visible, and a scent that said, 'I may not be Mata Hari but I am lovely to come home to.' The man must be mad. Maybe he wanted a woman moulded out of metal?

'I suppose he's shy. It takes a while for these yankee scientists to unbend.'

'Whenever he takes a bath, his mother goes in the bathroom and scrubs his back with a long-handled brush,' she said. Challengingly.

'You're still living with his mother. That's bad.'

'Yes. And she still gives him his bath. That's worse.'

McCormick backed off a little. 'Tell me, Helen, who wrote that Italian bit you recited?'

'Lorenzo the Magnificent wrote it, that's who,' she said grimly.

He came close to her and ran his clean hands down her sides. She stood quite still. 'You could tell me your troubles and I could tell you mine,' he said softly. 'I know a nice place over in the South Gallery behind that big door. That is, if you don't mind a certain amount of darkness. It's pretty late, but we could start tomorrow.'

She slipped her hand in his and drew him towards the door into the Deep Stack. 'I like the dark,' Helen said. 'Even though it is late, we could make some sort of beginning today.'

5 ☙

After four weeks, Dr Walski discontinued the radiation treatment. 'It was worth trying,' he said. 'At least we didn't burn her.'

McCormick wanted to know how Millicent would die. 'It's not morbid curiosity. I want to be heads up when she's going through it,' he explained, and hung his head.

Perhaps Walski was sympathetic but he did arch an eyebrow. 'What about the family angle? You're not actually married to her, are you? Or do you qualify under the common law?'

'Not at all. If you think that matters, you're not the man I took you for.' He added nervously, 'Strike that out. I don't take you for any particular sort of man. Anyway there's only a step-mother. She lives somewhere outside of Boston. Milly has been alienated from her for years and says she doesn't want to see her.'

'All right. You're the concerned person then. We'll let you know in plenty of time. But bear in mind you can't go through it with her. It's never like the ending of *La Bohème*.'

'If you don't mind, just tell me what happens. Roughly.'

Dr Walski frowned professionally. 'Various internal regulating processes of the body begin to fail. We introduce what counter-measures we can; however, certain

60

changes are irreversible. After that, stupor . . . deep coma . . . and so forth. Then respiratory failure.'

'She stops breathing.'

'That's it.'

'Are you the sort of physician who goes to any length to keep a patient alive? I mean when you know she'll die in a few hours or a few days regardless?' he asked flatly.

Dr Walski coloured. 'Am I the sort of Jew who goes around poisoning Christian wells you mean?'

Uncertain of the physician's drift, McCormick said, 'I'm sorry for sounding like such an ass. Maybe it's because I don't have any real rights in this situation. It puts me on edge.'

Walski took off his glasses and cleaned the lenses with a bit of surgical gauze. 'Be on edge,' he said wearily. 'We both can think of much worse places to be.'

During her years with the Back Bay nursing agency most of Millicent's cases had involved, according to the euphemism, 'terminal care'. In line of duty she had witnessed all the modes of holy and unholy dying extant in the Bay State. Now that it was her turn she had evidently concluded she had nothing to add. A side-effect of the radiological treatment was a severe sore throat which lingered after the series had been broken off. But her hoarseness seemed actually an excuse for a taciturnity which grew more marked each day. During the first month she had asked the day nurse to bring her a hand mirror every morning, so that she could put on some makeup and fix her hair. The morning after suspension of the radiation series she said, 'Christ! take it away and get it over with,' and turned her face to the wall. She never again asked for a mirror.

McCormick came to the hospital most evenings after work, ate supper in the big basement cafeteria, and visited Millicent until the night supervisor, a permissive giantess named Lloyd, who had graduated from Nursing School in Milly's class, came in to put the light out. Sometimes he brought her brandy in the little miniature bottles called nips. Usually he sat next to her bed quietly reading or else read aloud to her. He had stored a couple of volumes of the scientific romances of H. G. Wells in her invalid table drawer. They were very much her sort of literature, and they would probably see her out. Reading went better than talking when she had so little to say in reply. Anyway, what could he tell her? If they had been married he could have told how the children were getting along, complained about the extra housework, or reminisced about that day on their Niagara Falls honeymoon when she had insisted on his buying her an expensive parasol to keep the spray from spoiling her new hat.

She never complained about feeling pain. Sometimes while reading to her he felt that she was watching him. When he tried to catch her at it—as a preliminary to a genuine communication between them—her eyes were usually closed. It was stupid of him to be able to do so little for her as life, through the agency of a deadly disease, pushed her back and down and out. If only she were devout. Then a minister could have been brought in to help. Unfortunately, though raised a Unitarian, she was an unreconstructed atheist who supposed religion to be a racket much like Massachusetts politics.

Certainly he had no convenient fictions to interpose between the fact of her dying and the truth that he did not know how to comfort her. If the world were an immense, windy, rain-sodden English park in late November, then they were two loiterers in it out of season who had failed to hear the liveried attendant when he rode through on horseback blowing a bugle to signal the closing of the gates. Stumbling in the dark, they had bumped into each other, recognized a common plight, and crept together under a holly bush, each exploiting the other's warmth as a meagre substitute for a bed and a fire during that night only. Did this constitute a relation? The pity was it didn't. A pity too that the park conceit was so

62

unspeakably bathetic and incoherent. How could Millicent face death without howling, when every time she opened her eyes there was nobody there but a nurse or a Myles McCormick? A question not to be asked.

On weekends Prentiss Beal usually visited her: the disinherited Brahmin invert performing his corporal act of mercy at the bedside of the Yankee *nouveau pauvre* girl. He always came back winking and grinning like an old bawd, saying she was getting along fine, just fine, and raving about what a nice chat they'd had. It was good of him not to pull a long face, but McCormick couldn't understand why the old man chose to carry on so.

'What do you mean "a nice chat"?' he finally complained. 'We scarcely exchange a word. I want to ask her if she has any last requests but I don't dare.'

'She wants you to bring her back here afterwards. She has an understandable prejudice against funeral homes and morticians,' the landlord said, making his skinny fingers scamper on the hall banister railing.

McCormick gasped. 'She told you that? Why didn't she tell me? I've let her down, haven't I? All the way down.'

'Don't thrash about so, Myles. I'd advise you to continue in just the way you've been going. Otherwise she might worry that you were getting yourself seriously upset. Anyway, she's leaving you a message, and that ought to cover most of the things you imagine need talking over.'

'*She* might worry about *me*! My God!'

'Well, it's a little late for anyone to start worrying about her, isn't it?' Beal observed mildly. Then he took out a filthy handkerchief and hid his face in it.

They would go on as before at the hospital then, until coma rang down the curtain on the sessions of brandy-nipping and Wells. But it wouldn't be like Opera he reminded himself. He finished *The War of the Worlds* and began *Food for the Gods*, trusting that Milly was too hardheaded to make a personal application of the story's trope of uncontrolled wild growth. She did not seem to take it personally. She particularly liked the part about smoking out the giant wasps from their underground bunker, and when they came to the description of the forty-foot-tall German princess who walked lovelorn in Windsor Great Park clutching a huge limb of blossoming chestnut, she grinned and said, 'Barbara Lloyd'. Shortly afterwards Nurse Lloyd had come in and they had winked at each other behind her broad back.

At the library, between reading up the seventeenth-century religious wars, darting into the South Stack for sessions of self-induced mindlessness and for gradually-lengthening conversations with Helen, and the daily stint down in Cat. & Class. on the collection of Russian liturgical music, he was shoving ahead into the foul jungle of the Coxe Collection. A Puritan named William Prynne was running away with the title of most prolific pamphleteer. Brief assays of Prynne's prose revealed that he was also a powerful contender for Nastiest Mind of the Seventeenth Century—a century sometimes known as the Century of Nasty Minds. Prynne's style was a drivelling rant, his intelligence was mired in paranoid fantasies of Jesuitical plots, his pre-conscious *idée fixe* was that everything in the world, with the sole exception of his own boundless capacity for pseudo-moral indignation, was a put-up job. It would be amusing to recommend to Edgar Rooney, the crypto-Feeneyite file clerk in the Public Catalogue Department, that he read a little Prynne. Of sectarian persuasions historically at odds, both were actually blood brothers, vipers from the same brood, spiders working opposite sides of the same tattered puritanical web.

But he had begun to feel that it was all too lugubrious and dreary. The question was, how much time could anyone afford to lose to dreary horrors like Prynne and Rooney. There was no real reason to suppose that the fatuous Pee-Pee Pinkham would ever let him take over Petkov's cushy job. Wasn't it far more likely that he would end up at best like Roberta Colley, a drained soul with extinct eyes who, after giving each day full value for the few dollars they tossed her weekly, went home each night to a Brookline apartment that was empty of everything except furniture, snapshots of the nieces and nephews, a much thumbed missal, and last year's yellow and desiccated Palm Sunday frond?

These disconcerting reflections struck home late one afternoon when he was taking his occasional turn at closing down the deserted department. He tried to shrug them away. With the shades drawn and most of the lights off the Room always took on a graveyard air, the openings of the side-alcoves going inky black and suggesting the death-crammed monuments of the Capulets. So what? He sent a book cart crashing into Alcove H, locked the alcove gate and came up the line, checking the gate locks as he went. A last visitor stood near the front, the figure scarcely visible in the weak light of a single down-turned gooseneck lamp on the reception desk. Rattling the bars of Alcove A he snarled 'Closed!' without turning round.

A woman's voice said coolly, 'What do you keep in those things? Bodies?' And that was another thing. He was hag-ridden—had been most of his life in fact. What in God's name had become of all the men? They had gone off to do manly things, that was what had happened to them. What manly things? An example of manliness-in-action failed to come to mind. 'It's all pornography and cases of salt fish,' he said coming forward. 'I'd like to show you around but I've got to go see an undertaker.' And that was the truth.

The woman's tweed suit seemed heather coloured, although it was really too shadowy to tell: not new but so beautifully cut that the lines had held. He reached to the wall and switched on a front ceiling light.

Extraordinary eyes there. Would look purple under the weird daylight of Connemara or the Dingle Peninsula. Dense dark hair and high, prominent, almost Slavic cheekbones quite in keeping with the beyond-the-Shannon ascription. Yet tall and straight in the ruling class American manner. Who? Perhaps secretary of HOBOH membership committee giving onceoverlightly at F. Meat's instig? Or? . . . RICH CONTRACTOR'S DAUGHTER MARRIES YOUTHFUL APPEARING RARE BOOKMAN AND CRUSADING B.F.L. 'BULLETIN' EDITOR. Handsome couple. Fell for each other at Hon Hib Winter Ball. Neither in youth's first flush though. No matter. Her pattern so beautifully cut the lines had held. Extended wedding journey, details vague. Despaired of at Ste Anne de B., rumoured at Lourdes, anticipated at Fatima and Knock, secretly all the time at wife's family's castle in South Tip. Horses? Exceedingly. Centrally heated stables, Gold Cup winners, the lot. Castle draughty. Castle cozy in cozy castlebed. Ample four-poster, Adam ceiling above. Mature raven-haired beauty, limber long-legs, woman of the world. Could teach Venetian courtesans a few tricks. Honeymooning husband does damndest to show gratitude by keeping UP. Married before? Indeed. He—to misfortune. She??? To Mr Fortune, Chinese cookie king, slain in Tong war. Return in fall. Cohasset mansion on Jerusalem Road readied, bijou twelve-room pied-à-terre on Brimmer Street long-leased. Endow triptych at Holy Cross Cathedral, sit for side-panel donors' portraits, lead HOBOH well-heeled Benedicts through dazzling Social Season.

The woman stirred and put a hand up to her neck. 'I wish you wouldn't give me that glazed look,' she said.

McCormick started. 'Sorry. I was just wondering whether you were married.'

'I'm a widow.'

'No. Really?' He felt a vague excitement. 'Was he killed in a hunting accident? Pardon me! I was just thinking out loud.'

She quivered. 'They should have warned me about you downstairs at the Information Desk.'

66

'I'm usually kept chained in one of the alcoves. You came on me just as I was breaking out.'

'Sort of phantom of the opera, huh?' She added thoughtfully, 'I imagine a person gets pretty fantasy ridden in this sort of job. Watch out! You're liable to come unhinged.'

'Unhinged!' he echoed. 'You should meet the rest of the staff.' He sat down at the desk, shoved Miss Kearsarge's police truncheon to one side, and opened the Visitors' Register. 'Before we send you away empty-handed we have to ask you what you came looking for in the first place and write your name down. If we like you we suggest that you try the Atheneum, the Boston Public, or Harvard. I suggest you try one of those places. Name please?'

'I'm going to work with your maps,' she said briskly.

McCormick swung about and surveyed the farthest dim recesses of the Room. 'I don't see any maps. Have you thought of taking out an AAA membership?'

She dropped a note on the desk and said, 'Look again. You're supposed to have the most complete collection of old Boston maps in existence. The Olmstead collection.'

The envelope in which it came was standard B.F.L. inter-departmental brown, but the note itself was electrotyped on Brutal Bond so full of rags it gave off crinkling sounds like new folding money.

From: Pillsbury Pinkham
To: Rare Books Room & Graphic Arts Department
TOP PRIORITY
MRS GALLAGHER CIT PLAN STAFF BOS REDEL COMM GIV MAX
ACCS ALL MAT OLMST MAP GRAPHART AVAIL PHOTSTAT ETC
COPY
SERV FULL COOP BOTH ASKED PRETHANKED
PP
DIRSUITE

It was clear that the Director, despite the petition of protest signed by all chiefs and deputy chiefs of departments, was continuing his experiments with the minia-turization of inter-office memos. Well, what could they expect from a man who believed that prose was a pack-age? Pre-thanked, eh? The man should be post-kicked.

'Are you actually in favour of redeveloping Boston?' McCormick asked.

'Parts of it.'

'Ah, I see. When do you want to start working on this stuff, Mrs Gallagher?'

'I thought if I came by this afternoon and left the note, somebody could start getting out the maps early tomor-row, beginning with the oldest. Then if I turned up around ten, I could begin.'

'Most efficient. But eleven or twelve might be better the first day. I have to find the Olmstead Collection before you can work with it. We're a bit disarranged up here.'

She looked puzzled. 'You mean you'll be doing the hauling?'

'It is my pleasure,' he said suavely. 'We've been stripped of our sub-professional staff by the Director and I happen to be the only able-bodied man here.'

'Well. Much obliged. I hope I won't be a nuisance.'

'Not at all. I'll be your patient log man and we'll debate whenever you feel the need of a break. What could be better?'

'What do you suppose we're going to debate about?' she inquired drily.

'Oh—about redeveloping Boston, to begin with. Lots of other things if you stick around long enough.'

'My work here won't take long.' She pivoted towards the exit. 'Tomorrow at eleven then. Meanwhile have fun with your undertaker.'

'Not my undertaker,' he called after her. 'Just a friend's.'

The massive swinging door was faced with dark red up-holstery leather held down by large copper-headed nails. Its pneumatic stop was set so that it closed with ponderous dignity. He discovered that he had written in the Visitor's

68

Register, 'Mrs Gagger cit plan'. If she was a City Planner then she was probably not an Irish countess. Not even a Papal one. No coronet would ever coronet that splendid head. Recalling Baron Haussmann, the famous Paris boulevard and étoile man, he was pleased that it did not necessarily follow.

6 ∽

Helen called softly, 'Hey, psstt!' from the direction of the
Deep Stack. McCormick put down his work, sprang to the
sink for a quick wash of face and hands, took a fresh cotton
dust cover from a book truck, and went loping up the
aisle. He drew her through the open doorway, shut the
heavy metal door behind them and jammed it with a
wooden wedge. 'Did you jam the door at the other end?'
he asked.

She nodded and stooped to spread the cloth evenly on
the hard, chilly floor, then sat on it with her calves under
her. McCormick sank down beside her and reached for
her. She put her hands on his chest and said, 'Don't take
off my glasses yet, Myles. Today this place sort of gives
me the creeps.'

She was smiling a little constrainedly. While he kissed
her mouth and neck he helped her undress, peeling off
the blue work smock she had taken to wearing lately, un-
doing the snaps of her bra at the back, pushing her half-
slip and suspants beneath her hips and down her legs until
she stood up suddenly, heeling off her shoes against the
floor, and her garments went rustling in a heap. While
getting out of his own clothes he gave her long looks. The
way the crepuscular light of the Stack bathed her naked-
ness was always surprising, delightful and slightly spooky.
Today she wasn't taking long looks back.

Helen hung her glasses on the rung of a steel shelf, sat down, and with a deep breathing out lay back on the thin cloth. 'Go at it right away, Myles dear, but don't do anything.' Pressing her knees against his sides and holding down his shoulders she murmured, 'Steady. Just for a little while?'

Even lying still she was best at it. The amenity of Helen. He said enthusiastically, 'You must be the best screw in the world, Helen White!'

'Shh. Don't say "screw", say "making love". Don't say anything, Irishman. I have such a kind feeling for you. Do you know that?' She kissed his eyelids.

'Yes. Me too. Most natural thing in the world.' Something was different though. Maybe she thought she was falling for him, calling him an Irishman like that. Look at me I am loved. Rubbish. They could go into it later, he thought, burrowing in deeper against the warm pressure of her arms and thighs.

She was not yielding. 'You don't think it's been exactly sordid, do you?' she whispered.

McCormick laughed softly. 'No. Think of the lousy salary they pay a highly educated woman like you. It's a legitimate perquisite, like coffee breaks.'

'You never talk to the point because you don't know what the point is. Peculiar Myles,' she said, hugging him hard. Then she closed his hands over her breasts, tapped lightly with the tip of her tongue against the lobe of his right ear, and began a slow steady seethe under him.

Afterwards, when they were halfway through dressing, he took her on his lap, with his back up against a shelf of ancient statutes, and rubbed some of the places where she was sore from the stone floor. He wanted to know if things were generally all right.

They were not. There had been a frightful quarrel at Mrs White Senior's house in Hudson where they had been living all three since the marriage. The snooping mother-in-law had confronted her with the accusation that she was sneaking her diaphragm out of the house. Evan, the white-hot hope of Tech's Metallurgy Department, had stood white-faced and speechless by his mother's side in the over-furnished living-room as the scene continued. *Of course* she had denied it. Going further, with her hand on the door knob, preliminary to departure for an in-town hotel, she had reminded both of them of certain facts: of the mother's obnoxious presence on the singularly un-carnal August honeymoon in the most fog-bound and drizzly of the Canadian Maritime Provinces; then there was her habit here in Hudson of getting up ten minutes after the newlyweds retired to their bedroom and opening their door as well as her own, facing, door. Evan must come away *now* if he wished to salvage a marriage probably already unsalvageable. But what was life anyway if not risk-taking? Predictably, the old bitch had shrieked and staggered about, faking a stroke. Evan, weeping, had pursued his reeling mother with little, terrified cries while Helen executed a vigorous sequence of door-slammings on her way to the street. Now her clothes were out of the house and within the week she would go to New York. There would be a job in the U.N. Secretariat—something to do with her languages—the same job she had formerly turned down in order to marry Evan. A clean break was best. No doubt someone, in all probability the mother, would introduce divorce proceedings.

'Shocking!' McCormick said. 'I knew it was bad out there but not that bad. This clean break idea now—' He fell silent, stroking her perfect knees through a gloss of nylon. 'I feel some responsibility, you know. Maybe you and I could really get together . . . I mean after you've had a rest and a clarification and so forth.'

She got up quickly and began to put on her smock. 'Don't feel responsible. I'm responsible for me. Anyway, I don't see you. Us together, I mean, except here in the dark.'

'All you near-sighted people,' he said aggrievedly. 'Why don't you put your glasses on?'

72

She did in fact unhook her glasses from the shelf rung and put them on. 'I still see you as a blur. For all I really understand about you, you're just like Evan—with certain heady differences of course. I don't mean that.'

She looked at the line of her stockings and then bent to straighten them. 'Besides, you're for that Eithne,' she said half under her breath.

Of a sudden all ears, McCormick got up and began to put his work shirt back on. 'What do you mean? I drove Mrs Gallagher to her door twice and took her to lunch in the staff cafeteria once. All we do is argue.'

'And about two dozen coffee breaks,' Helen said quickly.

'She's my beard—my cover. Naturally I didn't want anyone to get on to our sessions in here. That's all.'

'And you're my perquisite,' she said smiling. She stopped smiling. 'Arguing's not such a bad thing. Evan and I never got a chance to do much arguing. That old bag was always in the way saying, "Now children, children".'

She glanced at her watch, then drew him over to a window slit and gripped his arms tightly while she looked up at him. 'I have to tell you something now, Myles. The hospital called with a message for you about an hour ago. Miss Meachum took it, but fortunately she asked me to tell you. You're supposed to be sure and go there this evening. They said you needn't hurry, but be on hand by your usual time.'

McCormick flinched. Feeling himself beginning to blush deeply he pulled free and turned his back on her. She put her arms around his back, pressed her cheek against his shoulder and said, 'Honey, honey, don't be scared.'

'I'm not scared, except of acting like a jerk. Maybe I'll start laughing. But it's her scene, not mine. Poor Milly! She deserves a better send-off.'

'You won't act like a jerk. Do what comes naturally. Anyway, she won't know, will she?'

'No.' He drew Helen in front of him, by the window

slit, and shook her gently. 'So many things seem to be breaking up at the same time. It's strange.'

'I hope I didn't—'

'Not at all. You make a lovely messenger.'

The late afternoon light had almost all bled away, leaving the depths of the Deep Stack nearly pitch black. They hugged each other tenderly, yet somehow remotely, like the shades of former lovers encountering in an Hawthornian wood. Blowing kisses off the palms of her tiny, sensuous hands, Helen was fading back towards the farther door to the Stack. From there she would circle around, by devious routes, into the main room of Rare Books. And from there, in a matter of days, out of Boston and out of his ragged life.

'Never surrender, darling Helen,' he called softly.

'Never. Or at least not until somebody who really likes me asks me to,' she called sweetly back.

Millicent's eleventh-floor room in the New England General Hospital main tower was a corner one at the junction of two quiet corridors. The nursing station for that sector of the floor, a narrow alcove with a counter, refrigerator, cabinets for medications and records, a typewriter and several steel swivel chairs, was located right next to it.

This night, coming along from the elevator, McCormick was relieved to find things peaceful, with everyone more or less tucked up, listening to radios or whimpering behind doors that were closed or at least screened. Nurse Lloyd, the Cardiff giantess, came out of the alcove to speak to him. 'I want you to meet Margie, she's on with me tonight,' she said, indicating a lean little student nurse with freckles and sharp shoulder blades who managed a nervous smile for a split second when McCormick said, 'Hi, Margie.'

Momentarily the librarian was at a loss. He looked at Milly's closed door and back to Barbara Lloyd. There was a narrow surgical cot on wheels standing along the corridor farther down. 'Dr Walski's in there now with an orderly,' the nurse explained. 'If you wait a minute, he'll be out.' At the end of the corridor, a young Negro orderly dressed in green and pushing a heavy floor-waxing machine came into view. 'Not tonight, Tommy,' Nurse Lloyd called down to him, and he went away.

McCormick said, 'So she's' and stopped. He said, 'I assume from the message that reached me at the library she's' and stopped again.

Nurse Lloyd merely nodded.

Elbowing the counter nervously, he said, 'Does Millicent stay where she is or do you have to wheel her down to some sort of dying room?'

Nurse Lloyd looked appalled. She said, 'That's all right. Milly isn't going to be moved. She's staying right where she is.'

'That's good,' he said dully.

She began to look a little bit embarrassed. 'A lot of her old friends on the staff visited up here today. You know, to pay their . . . to say so long. A couple of the girls wondered about a minister.'

'Well, I guess you know Millicent's viewpoint on that just as well as I do.'

'Sure. They were just wondering.' She looked as if she were glad to wash her hands of it.

Dr Walski, wearing hospital whites, came out of Millicent's room, leaving the door ajar. His flat feet made slapping sounds as he approached.

'Good evening, Mr McCormick. You got our message all right?'

'Yes. Thanks.'

'A cold night out?'

'Very.'

Dr Walski seemed faintly at a loss. Maybe he was put off by the fact that the dying patient's visitor was no sort of relation. Maybe the nurse was put off by that too. They would have been less bothered if Millicent were on the mend. In the vicinity of death people's sense of propriety perhaps became mustard-keen, because death was such a traditional kind of thing. Perhaps. He said earnestly, 'I just hope I can sit with her for a little while before it's over. You've all been very good to her and I can't thank you enough.' His eyes happened to light on Margie. She suddenly closed her mouth.

The resident brightened. 'Of course. But prepare yourself. The coma is now very deep and the breathing pattern is breaking up. There's been a build-up of chest and lung fluids. Measurable weakening over the last hour. I don't give her much longer. So we've removed the intravenous feeding tubes.'

McCormick shut his eyes and opened them. 'I'd like to see her right away. Alone if it's all right with you.'

Nodding, Dr Walski said, 'Just call out the orderly and say you'll take over for a few minutes.' Before flatfooting it off in the direction of the elevator he said to Miss Lloyd, 'Put me on call if I'm not back in ten minutes. I'll be bringing Dr Warren.'

The orderly, a pasty-faced white man with a big nose came out promptly at McCormick's knock. 'Don't let it get you down, Mr Rogers,' he whined. 'She isn't feeling a thing.'

'The name's not Rogers,' he said icily and entered. The room was softly lighted. There was grey froth around Milly's mouth and nose. He wiped it away with a soft cloth which was floating in a basin of hot water on her invalid table. Her breathing was very impeded. At half-minute intervals a rattling, strangulated breath from way down deep came and went. In between there were bubbling sounds in her throat and a suggestion of waves breaking far off that seemed to issue from her chest. The froth kept re-forming. She seemed to be drowning in herself.

The librarian felt that she should not die with her hair up and pulled out all the pins in her hair that he could find until it began to come down. It was necessary to lift her head off the pillow a little in order to draw the long plaits down so that they framed her face. The first time he'd seen her with her hair down she'd been naked and in a towering rage—like an angry Eve. That was the last time they'd actually had a serious quarrel, although with a strong-minded girl like Milly minor disagreements had been common enough. Milly looked pretty bad now, but she really had a comely face and a good figure too. Very un-Irish in general effect. There was that phrase in the book about Boston: the Yankee-Irish deadlock. Had they been that? Nothing like that. Yet Milly in her deadlock now.

McCormick, rising, leaned over the bed and brought his mouth close to her ear. 'I wish you could hear me, Millicent Rogers, R.N.,' he said hoarsely. 'I think you're the greatest and didn't we have some fun times?' He cursed himself for a fool and a driveller, but all his banalities were drowned out in the roar of her breathing. Beginning to cry he thought cravenly, 'How did I ever get myself into such a situation?' Even here he had to think of himself. Oh bitter bitter. Oh shame.

The student nurse had come in and was stumbling nervously about near the door. 'Why don't you bring in another water basin?' he suggested.

'Tha doctis' wanna come in hee-ah, Mista' Mahrcawmik,' Margie said, in a pristine East Cambridge accent.

He cleaned Milly's face one last time and retreated to the end of the bed. Dr Walski came in with Dr Warren, the elderly surgeon who had conducted the case from the beginning. Having operated on her twice and given her all her follow-up examinations between the first and second illnesses, he had excellent reasons for wanting to see it through. Walski switched on the ceiling lights and bent over the bed. Warren stood across from him watching. Then the resident straightened, took the ear-pieces of his stethoscope from his ears and with a faint note of irritation in his voice, asked, 'When did she stop breathing, Mr McCormick?'

'She hadn't stopped breathing! Unless it was just when you came in.'

Dr Warren, before bending over Millicent from his side of the bed, said sensibly, 'It doesn't really matter very much, does it?'

McCormick found it easier to stare at the twin peaks of Millicent's toes under the bedding than to pay close attention to what the physicians were doing. Soon, leaving final details to the resident, Warren came down and stood beside him. He was saying something in a loud, scratchy voice: 'A damned shame . . . overwhelming odds . . . several years she wouldn't have had fifty years ago . . . several years of practising her profession . . . several years of living. . . .'

The old man seemed to be awaiting an answer to a question. 'Pardon me?' McCormick said.

'I was saying you'd probably know better than I would whether the extra several years were worth it to her as a person. Did she have any fun?'

'Oh. As a person. Well, I've only known her a couple of years. But of course they were worth it to her. I mean do you know of any acceptable substitute for living, Doctor?' It was an odd query to address to him. Maybe Warren was troubled by doubts of the value of his work as his career drew to an end. His was a tough branch of the healing art certainly. So seldom one would be able to give a patient an unconditional discharge. Even when a cure did stick there was the business of discharging a patient minus a breast, or a lung, or a limb. Maybe Warren's nights were disturbed by memories of all those patients he had had to maim in order to cure, and those he had maimed without curing. Did he dream of the sunken, knowing eyes of childish leukaemia sufferers looking out from amidst the heaped toys which Santa Claus had delivered in mid-August because December would be too late?

78

'She had plenty of zest for life. You weren't wasting your time by adding several years to her life,' he hazarded. And if the first part of the statement needed some qualification, the statement as a whole was still true enough to say.

Dr Warren smiled, touching him on the shoulder lightly. 'Knowing that should make you feel better about this.' Then he bawled at Walski, 'If you're about through, Doctor, let's clear out and leave Mr McCormick a little peace and quiet.'

Alone again, McCormick went to sit on the edge of her bed. He took her hand in both his and squeezed it. It was not at all cold and stiff, yet there wasn't any heat in it either, and of course the pulse, assuming one knew how to look for it, would be missing. Why should it be missing? Why couldn't all the doctors, orderlies, nurses, technicians, with their medicines and tools and X-ray machines, make it come back again? There was a lamentable ineptness somehow involved in this death business. For instance, why only one heart, liver, vascular system, a measly single pair of lungs and kidneys and all those other important parts? Every third-rate designer of jet aircraft and ICBMs knew about back-up systems, yet life knew nothing of them. Why hadn't life been told? Why hadn't something been done about dragging life, kicking and screaming, into the present century?

He wondered how he would die, whether he would die alone, and knew that there was no other way of dying.

The face of Millicent Rogers, R.N., was clean and clear now, her mouth and eyes were closed. Facial colour, which had always inclined towards sallowness, was much as usual. She looked? Maybe as she might had she fallen into a doze on a dull afternoon when she had nothing to do and nothing to look forward to doing that evening. She looked all right, if that was looking all right. He curled her hand into a tight fist, as one sometimes does when giving a child a coin or a piece of hard candy, and laid it up on the pillow against her hair.

Nurse Lloyd came in. She went to the body and gently drew down the raised arm and unclenched the fist. 'She looks more peaceful now,' she explained. 'She looks nice.'

'She was nice.'

He went out of the room and Miss Lloyd followed him. 'You were very thoughtful to come see her night after night,' she said. 'You and Mr Beal. It's not as if you had to because she was a relative, I mean as if she belonged to you like a wife, or a daughter.'

'She didn't belong to anyone,' McCormick said. 'We were friends though, and Mr Beal was a friend of hers as well. It doesn't take any particular thoughtfulness to go on being friendly with a friend, does it, Miss Lloyd?'

Miss Lloyd went behind the counter of the nursing station and sat down. She looked tired. She said, 'What about the viewing and all that?'

'At my flat in the West End, tomorrow night. Where she was living. All you have to do is call Murray Funeral Homes, the one on Cambridge Street. The details'll be in the papers.'

'That's all right then. Now about her things that she brought with her to the hospital. We can gather them up and send them to you. Better still, I'll come by tomorrow night and bring them with me.'

'That's very decent of you, Miss Lloyd.'

He said good night and had started towards the elevator when he remembered something that Prentiss Beal had said and came back to ask whether Millicent had left a written message for him.

The nurse struck her forehead. 'I go and forget and I must have thought of it a dozen times tonight.' From her uniform pocket she drew out a small cardboard container and handed it to him. 'It's a tape. She couldn't write comfortably by then, and she didn't want to dictate, so we borrowed a tape recorder from the Aphasia Clinic down in the basement.'

McCormick shuddered briefly and shook the box. 'I wonder—'

'Nobody else heard what she said into the tape recorder, and I know she was easier in her mind afterwards,' Miss Lloyd said.

'If it made her feel better that's the main thing, so I'm certainly glad you remembered,' McCormick said politely, leaving.

7

ROGERS—March 11, at N. E. General Hospital, after
long illness, Millicent Louise Rogers. Friends may call
at Apt. 5, 65 Phillips St. (Friday only) after 7 p.m.
Burial private. No flowers please.

*No tears please and do not touch the microphone. Sorry,
Dr Anthony, I must have slipped.* The wording of the
notice had been long premeditated. McCormick mentally
filled in the date and time on the way down to the lobby.
From there he phoned in the information to two morning newspapers with a request for a repeat in the afternoon edition of one of them. If she was to be gotten to
the crematorium in Allston on Saturday morning before
the fires were banked for the weekend, then she had to be
waked on Friday night, the 12th. Otherwise it meant lying
an extra day and night either in the flat or in some root
cellar at Murray Morticians set aside for people who were
the object of inexpensive funerary arrangements. Both
alternatives were unthinkable.

Crossing the oval in front of the hospital's massive
central tower he noticed that the long cold had broken.
A warming damp southwesterly was shoving the filthy
winter overcast towards coastal Maine. Through scudding
cloud remnants the mid-March half-moon was intermit-
tently in evidence. Portents of spring? Just conceivably.

82

Boston weather, which in most respects modelled itself slavishly on Leningrad's, had of course this blessed capacity for sudden profound change. On a blazing mid-summer day the sky might blacken, a chill wind from the sea tumble the thermometer as much as 30° Fahrenheit in three quarters of an hour, so that business men in Dacron suits, lady shoppers in thin cotton shifts, hugged themselves while smiling thinly at one another. But some changes were irreversible, even in Boston.

The glad weather tidings had not yet communicated themselves to the interior of the Rambler, which retained an arctic chill, or to its engine, which resisted the starter's whining importunities, first by remaining rancidly silent, then by coughing and shuddering, before coming to a sort of half-life.

The librarian worked the bucking car through the parking lot and out into the stream of traffic on Commonwealth Avenue. Mainly in second gear and making frequent stops at traffic lights which appeared to be preparing to change from green to some other colour, he drove towards Charles Street and the West End. At the foot of Charles he muddled into the traffic circle next to the elevated station and went round and round while considering which way to proceed. At last he drove up West Cedar Street, past Phillips and Myrtle, and went up the hill along Pinkney Street. Eithne Gallagher lived at Number 42 in an apartment house and the questions were: was she in? if so up? if so apt to be annoyed at this so very necessary visit?

'It's McCormick from the library,' he said gruffly into the vestibule speaking screen. 'My friend died tonight and I was wondering whether I could use the tape recorder you take around with you when you're interviewing families in the condemned tenements.' For reply the earphone emitted cackling and crackling sounds, but the electrified door latch was clicking and he went in and began to run up flights of stairs without considering that

83

he was ignorant of what floor she lived on. As he reached the third landing a door halfway along the front hallway was opened and her voice said, 'Down here.'

'I'd just finished some painting in the kitchen,' she said, waving him in and leading the way through an open inner door into a long white living-room. It had the usual better-class Beacon Hill dark wood trim, wrought-iron wall-lamp fixtures and tall casement windows, with a wall of new-looking unpainted bookshelves supported by metal brackets in keyhole stripping at the end opposite the windows. Her hair was rolled in a bun at the back and her hands and face looked newly and austerely scrubbed. Her clothes, an old pair of dungarees and a faded black cotton jersey top, were encrusted with an accumulation of white and off-white spatters that seemed to go back for years and years. The top had pulled loose at the waist, revealing a fresh smear of white paint where her navel should have been visible. Dropping his gaze McCormick noticed among other things that her thighs were long and columnar, full but not fat, her feet paint-flecked and bare. Unusual in a woman, all the toes were well formed and properly independent of one another, looking as if they had spent much more time gripping the earth than crammed into pumps.

'You've painted a lot of apartments.' That was not what he had come here to say.

Her expression managed to be simultaneously concerned and wary. 'Yes, too many. Sit down, why don't you, and tell me what that was all about over the bleeper just now.'

He preferred to stand while reaching around for the full explanation and ended with an apology for coming in on her so late and not waiting until the next day.

'I couldn't have waited,' she said and went efficiently into action: bringing out her machine and setting it up on a coffee table in front of a couch, rewinding Milly's tape, after a quick examination, from its own spool to

84

one that fitted her instrument, explaining how one got the machine to play back, rewind and repeat.

McCormick took off his outer coat and sat down on the couch, staring apprehensively at the machine. It was ready to play and Eithne had gone out of the room again, but he felt shagged and desperate now that the problem of how to hear Milly's last wishes had been solved. She came back wearing an overcoat and winter boots and carrying a bottle of Old Fitzgerald, an ice tray, a tumbler and a small water pitcher. After putting these things on the marble-topped coffee table she said, 'I'm going out for a short walk. Help yourself, but I wouldn't finish the bottle if I were you.'

'Thanks, Eithne. Though I didn't intend to drive you out of your own apartment. Maybe I should borrow this thing overnight.'

'You might break it. Don't worry,' she added with apparent sincerity, 'I was going out anyway to get the smell of paint thinner out of my nose and throat.'

The librarian's stricken gaze returned to the machine. In his mind's eye he saw Millicent with grey froth bubbling from her nose and mouth. The living-room door and the hall door closed quietly. Almost cringing, he pressed the play-back control. During several seconds there was nothing but hum and woosh; then came the sound of someone, Milly, clearing her throat painfully and at length. In panic he jabbed at the stop and rewind controls and reached for the bottle of whiskey with his other hand. Certainly it was reasonable to take time to think oneself into a properly receptive frame of mind for the reception of this unsolicited post-mortem message? How tired he felt! He hoped that she had composed herself before speaking into the machine. Milly did have that drastic streak in her character though. Usually he had been able to put her off with various debating tricks when she wanted to make 'certain things very clear!' But how did one debate a tape recorder?

He lip-twisted, muttered, drank deep, stopped his procrastination, and restarted the tape. Milly cleared her throat and then said, 'Don't cringe, Myles'—more throat clearing—'Shit! It's the taste of it's so terrible'—pause—'I bet you didn't even kiss me, did you? Sorry dear, that's a low blow. I mustn't take advantage like a wife or something.' A longer pause while McCormick in a new, deeply submissive mood, considered that whatever advantage a person in Milly's position saw fit to take, other persons were bound to concede her right to take it.

When she spoke again her voice was clearer—husky certainly but not half-choked. 'Before I forget, I made a sort of will. It's in the tin valuables box in the bottom drawer of my dresser. I guess I don't know about the key. If it doesn't turn up you can break the lock . . . I like this talking from the next world. Better than a ouija board, ha!' A long series of deep wet coughs intervened, then silence. When she resumed she was not talking but weeping. She muttered something like, 'Wipe it off, wipe it—' then giggled and said, 'I'm drunk now, Myles. I've been hoarding your brandy nips and you never knew it. NOW LISTEN TO ME!'—she was shouting and sobbing— 'I bet you didn't know I was sick to death *all* the time we lived together, and I knew it? Doctor Warren may not have known it. *You* didn't know it. But I did. You thought I was cured! Well a lot you knew! How could you be so dumb? To live with somebody and not know the most important thing about them? . . . I'm not saying what I meant to say. Here's what I want to tell you. Here it is. I'M GOING TO SAY IT SLOWLY.'

McCormick stopped throwing himself about on the couch. He sat forward, pricking up his ears.

'Myles, I think you spend . . .' The tape went silent. The silence went on and on and on. Then it ended: 'Forgive me for standing you against the wall like that, honey. I wouldn't have done it if I weren't dead and if I didn't care what's going to happen to you. I wish I could've

86

stayed around a bit longer and watched. We were *good* friends weren't we, still and all? Don't forget me, Myles. Please?' . . .

And that was all? He pressed rewind and then play-back. That was all, except that this time he noticed how much her tone had softened after the last long pause. Whether by accident or design the main message had disappeared from the tape. And the blanked-out part went on for a very long time indeed: easily long enough for her to have delivered numerous shattering volleys by way of a final assessment of her situation, of him, of their relationship. What bad luck she always had. Maybe the lost message had offered some final reflections on that theme too.

So she had misled him about her sickness and on her deathbed was disposed to upbraid him for failing to see through the deception. Her logic was not only characteristically Millicentian but very human. On the other hand, had he known all the time in some foul corner of his mind that she was deceiving him? And had he been playing along with the deception because it was more comfortable that way? He could not be sure. Because when you came down to it you never knew what you really knew. An insight with Beispiel's name and mystery scrawled all over it. Besides, what good to have grasped the truth and unmasked her? What use and dignity for either of them in that? *This*: she could then have believed he cared about her sufficiently to notice what she was up to, and this realization might have made her dying less lonely. Yet hadn't she always insisted he didn't matter to her in that way? So what? What mattered was her thinking *she* mattered to *him* in that way. She could have died thinking, I don't care for him really—although he's been nice enough as a room-mate—but I see now that he's quite devoted to me and will be very broken up when I'm gone, poor man. He had missed his cue and denied her that much comfort. All those weeks of sitting reading to her or gossiping

87

abstractedly about the library while she lay there in silence watching and waiting for him to declare himself. He had *chosen* to leave her alone, with the foul taste of her dying in her mouth, while he lurked behind an invisible barrier of bluff pseudo-comradeliness. Yes, that was what his Good Samaritan routine, not to put too poisonous a nib on it, came down to.

'You don't look so hot. Maybe I should make some coffee.' Eithne had returned from her walk and was looking down at him concernedly.

'I'd love some coffee. But don't worry about me. I always show much more on the outside than I feel on the inside,' McCormick said with a pang of self-loathing so intense it almost doubled him up.

'I've noticed that. Sometimes at the library when you get bored your face turns utterly ashen, your eyes go wide and staring, your mouth gapes and makes suffocating motions like a fish out of water. The first time I saw you like that I thought you were having a stroke. Then you yawned.'

They went into the kitchen. He sat on a high stool while she put pulverized coffee into the paper filter of a Melitta coffee-maker and heated the kettle. She had been painting the insides and shelves of some hanging cabinets over the stove and sink. Dishes, condiments, cutlery and canned goods were sitting out on all the counter spaces.

When she heard how the main part of the tape had been erased she exclaimed, 'How maddening! Could I have done it when I was changing spools? I don't think so.'

'It doesn't matter very much,' he said brightly. 'I can guess the missing part: "Myles, I think you spend altogether too much time thinking about yourself— You're a marginal man, Myles— You don't think I'd have gone to live with you if I'd had any prospect of making a real life for myself, do you Myles?— No, Myles, I'd have found somebody decent and made babies— And so forth, Myles".'

88

Frowning and flushed, Eithne wheeled around and stared at him. 'For Pete's sake, please stop that phoney self-denigration. You simply don't know what she said. And *are* you a marginal man? What do you mean?'

He gestured vaguely. 'You know. Living on a ledge. Like halfway up a beetling guano cliff in the Gallapagos Islands. I mean diddling around the B.F.L. isn't exactly reaching the windswept sunstruck heights, crossing the purple plains, striking uranium—is it?'

She shrugged. 'If that's all you mean— The whole town's marginal then. Boston's definitely a ledge. But cute.'

'And you've come here from the great world to help clean off the guano and set up some middle-cost middle-rise nests for middle-class Boston boobies. Big deal.'

'I'm not planning to settle here. Are you?'

Her gaze was unusually direct. That, plus the fact that her eyes were the finest of her many fine facial features, discouraged him from looking away. 'I must have told you I was born here. In Cambridge actually.'

'So? You also told me you left. You haven't said what brought you back.'

'That's a tale that would take time to tell. Look, Mrs Gallagher—Eithne—why don't we consider becoming friends? You know, proceed very slowly and with dignity in that direction. As a matter of fact, I've completed my considering but you're the sort of decent honourable person who wouldn't want to rush into things. Do me a favour. Go listen to Milly on the tape while I finish making the coffee. Then tell me whether you'd consider a trial friendship. If you decide I'm too creepy and marginal a man, just say so. Don't worry about hurting my feelings. I tend to have the kind that need all the hurting they can get—keeps them from calcifying.'

'People who talk like that are usually lying,' Eithne said crisply, but she turned at once and went out the kitchen door, closing it behind her.

89

The kettle had come to the boil. McCormick read the directions for this type of coffee-making on the back of the container of paper filters, then lifted up the kettle and directed a slow trickle of fuming water into the centre of the funnel-shaped filter. When the pot was full, he took a quart of non-homogenized milk from the refrigerator and found spoons, mugs, and a pewter container of sugar amid the counter clutter. Eithne came back in. She took cream yes but sugar no. He sipped his black, sugared coffee and reflected that friends could be complements, the round and pointy ends of an egg immemorially ruptured. She put her mug down beside the sink and said, 'Poor woman. How awful. I couldn't be so brave.'

'You felt that. Her bravery.'

'Well no. She wasn't being brave exactly. She just went on being herself even when she was all used up—finished. I guess that's all I mean.'

'You mean her self-reliance. She had that all right.'

'I hope you weren't put off by her quick changes of mood. When you record a tape without a prepared script you keep pressing the stop button to think what you want to say next. That time she released the stop and started telling you the things she thought were really important for you to know she may have forgotten all about the mike. Maybe it got lost in the bedclothes. Maybe it was a loose connection in the microphone jack.'

'What about the trial friendship?'

She drank the rest of her coffee in a great gulp and stood at the sink with her back to him rinsing out the crockery mug. He was tempted to grab her from behind and pin her arms to her sides, squeezing her hard until she said 'Yes'. She said, 'I won't be coming to the library any more.' He sighed. 'But don't misunderstand,' she went on, turning around with a faint smile. 'It's because I've finished that part of my project. We live in the same neighbourhood, we seem to have lots to talk about—let's see more of each other.'

90

'Jesus!' he burst out, moving close to her, 'how beautiful and healthy you are.'

'Aren't we supposed to proceed slowly and with dignity in a certain direction?' she said, stepping back. 'It's late and you look utterly exhausted.'

They went into the living-room and McCormick put on his overcoat while she recovered the tape and put it back in its box. Pocketing it at the door he said cunningly, 'Now you've heard Milly's voice you may as well come to her wake. It's tomorrow night at my flat on Phillips Street. Number sixty-five, from seven on.'

This time too her gaze was unflinching. 'What *did* you feel for this Millicent Rogers? After living with her for practically years?'

'It wasn't love on either side,' he said quickly. 'It was an episode and it's closed. I liked her. She was sort of outrageous. And completely on her own. I liked treating her as if she weren't outrageous at all. That started even before I knew she'd been sick. We shared an apartment and slept in the same bed. We even had a joint bank account. And yet she was completely on her own. I don't know why that should impress me but it does. I'd take my hat off to her right now, only I never wear hats.'

'You treated her like a lady?' Her tone was a puzzle.

'I guess so. She *was* a lady. An eccentric, unfortunate, profane one. Prentiss—my queer landlord—saw that too. He was always very courtly with her.'

'I'm not unfortunate and eccentric and profane. I'm not sick,' she said rather sternly. 'If you need all that then you really are a marginal man.'

He shook his head. ' "The normal alone can overcome the abnormal"—J. Conrad. Maybe at one time I needed *some* of that. My Graham Greene period sort of. Not any more.' He thought for a moment. 'Anyway, I didn't know she was dying all along, and I'm not at all sure I even believe it.'

'All right then, I'll come. It may be rushing things, but there should be lots of dignity in a wake.'

'Especially a Boston wake,' McCormick said, with a blandness which failed to hide his relief and pleasure, and, in a sudden upsurge of energy, took the stairs going down five at a time.

8 ∽

On wake day the librarian rose early and cleaned the apartment thoroughly. After calling Miss Kearsarge at Rare Books to explain his absence from work he went out and placed modest orders at a package store on Cambridge Street and at a florist's on Charles. No congratulatory horse shoe please, no green Paddy ribbons. The day was perfect of its kind: the sky high, cloudless and brilliantly pale-blue; the buffeting March air spilling gusts of wind, some iron-assed, a few strangely redolent of warm spice islands—had there been a dust explosion at Slade's Spice Mill in Everett?—from all quarters of the compass. He sensed the stirring world wheeling to the East and walked swiftly to the Esplanade to discover whether the ice on the Basin was beginning to break up. It had gone rotten around the pediments of the bridges but no rifts of dark water had yet come into view.

Lounging on the dock in front of the Charles River Basin Sailing Club, he stared into Cambridge and remembered a bright summer twenty years before when he had strolled this same Esplanade many evenings with tall, slant-eyed Molly Lane, I.Q. 155, while the melting sun ran down the sky behind Harvard Bridge and the last sailing dinghies ran into moorings on the Boston side. Looking across the Basin at the elongated monolith of M.I.T. they had tried to guess behind which monotonous row of fiery windows lay the classrooms and laboratories in which, beginning that fall, she would prepare to surpass her idolized Marie Curie. On Labour Day they had taken each other to heart in the kindest way behind the closed hurricane shutters of her Aunt Ellen's vacant Cohasset cottage. Before catching the last boat back from Nantasket Pier they had clambered on the black Cohasset rocks, he pretending to show her the very spot described by Thoreau where two hundred Irish corpses, men, women, children and infants, were lined up along the beach, drowned when a famine ship from Cork drove ashore in a spring Northeaster. It made Molly cry to know of all that death. She had suddenly sprung away from his side and run along the shore. When he caught up with her, she shook back her short straight blue-black hair angrily and twisted her hand from his. Before that fall was out she had given him the definitive heave-ho. The heroine of an increasingly tawdry romance entitled 'Eleven-thousand Draft Deferred M.I.T. Engineers and a Girl', Molly had been swift to see her old high school lover as a mere point of departure . . .

Simple nostalgia, like pity, was an inferior emotion. A pity. Glancing along the bank he spotted a sidling West End pansy wearing a lemon-coloured wind-breaker, form-fitted St Moritz stretch pants in naughty maroon, and elastic-sided buffy-coloured fruit boots in the act of drawing a bead on him. One ferocious scowl sufficed to drive the man off in the direction of Storrow Drive.

Gulls were on the ice. She had said Think of me sometimes and How could you be so dumb? Think carefully. When did you know anything at all? After the first six months or so. In the sad store-front pad on obliterated Poplar Street.

The phone rang at a quarter to ten in the evening. It was Millicent, speaking in the hushed tones she used when calling from or near the sickroom of one of her patients.

94

She said, 'It's all right, McCormick. I'll be able to get in on Sunday. He isn't going to last the night.'

'Be sure you get his name on a will making you his sole beneficiary before he goes.'

'God damn you. That isn't funny!'

It was his little joke with her and seldom did she see the humour of it. As an R.N. who went out on private cases involving serious illness by preference—because of the pay, the freedom from close supervision, and the responsibility—she had to expect a few callow cracks. Many of her patients were rich old men and women in the phase of terminal sickness. By arrangement with her agency she nearly always took the night hours, when the will of the sufferer is weak and can be changed. This time she had been stuck out in a town northwest of Worcester for nearly two weeks nursing some mill-owner who had extended his holdings, during a business career of over sixty years, to include most of the industrial real estate of the Pioneer Valley.

He said, 'See you Sunday then. I'll even give the place a sweep and get a bottle of cream sherry.'

She murmured, 'Christ. I feel like ripping one off right now.'

'Offer it up, Milly. Keep your mind on your work. Unless there's a convenient footman lurking on the landing.'

She said tartly, 'You've got such a low mind, Myles. Why don't you admit I'm faithful?' He told her he was laughing silently into his hand. She said, 'Oh Mack, do an errand for me, would you?'

'What's that?'

'Pick me up a tube of vaginal stuff at the drug-store tomorrow.'

'Certainly not. It would embarrass me.'

The sound of a muted bronx cheer was wafted through the wire. Then she laughed, called him a stuffed shirt, said goodbye and hung up.

On Sunday, Millicent walked in shortly before noon

with a copy of the *New York Times* under her arm. After hanging up her coat in the bedroom closet she came back into the main room and lifted the lid of the big saucepan sitting over one of the burners of the oil stove.

'Is that our dinner? What do you call it?'

'Burgundy Beef Zinfandel. It'll be edible about two.'

'Why don't you do it on the gas?' she wanted to know.

'Because it tastes better if it does slowly.'

She dipped her fore-finger into the pot and sucked it. 'I like the taste. But I still don't understand why you don't use the gas stove. I mean, you could turn the gas way down and you'd know exactly how much heat the pot was getting. You can't do that on an oil burner ring, can you?'

'Nevertheless,' he said firmly, 'it tastes better cooked this way and in cold weather it represents a much more efficient use of fuel.'

'Oil smells.'

'So does this particular gas burner. Don't fight me.'

She replaced the lid on the steaming pot and came over to where he was sitting with his feet up on the table. She kissed him with a mouth still faintly and pleasantly cool from the wintry air outside. He put his feet down and took her on his lap. He said, 'So he died.'

'Around four in the morning that night after I called you. Near the end he held my hand and called me "Mummy". I slept most of Saturday.'

'Do you suppose it was a gag? That is, the old guy knew he was going and he thought, what the hell, I haven't handled a young broad since that Elks convention in 1936 because I was too busy and afraid for my health, but now I'm eighty-five and this is it brother so what the hell. Did he make a play for your tits?'

Milly took her hands out of his hair and tried to get up, but he had his arms belted around her waist. 'Honestly Mack, you think of the most disgusting things! Of course it wasn't like that.'

He said, 'Relax, honey. I really wasn't trying to shock.

96

After all, when old King David in the Bible was about to throw a seven they put a young girl in his bed to see if they couldn't heat him up a little. I'm really sorry he couldn't have enjoyed a few more years of coupon clipping and mortgage foreclosing.'

She sniffed and said, 'You wouldn't joke if you'd seen what I have. Dying's a very lonely affair. I do anything I can to help them through it. In line of duty, of course.'

He was tempted to say, 'At least the customers never complain,' but instead said seriously, 'It's a strange way to make a living. Why do you go on with it? I should think you'd be ready for a job in a maternity hospital. Think of all those wholesome pink and purple little buggers in the Lying-In.'

She lazed against his arm with her eyes closed. 'Actually,' she said, 'I like it. Think of it, Mylesey, all those rich, powerful old men with their mills and mansions and their unalterable trust funds. They can buy and sell you and me a hundred times over, and when they say "Jump!" the mayor or the congressman or the police chief jumps! And suddenly all that power is gone. There they are, all alone in a big bed feeling their fingers and asking me after the relatives go out of the room if I mind nursing them and is it going to hurt and do I believe in the after-life. Then their minds wander a little, and sometimes they talk to me in the queerest ways, and I try to stay with them and answer them the way they want. You remember Mr Welch of Fall River? I never told you this before, but just before he died he thought I was somebody else he called "Baby". At first I supposed he meant his daughter or his wife. He started out saying, "Remember when we went to Paris, Baby, and to Key West?" And I kept answering, "Yes, sweetheart, wasn't it nice?"—that sort of thing. But then he suddenly sat up in bed and shook his finger at me and snarled, "You bitch you! I saw you with that orchestra leader. You thought I was asleep but I was watching from the bedroom balcony, and I saw you go with him into that empty swimming pool!"'

'So what was your alibi, Baby?' he queried, keeping under restraint a strong impulse to bellow with nervous laughter.

'Well, I hardly remember. I'd been up through twenty-four hours and I was damned confused. It really got me. I was practically in tears. I said something like, "No, darling, it wasn't me. You must have seen somebody else who resembled me in the dark." Then he died, in the middle of this terrible pointless rage. His finger fell down on the sheet and curled up like a crab's leg and he fell forward on his face.'

'Jesus! And you like the work.' He was impressed. Passion, and the persistence of passion, were impressive, even in a grotesque episode of senile mania.

After a while he said, 'What sort of heaven do the Yankee tycoons go to anyway? I mean the ones who don't go straight to hell. It's probably full of golden mills. Every financier has his private State Street Trust and makes billion dollar loans to Texas oilmen at seventy-five per cent interest compounded semi-daily. The textile magnate lives in a big, Old Deerfield sort of timber mansion over-looking a village common with a rushing mill stream that never floods and never dries up. At his annual fête on the Green he has the B.S.O. to play while the decent poor do country dances and drink his watered cider at a quarter a glass.'

Millicent said lazily, 'Well, at least it's no worse than the Irish Catholic heaven, full of plaster saints and tin-selled Infant Saviours from Prague and a lot of Bishops and Popes riding around in litters with their girl friends fanning them. And the whole place stinking of incense.'

'You mean plastered saints, and you forgot the Jesuits with poison rings.'

He put her back on her feet and got up and dragged the beat-up old couch around until it faced the front of the big black stove. He opened the oven door so more heat would flow out, then settled down on the couch and began to pull apart the *Times*. Milly took off her shoes and pulled her grey woollen shift over her head. She was left wearing a long-sleeved white blouse, a black half-slip and green woollen knee socks. She pulled the pins out of her piled hair and sighed as it fell down her back in a great hair-coloured mass.

'This is the life,' she said, coming to the couch and lying down on her stomach with her cheek on his knee. 'Now or later?' she asked sleepily, her eyes half-closed.

'A little later and then later, nature girl.' He held the *Book Review* out over her head while he patted her bottom with his other hand. He was halfway through the front-page article and had moved his hand up under her blouse and was stroking her back when she gave a little start and said, 'Look out for that old scar. Sometimes it's sensitive—like pins and needles.'

He withdrew his hand. 'What was it again they operated on you for?'

'I told you. Growths.'

She was looking up at him with a certain amount of intentness, cradling her cheek in her hand against his knee. 'Growths,' he repeated. 'What sort of growths?'

And that was when she had told him exactly what sort.

Even though the sun remained unobstructed by cloud one got chilled sitting still. McCormick stood up and stamped his feet on the dock and then went to the edge and kicked at the pack ice. Perhaps he should have pursued the matter further. What for? You didn't go on bothering someone about the details of a former illness requiring major surgery unless you were a devotee of the estimable Sacher-Masoch or of the ingenious prisoner in the Bastille, Citizen Sade. And that same week, wasn't it? Mr Herman, the rental agent, had come by to explain that the whole of Poplar Street, along with the rest of the huddle of slum streets north of Cambridge Street, near

99

the Massachusetts General Hospital, was scheduled for imminent demolition by the Redevelopment Authority. During the next month he had been too busy, first with apartment hunting, then arranging the move to Phillips Street, across Cambridge and a third of the way up Beacon Hill's 'back side', then cleaning up and white-washing the new place, to do any brooding about what she had told him.

He had hoped that Millicent would want to move along with him to the new and much more comfortable flat but had rather expected she would seize the opportunity to go off again on her own, as she occasionally liked to announce that she was about to do; for she made much of being beholden to no one, and footloose and fancy free. So that he had been pleased and a bit flattered when she immediately took it for granted, at least so far as the quarter-mile move to Phillips was concerned, that 'whither thou goest I will go'. And this, hindsight now positively trumpeted, was the clue that the foul thing which had gotten hold of her once before was on the prowl again. He had missed it.

If hindsight in fact so trumpeted, then up hindsight's hindsight with a coal shovel. Their friendship had never involved hunting for clues about the other's state of mind, body and morale—like a couple of chimps exploring each other's pelts for fleas. From the first he had seen there was plenty askew with her—she undoubtedly making the same observation about him. Otherwise, once things settled down between them, they had let each other's oddities, short-comings, what have you, alone. . . .

They had met at a Saturday night party in Cambridge thrown by a mulatto former Harvard classmate who now made his living devising ways of increasing the amount drunk by the American Negro community of a certain nationally advertized blended whiskey. He respected with-out emulating the brisk way she was throwing down

Bourbon punch and asked her to dance after observing that she was by no means drunk. She danced close with some deep breathing below his ear and she followed well. One thing led to another, and when the party around them began to assume liberal-orgiastic features, he invited her to leave with him and come back to Poplar Street for a night-cap.

They necked in the taxi and went on to tosh-tosh number five at home. When it was over, she sat up and said energetically, 'That was good. I needed that.'

He said tentatively, 'Don't we all need as much of it as we can get? Or do we?'

'Of course, but I mean in a particular way. I told you I'm a nurse. Well, I've studied a lot of biology and physiology and I know much more about the workings of the body than most people. And I've noticed that when I don't have fairly regular intercourse my system is thrown off. It interferes with my periods. Other things go wrong too that I won't go into.'

He was fascinated. 'You mean *not* screwing throws your periods off?'

'Yes indeed. Before tonight I hadn't had a man for almost three months and I really haven't felt well lately.'

'You mean you've felt frustrated.'

'It's got nothing to do with frustration. I'm talking about body chemistry.'

'Well. What do you suppose it is?' he asked vacantly.

She looked at him coolly and he could almost see the ghostly outline of a white cap on her head. 'It's the male hormone, that's what it is,' she said in a tone admitting of no argument. 'I need the male hormone. There's a very slight hormonal imbalance in my system. The balance is restored through intercourse.'

He was startled and annoyed. 'So you were only having a hormone treatment just now. You make me feel like a hypodermic needle. Not very romantic for me, you know.'

She scratched her elbow and said, 'I don't see what you

mean. I certainly can't have romance if my periods are irregular and I have rheumatic pains in my limbs.'

He wanted to pursue the argument, only a great lassitude had come over him. It was compounded of ordinary fatigue, a touch of post-coital tristitia, and recognition that once again he had fallen in with a woman who was definitely odd. She would take her place in a line stretching out perhaps to the crack of doom, more likely to the cracking of his own soul. He slumped deeper into the pillow and shut his eyes. She went out to the bathroom, and he was almost asleep when she returned and got in the bed beside him. Running her hand down his side, she said, 'It was romantic too, McCormick. You have such fine white skin on your body. Finer than lots of women.'

In the morning he gave her more hormone therapy and an egg-and-sausage breakfast. She track-walked the railroad flat for a while, then announced she would have to go. She was starting a new case in Tyngsboro and had to get back to her room on Saint Botolph Street to pick up uniforms and thermometers. After a quick kiss at the door she said nervously, 'I often manage to get Sundays off.'

He was waiting for that. 'Nifty. Come back next Sunday then. I was afraid I'd have to send you the next treatment in an ampule.'

Millicent Rogers, R.N., went red and cocked her fist to strike a blow, but he caught her wrist and hugged her. She pulled away and was off along the street towards the Charles Street Elevated stop, walking fast.

He surmised he'd seen the last of her and wasn't altogether pleased about that, since he was fairly hard up himself, even if his body chemistry happened to work all right. Besides, he'd liked her. She had struck him as sort of *sui generis* although some might have claimed that her horrid dryness of imagination about hormones was generically Yankee. And he respected the way she managed to get along quite on her own. Most girls of twenty-eight living in a rented room near Mechanics Hall would have been half-crazed by panic fear of spinsterhood, or so frigid that they would have blighted the trees for miles around with chill. Not that Millicent was so tropical. Setting aside her obvious expertise, he suspected she hadn't gotten very much for herself, as distinguished from what she had gotten for her system, out of the encounter.

Surprisingly, a note came on Friday saying, 'All right you creep. Sunday at two. M. R.' As the time approached, he hardly knew what to expect, but was anticipating anything from tears, to a working over by a hood boy- or girl-friend whom she had failed to mention, to the business end of a derringer exquisitely inlaid with mother-of-pearl. If she came looking for real trouble his plan, half-seriously conceived, was to jump out a window and run shouting through the area-way alley where the garbage cans were kept.

Millicent marched in on the very stroke of two carrying a small valise and gave him a fraught glance that appeared to combine anger, resolution and fright. Without a word of greeting she walked into the bedroom, slamming the door behind her. As he stood waiting nervously he had visions of her ripping up the mattress with a long-bladed knife.

In about five minutes he heard the bedroom door open and strange clicking sounds from the middle room. When she emerged into the front room he gaped. She stood teetering on very high heels, naked except for black silk stockings and a garter belt. Her abundant hair was swept up above her ears and fixed in it was a large, rhinestone-studded tortoise-shell comb. She had put a lot of rouge and eye makeup on, and sketched Marilyn Monroe lips across her rather thin mouth with purplish-red lipstick. From a wide black neck ribbon dangled some sort of pendant jewel. (He later learned it was a masonic emblem formerly belonging to her father.)

He had seen nothing like her since certain sex dreams around age fifteen. He went towards her smiling a sickly smile and cudgelling his ingenuity for something appropriate to say. She reached out, taking his head in her hands, and pressed him into her breasts. A long moment passed while he fought surreptitiously for breath. When she released him he took a great gulp of gardenia-scented air. She muttered something unintelligible through the incongruous pucker of her painted lips, and went teetering off towards the bedroom in back while he followed, more or less at heel.

Thus was initiated the Babylonian Revels phase of their relationship, which endured six weeks or so. Millicent was out to convince that she knew how to romance, and she did convince him, although perhaps not exactly in the way she intended. She would arrive every Sunday with what he came to think of as her sex kit in hand, change immediately into the French stockings and the Toulouse-Lautrec hairdo and neck ribbon, and do her stuff.

She was very determined and ingenious. She gave herself and took him in exchange from all angles, and all over the flat from the bed to the bathtub. She had a special fondness for the bath, even though it meant removing her stockings and losing most of her makeup. Once she said to him that the great appeal of skin-diving must be the opportunity it affords for sex six fathoms deep with the grosser effects of gravity removed. He had commented that if gravity were the enemy of love, then a honeymoon on an inter-planetary spaceship under conditions of weightlessness must represent the supreme joy. Privately he was convinced that gravity, like sobriety, is an active ally in the sex act, a phenomenon of the earth earthy. In any case he wasn't mad about bathtub love. She always put in a half-cup of detergent powder to make bubbles; detergents tended to dry his skin and make him itch.

Millicent had a short neck and slightly rounded shoulders. Her bust was medium and sagged a little, and her bottom while shapely was pretty heavy. Her legs had pleasing contours but they were short, and, as with many women of her age and strenuous occupation, some capillary blowouts were visible on her upper thighs. The tall heels threw her weight forward, accentuating the roundness of her shoulders and pushing her stomach out. So described she sounded homely but she wasn't homely at all when you took her all together. She had a comely face —thin even features, light blue eyes and a fair unmottled complexion—and when she lay in bed or floated in the bath ungarmented she was beautiful.

One Sunday afternoon he was at the gas burner getting ready to cook some frankfurters and beans. Millicent stood next to the kitchen table reading the funny papers. Seeing her there with head lowered, holding her breasts in her hands while she pursued the fortunes of Mutt and Jeff, he felt a stirring of concern and wondered what she really thought she was doing in that get-up. It made such a final contrast to the girlish woollen dresses, knee socks and sensible low-heeled walking shoes she usually wore on the street. Or did it? She must have felt his eyes on her because she looked over and asked, 'Why are you staring at me like that, Myles?'

He said, 'Oh—for no reason.' Then he thought he understood something and continued, 'Milly, I guess you think you look like Butterfly Finkelstein, Queen of the Ginza, done up like that, and from one point of view you do. But you also make me think of a little girl who's clipped her mother's party shoes and plastered her mother's makeup on her face and goes clomping up and down the house pretending she's a grownup lady.'

Her shoulders seemed to go a little rounder when she let go of herself and turned towards him. 'Except for a bit of lipstick my mother never wore makeup and she never owned a pair of heels this high in her life,' she said and added flatly, 'What's the matter, McCormick? Don't you like the way I look? Too bad! Just because I don't go around the way you do in a filthy pair of chino pants and a T-shirt and Army-Navy store socks— Don't you like the way I make love?'

He answered hastily. 'Of course I like the way you make love, Milly. You've got all sorts of imagination. You're very ingenious. Only I wonder sometimes what you get out of it.' He was being a shit but it was too late to turn back now. And he was just realizing that things shouldn't go on in the way they'd been going. His nerves, and her nerves as well surely, were being eroded.

She sat down at the table and pushed her fists into her stomach. 'It's none of your business what I get out of it. Just because women don't— I get out of you what I want out of you and it's none of *your* damned business.'

He sat down near her, his knees just touching hers. Her expression was self-conscious and broody. 'Of course it isn't my business. But I think we should have this conversation out this one time. If I didn't like you very much, and if I didn't think you sort of liked me, I wouldn't bother.'

She swung her knees away and leaned her arm on the back of the chair while she stared off into space. She said tightly, 'What is it you don't like? My stockings and shoes and my cosmetics, or the way I make love?'

'You make spectacular love in a spectacular costume. I've enjoyed it. But have you enjoyed it all that much? We've had the fifty-seven varieties, and if we get any fancier we'll have to find some slaves and build some apparatuses based on ancient Pompeian working drawings. I suggest we try it a few times in the conventional hubbie and wifie manner. We have already, but only in passing. If we really put our backs into it—who knows?'

Milly got up abruptly and bolted. He heard the bathroom door slam and sat suspended for several minutes. When she reappeared she was several inches shorter, and the rest of the costume had vanished along with the heavy makeup. With her long, dull-coloured hair down she looked like an early Flemish painter's idea of an enraged Eve.

Hands on hips she said, 'You make me sick. You keep up

an unconventional front but you're nothing but an Irish-Catholic puritan underneath. Come on then. We'll do it your way, and then I'm getting out of here for good.'

'Don't you want to eat first?' he wheedled.

'No. You're a lousy cook anyway.'

Milly lay on the bed in the bedroom staring at the tawdry grape cluster designs on the tin ceiling, responding not at all to preliminary fondling. When he moved over her her legs flopped apart like those of a rag doll or a woman dead drunk. At first her profound indifference made him angry. He thought the thing to do was get it over with and say goodbye. Then he thought of how he'd hurt her feelings and decided to do what he could. Actually it felt a whole lot better without the slippery stockings tickling him.

He settled his nose under her ear and let his thoughts range. She yawned ostentatiously a couple of times and drummed her fingers on the headboard. He thought of Mahatma Ghandi and of Terence McSweeney, the lord mayor of Cork who died on a hunger strike in a British jail during the Troubled Times. He recalled nostalgically the round face and glossy dark bangs of a lady cellist he had been infatuated with at sixteen and considered regretfully the question of why he'd never gotten to Greece during his years in Europe. Brahmin men of high caste—of course of high caste because Brahmin meant high caste, didn't it?—often read a book or smoked while having intercourse with their wives or girl friends. Wait a minute dear. Don't come until I come to the end of this chapter ...A bad business that—smoking in bed. By now there was no sign of life from the arrangement of underlying soft warm tissue called Milly.

He lifted his head and scanned her face. She seemed to have fallen asleep. Rankling with defeat he had started to remove himself from her presence when she gave a sudden mermaid wriggle and he found himself more deeply involved than before. Almost at the same moment her eyes flew open and she said, 'Oh. I was dreaming.' She put her arms around his back and her whole body seemed to flow up and curl around his like a warm foaming wave. She closed her eyes again and an expression of enormous concentration wrinkled her forehead and tightened her mouth. She sighed and muttered, 'Don't stop now.' He had said, 'Don't wait for me.' Within seconds they had really gotten together and been very happy.

The sky was greying, the wind had steadied to an easterly and put its steel teeth back in. The river shore, from the base of the nearby bridge to the little lagoon where well-born children sailed their finely tooled model twelve-metre yachts in summer, was entirely deserted. No chick no child. No watchful gulls wheeling and whimpering overhead. Not even a policeman.

With head down and hands plunged deeply into overcoat pockets McCormick walked slowly back to Charles Street Circle, crossed to the jail wall, continued a little way up Cambridge Street and stood still, contemplating the devastation of renewal. The old neighbourhood, a couple of dozen narrow twisting streets around and behind the hospital, which had been lined with jerry-built brick tenements and populated by elderly Jewish couples, Ukrainian fascists, thaw-resistant Stalinists, dipsomaniacs, drug addicts and policy game agents, students, jail-house widows, pimps and whores, grifters and drifters, and the occasional homely philosopher, store-front revivalist and curbstone sitter, had given way to a vast mud plain extending with little interruption all the way to the North Station. On Planners Plain there was just now no activity at all; for, after clearing away the rubble the demolition crews had taken their battering instruments and bull-dozers into the North End to undertake the unbuilding of Bowdoin, Dock, Scollay and Haymarket Squares. In the West End they had left several monuments behind as mute testimonials of their devotion to a certain order of

108

humane values: the General Hospital, the jail, the Fruit Street Morgue, a boarded-up public elementary school, its asphalt yard now littered with rusting automobile transmissions, and the hulking brick basilica of St Joseph's Catholic Church. And if they had neglected to preserve the Russkaya Banya on Green Street and that excellent Jewish restaurant on Leverett which used to purvey great slabs of derma and fruit pudding for nickels and dimes, no doubt they understood their civilizing mission better than a librarian of idle habits who would not, if pressed, have given two cents for manorial rights to the entire district.

No, these tenements, built originally by Yankee speculators to house, to hovel rather, the heavy influx of Irish immigrants after the Famine, had never contributed a jot to the sum total of human happiness, and it was appropriate that all trace of their former existence should be wiped off the Boston townscape. Let the redevelopers erect their richly rateable apartment blocks interspersed with light industry of the 'research' type and a shopping plaza or two. Or, if they preferred, let them grass the entire acreage over and set a sturdy breed of Connacht peasant to tending long-haired black-face sheep there at top-dollar American wages, with overtime for after five and double time on Sundays and holy days of obligation. It had nothing to do with him.

If this large-scale change, if this brisk cycle of destruction and construction had nothing to do with him, why did he find it so unsettling? He remembered how Dr Beispiel had gone on about his distrusting purposive activity of any sort and how he had tried to trace it back to the pre-weaning stage by means of shrewd questioning and word association games. That part of the treatment struck him now, as it had then, as pretty unconvincing. There are more purposes in heaven and earth than are dreamed of in your system of psychopathology, Sidney. Certainly he had his hands full of purposes these days:

to accomplish the destruction of Milly's remains in all decency, to blow the little spark between him and Eithne into a warming fire, to ease Panayot Petkov out of his directorial chair and himself into it over the next few months; in a word, to hold certain rough beasts of ill-chance frozen to their perches in the world cage by dextrous manipulation of whip and chair. Time enough later, if all went well, to subdue them to the art of leaping through flaming hoops and over one another's arched backs.

With head erect and arms swinging largely McCormick strode towards Phillips Street to complete preparations for the evening wake.

9 ⌒

'Bring out your dead!' That had been the cry in old-time plagues and a wake nowadays was also a way of bringing out your dead. McCormick set up a card table at the rear of the living-room, near the closet kitchen, and laid on it plates of sliced salami and liverwurst, Swiss, Cheddar and Camembert cheese, green and black olives, sliced Jewish rye bread, a two-pound party assortment of cookies, a slab of butter and some knives, and some glasses for the whiskey. There was sufficient room left for two quarts of bourbon, four bottles of Hungarian red wine, a pitcher of water, a bottle opener, bottles of soda water and the wine glasses.

The wine glasses. Prentiss was calling from the other side of the hall door to be let in. He came in gasping, with a large cardboard carton in his arms. After lowering it to the floor he clutched his chest and said: 'I warned those dry-cleaning establishment girls downstairs that if they come rolling home from the taverns with their usual Friday night collection of thugs in tow I would put them out in the street. I told them this is a house in mourning.'

'They understand that. They even loaned me this card table. By the way, I've never seen you in a regular suit before. On you a double-breasted jacket looks positively elegant.'

Prentiss hitched up his light grey flannel trousers by

grabbing handfuls of loose fabric at the knees and said, 'I'll bet you've never seen me in shoes like these before either.' They were black pumps of antique design with large silver buckles and blunt toes, the sort of shoe that young Jim Hawkins might have worn after making his fortune on Treasure Island. 'Many the night I danced away in these, in the dear dreadful days beyond recall,' he remarked. 'And now to business.' Lunging downwards he began pulling newspaper wrapped objects from the carton.

He had brought a couple of dozen long-stemmed wine glasses, two large silver candlesticks, assorted glass vases and several white and yellow candles. Lining up the glasses on the card table he gave the rim of one of them a musical tap and said 'Crystal.' Waving disparagingly at the vases he said, 'Junk except for that one Waterford piece.' Then he picked up the candlesticks and flourished them like bar bells. 'Early Georgian or Queen Anne—they were once the property of General Gage.'

'Marvellous.'

The landlord dashed from the apartment holding the empty carton. An instant later he popped his head back in to say, 'I think the photograph is a good idea after all.'

McCormick nodded. It was about time to do something with the flowers. The local shop had come up with camellias, a bouquet of tender young red roses, a spray of gladioli, and a lot of green fern stuff. Miss Colley and Miss Dwyer from the library, ignoring the obituary notice on this point, had sent a mixed bouquet of gladiolas and sweet pea accompanied by a black-edged card that said, 'Our deepest sympathy.' Helen White's card, attached to half a dozen gardenias wired together in a line, read, 'I'm off to *U NO* where. Let's meet after our respective ships come in to weep, gloat and laff. Ur frend DU-EE.' It was a nice thought, provided one could believe that one's respective ship had ever managed to up-anchor and clear the harbour mouth in the first place.

The flowers with stems went reluctantly but finally into assorted vases. Slinging the gardenias over his shoulder he stood pondering until the noise of trampling on the stairs and the landlord's voice from lower down crying, 'Watch the corners, if you please!' brought him to the hall door. The coffin was carried in by four men in dark clothing followed by a fifth man carrying a collapsible device of tubular metal which he began to open out into a wheeled catafalque.

'I don't want that thing. You're to put the coffin on that trestle table over there in front of the windows.'

The fifth man looked at the librarian's flowery shoulders somewhat scornfully. 'This carriage is scientifically designed to support the casket.' He glanced at the table and said, 'I wouldn't want to take responsibility for those saw horses.'

'With a couple of chairs under the centre they'll hold. Anyway it isn't your responsibility.'

'It's your funeral,' the fifth man said and began to disassemble the base.

'What about those chairs, huh?' said one of the other men. 'This box don't have no handgrips, it's startin' to slip.'

McCormick darted into the bedroom and brought out two straight chairs. He slid them under the edge of the table midway between the saw horses and added books to fill the gap between the chair seats and the table. The men eased the coffin down. The table top took the weight without perceptible buckling. The men started to file out of the room. The fifth man had already gone. One of the carriers came back in. 'The other fellow should have gone into this,' he said. 'Now sometimes, even at a closed casket viewing, you get a relative or a friend wanting to have the lid opened for a last look. Now this lid is fixed down and—'

'That's all right. There won't be anyone wanting the coffin opened.'

'Oh. Well, goodnight then.'

He fetched from the bedroom a large framed photograph of Millicent, showing her in uniform at the time of her graduation from nursing school, and set it on the coffin lid. He put candles into the two silver candlesticks, lighted them and put one on each side of the picture. He unslung the gardenias from his shoulder, bent the wire into a semi-circle, and wreathed them around the lower part of the frame, where they created a miniature bower effect without hiding any essential part of her portrait. The candle flames were reflected in the lustrous blackness of newly polished window panes. Stepping back and looking around the room McCormick felt a dim satisfaction at his handiwork.

The new letter from Julia Ward Mack, surely written in reply to his brief note explaining how things stood with Millicent, wasn't exactly burning a hole in his pocket, but there should be sufficient time to read it now before any guests, assuming there would be any apart from Prentiss and Eithne, began to arrive. He took out the letter and went to sit on the couch to read it.

My Dear Son,

Dying!! I just can't believe it. You have never said anything about her having as much as a cold in any of your letters to me this winter. How sad. How terrible.

It isn't fair. People down here die all the time but you expect that in a town full of retired people and invalids. They're old and worn out and bored. Oh yes, it is *boring*—never mind the cook-outs and bowling and so forth. Just a bunch of old nags sitting around in these grubby trailers showing each other snapshots and maundering on about grandchildren. For me New England winters would only mean a broken hip sooner or later. Otherwise I wouldn't stay down here a minute longer.

Your letter doesn't say what hospital she's in. You

114

couldn't be so careless unless it was too late for me to write to her or send her something.

It pains me to say this but now is the time for you, Myles, to get your life straightened out. Or else suddenly *you* will be ready for the boneyard, like this bunch in the trailer park, like me, only without anything having happened to you worth remembering. Nothing to look forward to and back upon. Not even some snapshots of grandchildren to pass around.

What will be done about the funeral and burial? I have made my arrangements, you may be sure of that, but young people often neglect to. But there must be relatives. Now is the time for you to fade out of the picture 'gracefully' and let them take over. I imagine she was brought up Episcopalian or Congregationalist. Protestants have their own beautiful way of saying goodbye to the dead—no waking for instance.

About your father. You say you want to know what happened so you won't waste time sitting around 're-inventing family history and getting it wrong'. This is the first time I ever heard you worried about wasting time. Perhaps you *have* changed.

Joe got home from France quite late—it was 1920. His commander had wangled a commission for him after he wrote and produced the squadron's minstrel show (apparently a great hit). He was idle all that summer, running through his severance pay and savings, swapping war stories with the other veterans, and pretending to be looking into various 'business opportunities'. Finally I gave him an ultimatum. No steady job no wedding—so he agreed to go back into United Fruit and we were married in the fall. For our honeymoon he rented a huge open touring car and we went up to an inn in New Hampshire for a week. It was glorious riding around the countryside all bundled up looking at lakes and mountains, and the Belknap Inn was warm and comfortable and served excellent food. When Friday night came, Joe suddenly proposed we go down to see the Harvard-Yale game which was being played next day. So we rose very early on Saturday and started out. After a couple of hours on the road I saw he wasn't taking the proper route for Cambridge and I asked him if he knew the game was at Harvard that year. He said Nonsense! it was at New Haven. I was certain he was wrong. I urged him to stop along the road and pick up a newspaper. He refused. To make a long story short we arrived in New Haven a few minutes before kick-off time, only the game was being played in Cambridge!

Now you can believe me when I say that this is the story of our marriage in a nut shell. I don't mean he was always wrong. I do mean he had the habit of going off half-coked, and he never was so stubborn as when he *knew* he was in the wrong. The 1920s were a bad time for a poor Boston boy with that sort of attitude to get ahead in. As the years passed we suffered for it, let me tell you. I'm not going to tell you now though.

Don't get morbid about Millicent's passing away. She has pulled her load and God will see she gets a fair share in the after-life. Believe it or not, that is how He works, all opinions of smart-alec Harvard professors of philosophy to the contrary notwithstanding. You should get on your knees, my son, and pray for your poor, dying friend.

Your loving mother JWM

. . . 'Half-coked'? It sounded like a state of intoxication induced by drinking milk through which cooking gas had been bubbled. She must mean half-cocked. The only surviving picture of Joseph, so far as he knew, dated from about 1905 and showed a short sturdy youth with a Jimmy Cagney face, standing on an unpaved street in corduroy knickers and a shapeless cap holding up a fungo bat. But by 1920 Joe was hiring immense touring cars,

116

had written at least one minstrel show, and was motoring hundreds of miles to attend Harvard-Yale games without even the excuse of being any sort of college graduate. Maybe he had hoped to encounter the former drop-kicker in the stands and triumph over him. Would he have been wearing grey spats and a racoon coat and flourishing a slim, ivory-headed cane? What had he smoked? The boy with the bat looked destined for a life of tobacco chewing but the honeymooner in New Hampshire sounded like he would prefer long cigars purchased a box at a time from Ehrlich's. Who had Joseph McCormick admired and attempted to model himself upon in early manhood? George M. Cohan? He suddenly wished that Julia Ward Mack was better at supplying sensuous details and less concerned to bring the past to the bar of rational judgement. Take the stuff about going to the wrong football stadium. Maybe it was a key to something or other; yet if the old man had not decamped, leaving her (and him) high and dry, it would have been just another whimsical anecdote about the inevitable contretemps of honeymooners. However. At least the idea of Joseph Anthony McCormick, 1890—?, was a lot less wraith-like than before.

He put the letter away and went to pour himself a drink of bonded bourbon. While he was getting icecubes from the bag in the sink the hall door opened. Angelina Stratis came in, followed by a stocky swarthy man wearing a charcoal grey flannel suit, thick-soled shell cordovan shoes and a dark tie spotted with tiny red sailboats over a white button-down-collar shirt.

'Hello Angel,' McCormick said, taking their coats to the couch. 'What a nice surprise.'

'Dabroye vecher, Meals Ossipovitch. This is my Uncle Lou Doxiades, my mother's brother.'

The uncle smiled broadly, showing good white teeth as he extended his hand. 'Nice establishment you have here. Simple. In excellent taste.' He added, 'Don't think I'm

117

making a snap judgement. I've trained my eye to take in a setting in a flash.'

'Oh for Pete's sake, Lou. Spare Mr McCormick the routine until he knows you better.'

The uncle laughed indulgently while Angelina crossed the room and looked closely at Millicent's photograph. Then she knelt down with one hand holding onto a chair back and inclined her dark head. If the room had contained torches she would have taught them to burn bright. Doxiades had gone prowling off to have a closer look at the Piranesi Vatican. Now he came back. His prominent dark eyes followed the librarian's gaze.

'A beautiful kid,' he announced. 'And a genius. The sister and I are working on my brother-in-law to send her to the Sorbonne. Université de Paris.'

'What's the matter with Radcliffe?'

'An excellent school. Too close though. Old John'd want her to work in the family spa after classes. A fatal mistake. By the way, I admire your taste in coffins. A simple box of fitted pine planking. Right in the tradition.'

McCormick found himself beginning ever so slightly to goggle. Uncle Lou spoke with the easy assurance of a man who had powerful friends in the admissions office of both the institutions of higher learning mentioned, with the assurance as well of a leading trend-setter in the field of funerary equipment design. 'What tradition is that?' he asked cautiously.

'The tradition of the pilgrim fathers, of the New England village, of the Salem Clipper captains, of the Boston merchant princes.' His strong brown hands shaped a long rectangle in the air. 'Shall we call it the tradition of noble plainness?'

The last phrase issued from his lips as if newly minted. McCormick began to feel more cheerful than he had in some time. He hoped there would be many guests and that Uncle Lou would stick around to turn his self-trained eye on all of them.

118

'Look Lou—you don't mind if I call you Lou?—come have a drink,' he said, drawing him towards the card table. 'Not at all, Myles. Make mine bourbon on the stones.' He tilted up one of the wine bottles. 'Bull's Blood of Eger,' he read. 'Arresting. The exotic touch in the simple setting. It rings true.'

Angelina rejoined them and agreed to take a glass of wine and a cookie. Lou raised his whiskey tumbler and said, 'To the memory of the deceased,' and they all drank to it.

'Uncle Lou wants you to guess what he does. He's got that look.'

'Now Angelina!' He raised his hand in protest then turned his eyes expectantly on McCormick.

The librarian stared at Doxiades' richly fashioned neckware. A happy thought struck him. 'I've got it,' he exclaimed. 'You're Aristotle Onassis' man in the Boston shipping world.'

'Keen but incorrect. You make the inductive leap and land in the soup.'

'I know why he guessed that,' Angelina said.

'So do I,' a new voice struck in. 'It's that yacht club tie.' It was Eithne Gallagher. She had come in through the open door, leaving her coat on the railing in the hall. Tall and high-bosomed and wearing basic black with a double strand of pearls at the neck she looked every inch a queen. McCormick flushed with pleasure. He made introductions and went to get Eithne a glass of wine. She followed to the card table and said, 'I'm impressed. The flowers look lovely. And you've even got a sweet elderly man opening the door downstairs. Maybe you'll wake me some time.'

'Don't talk like that. And wait a second—' He rushed to the hall door and bellowed down the stairs, 'Prentiss? Please don't bother about letting people in. Come up and meet people.'

Eithne had gone to the coffin and was looking at Millicent's picture. She lifted up the wreath of gardenias, re-shaped it, and put it back. McCormick rejoined Uncle Lou and Angelina after pouring himself a fresh drink.

Lou said, 'That Mrs Gallagher, she's what I call to the manner born. Perfectly turned out.'

'She's very handsome,' said Angelina, a small beauty cutting a large one down to size. 'I've seen her around the library.'

'Where were we? I was trying to guess what you did, Lou. I think I give up.'

Lou rocked back on his heels and half-closed his eyes. 'What am I?' he interrogated himself sternly. 'I'll tell you what I am. I'm a close student of society in all its strange and fascinating forms.'

Angelina groaned, muttered something in demotic Greek or Lowell Institute Russian and walked off in Eithne's general direction. McCormick fetched the whis-key and freshened her uncle's drink. 'You Myles,' he continued, 'have inherited your position in society. You take it for granted. I am a Greek. I was born there, in Thessalonika. If I wish to join the Boston establishment I must analyse it, see what makes it tick. I'm not saying I want to but I am saying that the pleasure some people take in remaining buried in the hoipolloi, like John Stratis for instance, isn't for me.'

'But I have no position in Boston society,' McCormick expostulated. 'I'm Irish not Yankee. My grandfather was a teamster from County Cork. Not only was he non-U, he probably couldn't even pronounce that vowel sound' (Aroo from Cork? I am, aroo?).

Lou shook his head. 'Wake up, Myles, and claim your heritage. Society is change. What do you think has hap-pened since your grand-dad came here? Who at present is the upper-crust in this town? The Cabots certainly but who else? My lord Archbishop Cushing and the Kennedys. A Yankee-Irish blend. And of course it doesn't stop there. The door is open and the Italians are coming in, followed closely by the Armenians: the Colettis and Bragiottis, the Hagopians and the Hovanessians. The Albanians are next.'

'Come on, Lou. You're pulling my leg. There aren't any Albanians in Boston . . .'

'You'll be surprised what you find in Boston when you look around. You'll pardon me, Myles, but you don't understand society. Its nature is to accommodate, not to exclude. Look at Britain, study *Burke's Peerage*, read Debrett.'

'What about Jews and Negroes if it's so accommodating, huh?' McCormick asked.

'What about them? Haven't you heard of Arthur Fiedler and Ralph Bunche? Each group needs a bellwether. They lead, the rest follow.'

'Ha! In about ten thousand years time.'

'You're fighting me,' Lou said almost wistfully. 'Look. What is society anyway? It's a manner, a style, a tone, an inflection, a set of techniques. Master those techniques and it'll fall all over itself making room for you. Society is a push-over.'

He looked quickly around, moved closer and said in a hushed voice, 'Do you realize there are people in this town who give dinner parties where they dress up in eighteenth-century costumes with powdered wigs? I have an acquaintance, a chauffeur, who works for such people. They've had champagne, steak, *crêpe normande* and Gaelic coffee. They do minuets. About four a.m. Eddie enters from the kitchen, as previously arranged, to see if anyone needs driving home and discovers that a sexual frolic is under way. A dozen people, including the hostess, invite him to join in.'

And Eddie without a wig. 'Does he?—I mean did he?'

'Never!' said Lou, twitching his shoulders. 'Eddie is a married man. But you get my point, I'm sure.'

Was Lou's point simply that society was lonely and needed Eddie more than he apparently needed it, or was his point something larger? McCormick closed his eyes, picturing the races and nationalities of Greater Boston according to their conventional distinguishing traits: lean, sharp-nosed Yankee money-changers, olive-hued Salem Street beauties with flashing Neapolitan eyes, dark Levantine rug merchants from Newbury Street, perspiring raw-boned Irish police patrolmen of Achill Island antecedents, thin-legged, swivel-hipped coloured girls from Columbus Avenue, the stout inscrutable proprietor of the Green Dragon Restaurant in Chinatown—the whole bunch attired in powdered wigs and dancing a minuet while Lou Doxiades conducted an ensemble of Polish accordionists, Greek clarinetists, and ceilidh band tin whistle virtuosi by beating a long staff against a gleaming marble floor. Like heaven, it might be a desirable consummation and, like heaven, it didn't quite make sense.

Before he began to want to open his eyes he heard Lou say, 'I seem to have put my host to sleep. The name is Doxiades, sir,' and Prentiss saying nervously in reply, 'I own the building. Prentiss Beal is my name.' There was a brief, calculated silence, then Lou's voice resumed.

'Beal? You would be connected with the Beals of Dover. The large estate not too far from the Saltonstalls.'

McCormick's eyes flew open. Pink with excitement, and leaping from one foot to the other, Prentiss was beating lightly on the chest of Angelina's uncle.

'Not on your life the Dover Beals, Mr Doxiades. My family came from the west of England, around Plymouth, and the main American branch settled in Essex County, where was I born. I imagine that the Beals you mention —from Dover—are by no means parvenues, however.'

Lou struck himself on the forehead. 'It was there nagging at my mind all the time. The Beals of Plymouth, England, settled on the North Shore, in Essex County. What could I have been thinking of?'

Before the landlord could drag him off into a corner to go a little deeper into the question of pedigrees, Lou managed to swivel around facing his host. A large slow wink creased his right eye.

'Why don't you go get yourself a drink, Prentiss?' The librarian looked doubtfully at Doxiades. 'You shouldn't,' he said quietly. 'You'll just get him worked up to no avail. He was jailed years back for homosexuality and his family threw him out. All he's got is this house and a few Georgian candlesticks.'

'Fascinating. So he used to move in the weird woo set. An aristocratic failing. Maybe we can get him reinstated. Society always forgives, provided the black sheep makes his petition in proper form,' said Lou, following the landlord to the card table to renew his glass.

10 ~

Eithne and Angelina stood talking together in the middle of the room. Prentiss and Lou paced to and fro along the longer axis of the room, sipping their drinks and exchanging societal views. The wake ran on.

McCormick handed round some snacks then toured the flower vases, pulling up a reticent blossom here, thrusting back into line an occasional forward specimen there, abandoning the effort to sniff with the thought that most of the flowers were scentless and that he was not very fond of the odour of flowers indoors anyway. He went to the record player and hunted through a pile of LPs lying on a bookshelf beside it. 'The Best of Fats Waller' would certainly not do; perhaps something in the two-disc set of Bach Cantatas would. He turned the album over and scanned closely printed columns of commentary . . . 'the soul, prepared for flight into death, addresses the Creator'. It covered the case, broadly speaking: 'Ich habe genug' which was to say, 'My God, I have had it'.

The orchestral part and the organ continuo came up softly as he went forward to the coffin to fuss with the candles, and the male soloist entered on cue to express predictable sentiments according to a perfectly reasonable tonal, contrapuntal and theological scheme. And, how, nowadays, did the soul prepare for death? What

124

would Milly's soul have to say (or sing) to its Creator on the theme of cancer? 'Thank you very much, Sir, I had it coming to me'? How about 'Oh thou nasty Man, spreading death on the Belsen plan'? Or 'Nothing: A Non-Address to its Non-Creator from a Non-Soul'?

At graduation time she had faced the camera with an expression both wary and quizzical, with her head ducked down a little, with a side-long glance and a tight smile. That look was characteristic and familiar to anyone who had known her well. It made the rather third-rate Tremont Street commercial studio portrait a superior one of its kind. What could have been done for her to encourage her to exchange that look for a more open, confiding one? Nothing that he had known how to do. 'She has pulled her load,' indeed.

Momentarily distressed, he turned around, walked away from the coffin, and saw Barbara Lloyd, wearing the New England General blue cape over her white uniform, come in. She whispered that she could only stay a moment before going on duty at the hospital. He thanked her for coming. She went to the coffin and stood by it with her head bowed.

He went out on the landing and looked down the dimly lighted stairwell. Someone was plodding up the stairs. 'Only one more flight,' he called to a hunched figure in a dark suit, an open gaberdine topcoat and a narrow-brimmed hat. The man reached the top of the flight and turned towards him. 'Ronnie Davis!' he exclaimed. 'Aren't you supposed to be out in Cincinnati peddling brand-x booze to the coloured community?'

Davis, a mulatto with straight black Naragannsett Indian hair and a wide mouth, removed his hat and rubbed his forehead. 'National sales conference at the Statler this week,' he explained. 'Maybe we should do a line called brand-x at that and get those sons of bitches in the Nation of Islam off the wagon. How's the boy, Myles?'

Ronnie looked a good bit more gone around the eyes and generally than eighteen months before, when he had given the party in Cambridge at which Myles and Milly had met. But didn't they all? 'You look bushed. Come in and have a drink.'

Ronnie drank a long strong bourbon in two swallows. 'Much better. I had a tough night last night and the banquet lunch today didn't help any either.'

'How's business?'

'It's a bad business and it's good.' He nodded sadly towards the coffin. 'Gee. You and Milly. I didn't even know you knew her. And now she's dead. I read it in the paper this morning. Were you and she going to get married? She and I almost were engaged once. Anyway, I'm very very sorry.'

'We hadn't gotten that far,' McCormick said uneasily. 'What about your romantic life these days? I remember your girl at your party over in Cambridge, before you went west—she was working in an art gallery, wasn't she?'

Ronnie finished a second drink. He looked depressed. 'I married her and she turned out crazy. I mean certifiable. I thought she had a thing on me but it seems she had a thing on Negroes in general. A very unstable thing.' He seemed to shudder and then collected himself. 'We're divorced now.'

'I'm sorry.' He poured new drinks for himself and Ronnie.

'Such beautiful music. You always went for the classics, didn't you? Beethoven and Greek and all. I remember you in high school playing that flute solo. The kids laughed but you played all right.'

'I played Gluck that time,' McCormick said. 'It was too slow for the jive set. A lot of water under the bridge since then.'

'And a lot of strong drink. You teach, don't you?'

'I work in a library.' They walked side by side to the
126

coffin. He signalled goodbye to Nurse Lloyd as she passed them on her way to the door.

Ronnie studied the photograph. 'I'd almost forgotten she did nursing,' he mused. 'Useful work. You know, Myles, once she drove me out in the country and spent hours walking me around a big chicken ranch that belonged to some woman she knew. She thought I might prefer chicken farming to thinking up booze campaigns and hanging out with the black bourgeoisie. Can you beat that?'

'Were you taken with the idea at all?'

Ronnie closed his eyes and looked sick. 'Christ. Wading in that hen plop and me with a bad hangover. The idea was you could gross a dollar per year per bird if you broke your ass fifteen hours a day, seven days a week.'

'Not very challenging.' There seemed to be nothing more to say. Uncle Lou gave signs of being about to close in, but he was having difficulty pulling free of Prentiss. 'Are you going to the Harvard class reunion this year, Ronnie?'

'Are you?'

'I might go for the free lunch in the Yard,' McCormick lied.

'Maybe I'll make it myself this year. The firm may want me to transfer back to the New England district. It seems the local dipsomania rate south of Huntington Ave. is declining.'

McCormick remembered that Ronnie Davis always talked about his work in that bitter way. But if it was a bad business he should get out of it. On the other hand, if there was a valid argument that Negroes, like other sorts of people, drank a certain amount of whiskey anyway and you were entitled to make a living influencing them to drink your brand instead of your competitors', then he should stick to it if he wanted to, and stop feeling sorry for himself. 'I heard from somebody you got a full-page write-up in Bronze Tatler magazine,' he said rather spitefully.

Ronnie smiled rather plaintively. 'Don't mock me, Myles, not you.'

'I'm not mocking you. Look, if you hate your work, why don't you quit it?'

'And do what?'

'I don't know. You could always teach math like your old man. Or become a leader of your people—N.A.A.C.P. work. You might even like working in a library.'

Ronnie looked again at Milly's portrait. 'Is your work useful? What the hell are you up to anyway?'

'I don't know what I'm up to. Rather, I know sometimes but I keep forgetting.'

'You know what I think?' Ronnie said.

'What?'

'I think we're both in the shit.'

It was a depressing thought and quite possibly true. Uncle Lou had now moved within social range. McCormick said, 'Lou Doxiades. This is Ronnie Davis.'

'Swifty Davis,' Lou amended genially. 'Shall I ever forget that run-back from kick-off at the beginning of the Army game some years back? You must have covered ninety-yards. I forget how that game turned out.'

'We lost thirty-five to nothing and I was out for good after that one play with two bad knees. I've still got the bad knees,' Ronnie added, looking pleased to have been remembered.

The librarian slipped away and went to turn the cantata recording over. A gangling, weakly built man of about forty-five with bony knees, round glasses, a fresh complexion and hair the colour of wet cement came in accompanied by a tall, powerfully built Negro. The first man carried a bamboo swagger stick tucked up under his arm, and both were wearing kilts, military tunics, and Scottish caps with ribbons falling down behind.

'My God, Myles,' the white man brayed. 'What have you got in that box? What's going on here?'

McCormick noticed Prentiss Beal beginning to wring

128

his hands and took quick action. 'Stop bellowing, Frank,' he sternly enjoined. 'And I suggest you take your hat off. Milly died and you've blundered into her wake. Don't you read the papers?'

'Millicent died? How shocking! Why didn't you let me know? I *liked* that girl.' He removed his hat and threw it, along with the swagger stick, on a nearby chair. 'Uncover, adjutant,' he commanded. The Negro took off his hat and thrust it between two buttons of his tunic. 'This is my adjutant, Parkhurst,' Frank Meat explained. 'Stand at ease there, Parkhurst.'

'Yes sir. Thank you Captain Meat, sir,' Parkhurst said, moving his legs apart and joining his hands behind his back.

'How could I let you know when you've never given me your local address? Besides, I thought you knew everything happening everywhere all the time.'

Meat ignored these gibes and went pacing towards the coffin. Ronnie came over and said he would have to go. On the landing he said, 'I don't know about the field marshal but I do know something about Parkhurst. Keep an eye on him. He has a bad character in certain circles.'

'They were both in the same Canadian Army unit during the war. There's a bunch of them that like to get dressed up in those fancy costumes once a month and meet. Just another local veterans' group, only flashier dressed than most.'

Ronnie stared in disbelief. 'Are you kidding? Parkhurst's a veteran all right, but not of any wars where they wore uniforms.'

The librarian went back inside. Meat seemed to be introducing himself to Angelina, Lou and Eithne, who stood together looking collectively bemused. Prentiss had gone to the end of the room. He stood nervously tapping his fingers on the coffin lid and looking into the black night outside. Parkhurst was standing as before, at parade rest.

'I'm pleased to meet you, Mr Parkhurst,' McCormick said. 'Can I get you something to drink?'

'Wine, if you please, Chief.'

Wasn't 'Chief' supposed to be a rather hostile form of address when used by a coloured person in conversation with a white person? Perhaps it was, but it was certainly easier to take than 'varlet', 'shitbum' or 'you rotten social-chauvinist, you'.

After tasting, Parkhurst extended an arm and put the wine glass back on the table. 'Not my kind of wine, Chief,' he offered tonelessly.

Meat came near with Eithne, made a fuss about not being offered Scotch, then settled for a neat bourbon. McCormick freshened his own glass with more whiskey and new ice. Meat said, 'This has been a great shock to me, you understand that don't you, Myles? However, I recover quickly. I came to tell you that I've got it all fixed up with the membership committee of the Honourable Order of Boston Hibernians. We meet Monday and you'll be entered on the books, barring the unlikely black-ball, in time for the big St Patrick's Day spread.'

'What are you doing in an Irish club?' Eithne asked. 'Aren't you supposed to be Scotch or English or something?'

McCormick snickered. 'Something is right. He's the last of the Orient Heights Brahmins.'

'Ignore him, dear lady,' Meat said rather grandly. 'I hold the B.Litt. degree from Trinity College, Dublin, where I first met Myles when he was pretending to be a graduate student in Classics. The overwhelming majority of Honourable Hibernians are descended from Papist famine victims and bogmen. I try to supply the Order with a little Protestant Ascendency flavouring. A little leavening of the heavy Irish soda bread, as it were.'

Eithne was looking at Adjutant Parkhurst with interest. 'His uniform's very becoming, isn't it?' she whispered.

'Yes. But I wish he'd unbend a little. Get yourself some

more to eat and drink. There's something I want to ask Frank about him.' He led Meat apart from the others. 'Forget about HOBOH, Frank. I don't want to join this season—what with Milly's death and all. Now tell me about your little group of Highlanders. What actually are you up to if anything?'

Meat beamed and chuckled. 'Can you keep a secret, Myles?'

'Absolutely.'

'Well then, come here.' He bustled him to a position beside the impassive Parkhurst. 'Watch this,' he said confidently. 'Now Parkhurst, listen attentively. I'm going to put some questions to you.'

'Fire away, Captain,' Parkhurst said.

'Who was the father of our country and why?'

'Sir! Alexander Hamilton fathered the country because he best embodied the aristocratic ideals of the founding fathers and because he laid the foundations of a sound fiscal policy.'

'What is your opinion of FDR?'

'Sir! He was a traitor to his class, he practised unsound fiscal policy like NRA and the graduated income tax, at Yalta he was stoned out of his mind and delivered the fruits of victory to Russian communism.'

'Harry Truman?'

'Sir! He was soft on communism, a tool of the Missouri cracker bosses, and he hated the black man.'

'McCarthy?'

'Sir! Though misguided in his methods he was an old-fashioned American patriot alert to the dangers of creeping socialism and the communist conspiracy within the State Department and the Department of Defence.'

'Fulbright?'

'Sir! He hates the black man and is soft on the international communist conspiracy.'

'Is America properly a democracy?'

'Sir! Democracy is demagoguery. America is an old-fashioned Hamiltonian republic with justice for all and freedom for the best.'

'Who may aspire to enjoy the privileges of the best?'

'Sir! Any man, regardless of colour, may aspire to the privileges of the best so long as he is not soft on the international conspiracy of communists and so-called liberals practising unsound fiscal policy.'

'Jesus Christ!' McCormick ejaculated.

'Sir! Although he personally preached a form of creeping socialism, wiser heads prevailed in later times and made his religion suitable to the ideals of old-fashioned Hamiltonian republicanism.'

Meat caught sight of McCormick's face and dragged him towards the hall door talking rapidly. 'I can tell, you don't grasp it. Or else it seems fearfully low-level to you in your ivory tower. These men worship me. After a few more weeks of indoctrination each one will be assigned to infiltrate one of the major Negro civil rights organizations. Parkhurst will be seconded to N.A.A.C.P., another to the Urban League, and so forth. Their job will be to establish secret cells and study groups. My aim is to free the entire Negro civil rights movement from its bondage to Peiping, Moscow and Accra and bring it back into the mainstream of American conservatism. It might not sound to you like the greatest thing since Lincoln's Emancipation Proclamation, but we're going to grow and grow.'

'Why—'

'Why am I doing this? Because I'm directly descended from a distinguished Abolitionist family. We Meats have always loved the Black. That's God's truth, Myles.'

McCormick laughed briefly. To his own ears the laugh resembled a snarl. Raising his glass he proposed, 'Glory glory hallelujah.'

Meat's owl-face fell. 'You imagine my plan can't succeed.'

'I imagine your plan is . . . revolting. No . . . dippy. No! Fat-headed. I don't think it is. IT IS.'

The owl-face came nearer scowling. The scowling owl. 'When are you going to wake up out of your trance and see what is going on around you? Haven't you heard of the Montgomery bus boycott? Where do you suppose that man King is getting his money from?' Meat drew back. 'But you won't say anything, Myles?'

'I wouldn't insult an old blind wall by throwing such gibberish at it. Go away now, Frank. I'm tired and I want to close down this wake. Go away and play with your toy soldiers.'

Frank Meat soon left followed smartly by his adjutant. Prentiss had already slipped away unnoticed. Lou and Angelina said their goodbyes and when the librarian came back from showing them down the badly lighted stairs, Eithne had her coat on. He asked her to stay for a little while, until he got used to the idea of spending the rest of the night alone with a dead body. She sat on the couch and agreed to take a bourbon nightcap but kept her coat on. He joined her, groaning with fatigue as he sat down.

'You don't believe in ghosts, do you?' she asked.

'I want to—I've tried to—but I can't.' He looked at the rich curve of her thighs where the skirt of her overcoat fell open, put his arm along the back of the couch, took some drink and suddenly felt mustard keen. 'What did you think of my mourners?'

'Those highlanders—wow! Uncle Lou—wow!'

'What is this "wow"?'

'That was Angelina's comment on Mr Meat.'

He put his hand on her hair and she turned towards him. 'A cute kid that Angelina,' he said shakily and kissed her on the mouth.

'She's very bright too,' Eithne said and put her hand on his cheek. Then she stood up.

'Don't go away,' he said quickly.

133

'We're being watched.' She pointed to the picture of Millicent. Then she walked over and picked up the gardenia wreath.

'Take it, it suits you.'

'Just one if you don't mind.' She pulled a blossom free and put it in her dark hair on the side. 'Now how about my helping you clean up?'

'Not tonight. Milly won't mind the mess. At least she never used to. But since you're up, why don't you go in and rummage in the bottom of the bedroom dresser and bring out a little tin strongbox you'll find there. She put some sort of will in it.'

Eithne brought it out and set it on the couch between them. McCormick turned it and shook it, imagining a sort of woman who would put a flask of nitroglycerin in a flimsy green strongbox, lock it, throw away the key, and leave instructions that it should be broken into after her death. He put the box on the floor and aimed a sharp blow at the lock with the toe of his shoe.

'That did it,' Eithne said.

He put the box back on the couch. He wanted to hold her, involve her. He would hold her by involving her. 'Do me a favour, Eithne, you make the inventory.'

'All right, let's see . . . One diaphragm, not new, size 70.'

The librarian eyed it and put it away in his pocket. 'I guess that's what was rattling.'

'Item : a bill of sale for a rambler station wagon, model year 1952. Seller Millicent L. Rogers, buyer Myles McCormick. For the sum of one dollar.'

She had signed the paper, dated it, and indicated a place for the buyer to sign. There were similar bills of sale for her clothing, her record player and 'records miscellaneous', and for her old Raleigh bike, which had been stored in the cellar ever since they had moved over from Poplar Street. In order to become sole owner of her slender stock of possessions he merely had to sign his name four times and transfer four dollars from one pocket to the other.

Each bill of sale bore the same date, January 25. She had gone into the hospital on the morning of the 26th, driving herself there in her own car and leaving the car keys at the reception desk for him to pick up when he visited her.

'She was generous,' Eithne said.

'She didn't have any interest in owning things. Anyway, she had no one else to leave her stuff to,' he added gloomily.

'There's a letter. Dated January 26. "Dear Myles—" Shall I read it?'

'What else is there?'

'Nothing. A hair pin and an elastic band—broken. You'd better read the letter.'

He read it to himself:

Dear Myles,

This is the morning I go into the hospital and it's just possible I won't be coming back alive. If things work out you'll never see this. You've heard me mention my step-mother, Margarite, but you don't know I also have a half-brother. He's quite young—nine about —and his name is Gerard. I used to keep an eye on him but these past few months I haven't felt up to it.

You would be doing me a big favor if a week or two after reading this you would go down there and see if he is all right. I mean relatively all right. The situation is pretty unsavory but he is used to it more or less. Margarite likes him, at least she did the last time I was there.

The address is 9 Worthington St., Walpole. Directly opposite the house there is a tavern called the Nip-Inn. The owner knows my step-mother's ways and could fill you in on the set-up if you didn't want to walk in cold.

I'm due at the hospital before noon so will close.

As ever,
Milly

135

He passed the letter to Eithne. She read it through slowly. She said, 'What do you think?'

He thought that he was tired of playing the Good Samaritan of Rat's Alley. 'I think I'm tired of receiving letters and messages,' he answered. 'For tonight anyway.'

'Do you know what I think?'

'What?'

'It's a life-long involvement.'

'With what?'

'With her. You see how she signed off—"As ever".'

He stood up and began transferring used glasses from the card table into the sink.

'Well isn't it?' she persisted.

'Milly Rogers goes into the fire at the crematorium tomorrow around ten a.m. I guess that answers your question.'

'Oh no it doesn't,' Eithne said.

II ◇

Eithne was a Philadelphian, from Bala Cynwyd, and her father, a second-generation American named O'Malley, now ran the automotive accessories department of the main Philadelphia Sears Roebuck. He had always worked for that company. Her mother, a Pennsylvania German from the Perkiomen Valley, chose the name Eithne thinking it Welsh and therefore in keeping with the pidgin-Welsh designations of several of the city's more prosperous suburbs. The father was Catholic, although not devout, and the mother Lutheran. Each kept to his and her own faith but the children were brought up Catholic. For the older brother, Andrew, now an attorney practising in Harrisburg, religion had remained important. Eithne had drifted out of the Church during her second year at the University of Pennsylvania, about the time she began going out with Jimmy Gallagher, an architectural student from Germantown. Gallagher had dropped religion altogether after exposing himself to a course of sceptical reading in cheap editions of Hume, Gibbon, Santayana and Dewey during the summer before he entered Penn.

At the university she had studied English and Fine Arts and had thought about becoming a reporter or a teacher, until she reached an understanding with her boy friend that they would get married immediately after graduation. Gallagher was the top student in architecture of his year, regularly carrying off whatever honours and prizes were offered at each level of the course. Beyond architecture he was interested in landscape design, urban and regional planning, and economics and sociology insofar as these disciplines entered into problems of design and planning. As she became more identified with her fiancé's ambitions and began to understand something of what he and his friends were talking about when they rang the changes on 'Le Corbu', 'Mies', 'Ebenezer Howard', 'Sert', and 'Grope', her interest in English and Fine Arts declined somewhat. In her third year she took an elective course in elementary architectural design given by the School of Architecture and did poorly at it. She was able to handle the drawing part all right but discovered she had little aptitude for imagining in terms of three-dimensional space.

In her last year she took a lecture course in the history of urban planning. This went much better. She found she could imagine and define the historical, social and economic relations which the look and shapes of a town, a neighbourhood, an industrial clutter like nearby Camden, concretely expressed. Cities ceased to be mere heaps and congelations, became complex orders of ideas, exposed through the centuries to modifications caused by measurable phenomena such as population growth, foreign invasion, technological and industrial development, famine, plague and prosperity. The planner, who in former times might have been a Chinese emperor, a French archbishop or a Lombard master builder, always sought to impose a controlling idea of order for reasons that varied: for self-glorification or the greater glory of God; for increase of business or to increase the sum total of human happiness. And the city, recalcitrant and unpredictable, perpetually fought back to resist, overwhelm and render nugatory the controlling idea.

The planner's weapons were rationality and a vision of the future. The city's strength lay in its vast energy and in the immense pressure of immediate human need which it brought to bear upon the urban plan. Since the Industrial Revolution this 'dialogue', as the lecturer oddly named it, had become more agitated, as the factor of energy and the pressure of need increased geometrically with the growth of urban populations and industrial power. But in the twentieth century the planners, by learning to develop complex compromises between long-range goals and immediate pressures, had begun to make the factor of energy work for instead of against them.

The great aim of modern planning was design of the total human environment, provision of an ultimate space where everybody could enjoy the good life to the limit of his capacity for wholesome happiness. Planning, then, was not only more important than mere architecture but also more important than mere statesmanship and the captaining of big industry. For the planner reached all people where they lived and worked, where they actually had their being during their short span of years on earth. And only the planner was working directly to create the better life which all men wanted for themselves, their children and their children's children. Or so the youthful and enthusiastic lecturer insisted in the opening and closing lectures of the course.

When Eithne took walks around Philadelphia, stopping to look at a new parking garage, bowladrome, shopping centre, or jumping back onto the kerbstone of a new roadway as a hot-rod full of leather-jacketed J.D.'s went roaring past with a skull-and-crossbones pennon streaming from the radio aerial, she found it hard sometimes to share the lecturer's enthusiasm. For instance, here a company had bought an old business building, demolished it, erected a thirty-storey office block of steel and glass, and moved in. The Planning Board inspected plans, issued a permission, made an alteration on the Centre City Master Plan and then sat back to wait for the next proposal.

Anyway, that was how it seemed. Perhaps the new Urban Renewal legislation would change things.

Meanwhile, she found her own reason to get excited about City Planning. Looking at slides, drawings and maps of old and young cities for her course work she began to see cities as works of art of a unique kind. They were works of art that changed. They opened backwards into the past and forward into the future. The city was buildings, thoroughfares, parks, precincts, neighbourhoods, but it was also inhabitants. So that these works of art, unlike any other kind she knew of, were alive; not merely set over against life and representing it as with a painting or a poem, but inhabited by flesh-and-blood creatures—the young and the old, the poor and the rich, the sick and the well, plus dogs, cats and a minority of more unusual animals. Moreover, the inhabitants were a part of the city's form and not merely its content. Cities could die by losing their inhabitants; those of the Mayans, and the desert city of Petra in Asia Minor, had done just that, dying into shapely architecture, which was another art altogether from the art of the city. Or they could settle into a more or less fixed form, like Siena or Annapolis. These museum cities, where the citizens probably went on tiptoe, spoke *sotto voce*, and breathed with some of the diminished vigour of an elderly gallery attendant, held their appeal, but it was precisely that of the museum. She felt that if cities were immense, populated works of art that changed, then the greatest cities must be the greatest changers. New York, London, and Chicago seemed to support her ideas with some specific evidence.

At graduation Jimmy Gallagher surprised no one by walking off with the Hicks Travelling Fellowship, which provided enough money to support one person during a full year abroad. The day after graduation he and Eithne were married at Philadelphia City Hall. When they returned from a brief honeymoon and architectural tour in New York they successfully fought off the suggestion of

140

Mr O'Malley and the senior Gallaghers that they repeat the ceremony at a Catholic rectory in Germantown where the priests, Mr Gallagher averred, would not ask any searching questions about religious belief. In the end, after all four parents had grumbled and Mrs O'Malley had fretted about not having the fun of planning a proper wedding for an only daughter, they got up a purse of fifteen hundred dollars among them and settled it on the young couple in lieu of the usual catered affair. Eithne and Jimmy sailed tourist class on a Holland-America liner bound for Rotterdam in the last week of June, determined to make the most of their year abroad.

As it happened, the one year stretched into four, even though they began with so little money and used up the marriage present in an initial glorious summer of touring Europe on a Vespa motor scooter, from the cities of northwestern Europe to Venice and Milan in the south, and as far east as Warsaw. That fall they holed up in London, taking a cheap flat in The Cut, near Waterloo Station, and furnishing it from several second-hand furniture stores along their own street. Jimmy was not supposed to work, according to the terms of his fellowship, but he managed to pick up extra money on the sly free-lancing for the New Details department of a London architectural journal with offices in Birdcage Walk.

Eithne wanted to work too but did not know how to begin looking for the sort of teaching or library job she felt she had been half-trained to do. Then a young housewife living one landing down, whose husband covered minor sports for *The Observer*, suggested she visit a Citizen's Advice Bureau to see whether she would run into any problems over labour permits. The young woman at the Bureau saw no difficulty in that direction and went on to offer her work as an interviewer in an East End branch of the same agency. She would have to learn the London welfare set-up and enough general information about English law to make intelligent referrals but it was all down in the handbooks and the shortage of educated people in this work was acute.

On and off Eithne spent about a year and a half as an interviewer in an Advice Bureau in Stepney. She worked about twenty hours a week. A majority of the problems concerned evictions, alcoholism, juvenile delinquency, deserting parents and hire-purchase debt. Jimmy kidded her that her Philadelphia background helped her to spot professional litigants swiftly. She did not delude herself that she was acquiring profound knowledge of the intimate lives of the London poor; yet it pleased her that after the first few months she could do her job about as efficiently as the native born interviewers. She loved London more than she had ever loved Philadelphia; because it had more flavour and variety; because it had more of a past and more of a future; because it had more achievement and more hope; because it was a wonderfully complicated work of art that teemed and changed. Even after four years she was not able to pretend that she knew the city well, but without the eighteen months of commuting to Stepney her sense of London would not have included much to the east of St Paul's apart from the Whitechapel Gallery and the Old Friends Chinese Restaurant. Stepney had given her among other things the Yiddish Art Theatre on Mile End Road, the bomb sites where derelicts drank methylated spirits and sometimes died of exposure in the freezing mid-winter drizzle, and the people—of all ages, races and dispositions—who came in for advice. These acquisitions were scarcely beautiful in themselves. They were, nevertheless, a part of what she meant when she said to herself that London was beautiful.

At the end of his first year abroad Gallagher won a Fulbright scholarship for the study of advanced architectural design and planning at London University. At the end of this year at the university his design thesis for a graduate degree, consisting of plans for a projected overflow airport in the Midlands, passed with high distinction.

142

One of the external examiners, a senior architect in the Planning Department of the London County Council, liked his thesis well enough to offer him a good job in his own office. And an American firm doing contract work for the U.S. Air Force bases in East Anglia asked him to consider coming to work for them. Without hesitation he chose the L.C.C. He wanted to see for himself whether the practice of design in an atmosphere free from commercial pressures, and where there was regular consultation between planner and architect, was as effective in producing good design as several of the London lecturers claimed it was.

He was given work developing new design schemes for primary and secondary schools. Over a period of two years a number of his ideas were adopted, with modifications, and were incorporated in the building of a dozen or more school buildings in the London area. He was reasonably well paid, his creative flair was freely admitted and respected by the people he worked with, but in the long run it was frustrating never to get a building all one's own to carry through from drawing board to on-site supervision. He began to think about going into private practice. And since the quality of creative practice in American firms which did contemporary work seemed to him superior to that of their English counterparts, he began to think about returning to the United States.

During their last two years in London the Gallaghers rented a centrally heated maisonette in a modern development in Highgate. After Eithne herself went to work for the L.C.C., doing interviewing and research for the Council Housing Department, they began to put money in the bank. Their friends tended to be young architects and social workers and their wives. They would meet them in the pub and exchange occasional dinner invitations with them. For a young married couple their lives were probably more routinized than either would have tolerated in the States. But living abroad made a distinct difference. When even small experiences and fleeting impressions were full of novel disclosures and unfamiliar perspectives, routine itself held an element of adventure.

Just the same, when the decision to go home was taken, Eithne felt herself suddenly relax. She asked herself whether she had been trying too hard to be a good American visitor abroad, and whether English people on the whole gave a damn for the difference between the good and the other kind. She wondered what her friends in Philadelphia were doing with their lives and fired off half a dozen letters announcing their return. She and Jimmy talked about starting a baby. A few weeks before sailing day they liquidated most of their savings and bought a car, their first, to bring back with them.

Full of hope, filled with premature nostalgia over the loss of London, and burdened with a good deal more luggage than they had brought to Europe four years before, Eithne took the boat train to Southampton. In order to reach the French Line pier before the noon deadline for receiving automobiles Jimmy had set out very early that same morning with the tiny car loaded with the few pieces of their furniture that seemed worth bringing home. In the departure shed on the pier she changed some English money into francs, saw her luggage being moved to the deck of the cabin class tender, and began to look around through the crowds for her husband. She was unable to find him.

After a half hour she asked her way to the company offices and went in to explain her dilemma and seek advice. She was immediately shown to an inner office where an elderly police officer was sitting drinking tea and was left alone with him. Calmly, kindly, and looking at her steadily the whole time, he explained how things stood. There had been an accident. On the narrow bridge over the Thames at Staines, a few miles outside London, early in the morning when traffic was still light, a London-bound lorry heavily loaded with steel girders had gone out

144

of control and swerved across the road when a chain snapped and the load shifted. The lorry had toppled on its side, pinning a small car in the west-bound lane against the bridge railing. Perhaps it would have been better if the car had broken through the railing and gone into the river, for as it was, two of the girders had slid down from the top of the load and crushed it.

Eithne had asked, 'Is my husband dead?' The officer had nodded without looking away and said, 'Yes. He is.' She remembered saying 'Thank you' and declining his offer of a cup of tea. . . .

'On the very day you would have sailed,' McCormick said. 'You weren't spared very much, were you?'

'Not an awful lot,' she agreed. 'One of the papers was running an anti-accident campaign at the time. They featured it on the front page. They said that blood dripped down onto the back of a swan swimming in the river. My Jimmy.'

The waiter came over to sweep crumbs from the cleared table with a loosely rolled napkin. She bent her head. 'How about a brandy?' McCormick asked.

'All right.'

'Two XOs please.'

'Snifters, sir?'

'No.'

He put his hand on one of hers. 'So then you came back by yourself and did the Planning course in the Penn. grad. school. How long did that take?'

'Nearly three years once I got started. At first I lived with his parents.'

'Taking that up as a profession was a way of keeping the connection with him alive, wasn't it?'

'I didn't think of it that way. It's something I always would have wanted to do if the chance came up—not that I'm very good at it. But I expect you're right.'

The waiter brought the brandies and retired into a dim

corner of the nearly deserted dining-room where a second waiter was eating a late snack of what sounded at this distance like Spaghetti Bolognese. She pushed a lock of hair back from her forehead and picked up her drink. 'And it isn't that much of a profession anyway. Just a lot of different people doing various things—from master plans to sewage system analyses. I've been lucky in this job—getting to do the old maps and asking people in the condemned neighbourhoods how they feel about being moved out.'

'When I lived on Poplar Street there was an old Jewish lady who lived five floors up. She used to lower her market basket at the end of a rope. There would be money in it and an order for the corner delicatessen. Sooner or later somebody came along and did her shopping for her. I wonder what she felt when they moved her out.'

'Did you ever think how she felt about living five steep flights up in a fire trap with no elevator? The point is, districts do decay. Urban renewal is a very old idea and a good one. But you mustn't start clearing away without taking a good long look at what's there and at what was there before that, for as far back as the record goes. Otherwise it isn't going to be any good. You can't just push people aside, or push the past aside.'

'I certainly believe that,' McCormick said. She sat in silence for a while, looking absorbed in her own thoughts, tilting the tiny glass so that the liquor caught the light from changing angles. Was she thinking about her daily work or communing with her dead?

At last he said, 'Forgive me, Eithne, but I just can't understand why, after all these years, you're still on your own. You're very beautiful. Everything about you is rich and vital. You're not odd like Millicent was and you've got a nice disposition. I thought happily married people who lost a spouse tended to remarry easily and quickly. I mean they would know that the person they lost would have wanted them to be happy and lead a full life.'

She flushed and took her hands from the table. 'How can I explain? . . . Look. We had a wonderful life in England. There was so much to do and see and talk over. He was absorbed in his work, and his talent was growing over every month we spent there. He was going to be a great architect. Everyone knew it. A boy from Germantown! Have you ever seen Germantown? It's the absolute negation of architecture. Well, anyway. We knew London wasn't going to last forever. So we put a lot of things off. In a way we were saving it up for when we went back. We knew we loved each other. The time flew by and we both thought we could afford to postpone a lot of what *that* meant. Because we had all the time in the world. And suddenly all the time was gone.'

She put her hands up against her face, covering her eyes, and McCormick stared fascinated at the wide gold band on the third finger of her left hand. 'That's too high-flown. You probably don't know what I mean. It's really quite simple. For instance, putting off having a baby. Not lying in bed late. We almost never did that. There was so much to get up for and there was going to be so much time later on when we could relax and love each other.'

He felt all the blood drain from his face at the thought of a late lie in bed with Eithne. He said, 'I do know what you mean. I think I know something about the consequences of putting things off. I think he'd want you to start enjoying some of the experiences you and he never got around to—including lying late in bed with someone who loved you. I mean after all this time.'

She struck her breast with her clenched hand. 'He had such joy and intensity. He poured it into his work. Of course I've had to do with men since then, but I still feel I'm cheating him. *He* had the talent. I should have been the one to drive that car to Southampton.'

He remained silent, reflecting. The genuineness of her grief was beyond question; yet he wondered at the self-punishing trend of her last remarks and of the gesture which accompanied them. Sidney Beispiel would have made short and nasty work of these cues—grief equals guilt equals suppressed envy equals infantile penis envy or some other equally puerile equation—but the trouble with Sidney's system—of what in former Pilchard Clinic days McCormick had labelled the psycho-bicker viewpoint—was that it made insufficient allowance for faith, hope and charity. This woman inspired the first two and certainly was in no need of the last. He said, 'You ought to try and work some of that joy and intensity back into your own life. That's all you can do for Jimmy Gallagher now.'

She looked across the table, smiling faintly. 'It's hard to do by yourself.'

'You know you don't have to do it by yourself. Now how about coming back to my place for a nightcap? I want you to listen to Fats Waller playing the "B Flat Blues" and then an old New Orleans version of "I've Got a New Baby" by Tommy Ladnier and Sidney Bechet. It's full of pain and joy and discipline and excess.'

'All right. But what about *your* obligations to the dead?'

'What? I told you. There's nothing left except an urn full of ashes.'

'I was thinking of the little boy.'

He started. 'You mean Gerard. I've been waiting for the spring weather to get settled. It's sort of a long drive down there and I haven't got a driver's license. Let me get your coat.'

12 §

Mr Joe Walter, proprietor of the Nip-Inn, sat at a round table eating cube steak and french fries. He said, 'The last of the Rogerses—the best.'

'It's rotten she had to die, but there's this boy named Gerard?'

'Gerard's only a half-Rogers. The first wife died. Then old man Rogers met Margarite while Millicent was up in Boston at nursing school. Immediately he married Margarite he started to fall apart. Pretty soon he died and Gerard was born.'

'What happened to him? Did he drink too?'

'No he didn't drink.'

'So he just died like anybody might.'

Walter's face twisted oddly. 'Look. The guy was a thirty-third degree Mason and almost a C.P.A. A man like that when he marries a woman like Margarite might just as well go buy a pistol and stick it in his mouth.' He pushed back his chair and plate, took out a cigarette without removing the pack from his pants pocket, lighted it and blew smoke at the dingy ceiling.

'I'll tell you about Margarite,' Walter continued. 'This is a pretty dull place. She is a subject people around here never get to the end of.' He interrupted himself to call out to the bar waitress, Lucille, for a Calvados and ginger. After she had come and gone, squatly and silently, he

149

resumed. 'Margarite is French. She speaks languages. She used to be married to a professor at a college in France and then she ran away with a professor at a college in Indiana. She says the second professor ruined her. He knew all about witchcraft and black magic and he practised it on her, or so she claims.'

'This is all new to me. I'm mainly interested in how she gets along with the boy though.'

Walter waved his cigarette impatiently. 'As I was saying. Margarite's the worst boozer for a woman I ever saw and I've seen plenty. She can sit lapping it up in her kitchen for a week straight with her hair a mess and her tits hanging out of her wrap. And at the end of that week she'll get a little sleep, take a bath, go get a facial and her hair fixed. She'll come out of the house all dolled up and taxi straight into town for a date at the Parker House Restaurant. You would see her there talking French or ginzo with some big spender in from South America and you wouldn't know what to make of her.'

Without ever having glimpsed her speaking languages at the Parker House McCormick didn't know what to make of her. 'She has quite a following among South Americans?'

Walter laughed hard and briefly. 'That Margarite. She fixed it up so she's honorary consul for some crummy banana republic. So she gets about a dozen big nights on the town for free every year.'

'Lots of vitality. I mean she has.'

The proprietor of the Nip-Inn looked dubious. 'In her time, sure. Lately she's been going downhill a bit. Rebuilding the house since the fire took it out of her.'

'What fire?'

Walter drank from his glass, squeezed out a belch by pressing hard against his stomach with both forearms, and said, 'Some months back the house went up like a torch one night. The engine company came quick and got her out but both storeys on the front were a write-off. Maybe Milly never heard about it. Margarite was passed out so she didn't know about it herself until the next day.'

'What about Gerard?' This grimly.

'He sleeps in the back part where the fire didn't get.'

'I bet she started that fire!' McCormick said agitatedly.

'Uh uh. She knows what she's doing. You might just say all heavy drinkers are a bad risk for fire insurance. I should know, I'm in the business. What do you expect to do about Gerard, if you don't mind me asking?'

'I have no plans. Milly simply asked me to take a look and size things up.'

He grunted. 'Well, go and have a look then. A lot of people around here have their eye on the situation. One more can't hurt.'

'Or help either you mean? Everybody watches but nobody does anything?'

Walter shrugged inexpressively. 'What's to do? Margarite has money, or at least she still has a few parcels of real estate. Nobody could ever handle her, not even Milly. Of course there's this lady living around here who keeps mentioning getting a court order and having Gerard put in a home.'

'Christ!'

'Don't worry. If it came to a fight between Margarite and the whole town I'd put money on Margarite.'

'Does that mean you're on her side?'

'There aren't any sides. Look, I run a boozer. For years she took half my late night business. My regulars'd hang in here a while and then go across the street and kick the gong around in Margarite's house until the small hours. Did I resent it? Sure! So after a while I started going across the street myself after I closed up. We had some wild times, let me tell you, until lately when she started going downhill.'

'No more open house?'

'Only once in a while. It used to be four or five times a

week.' He stood up, apparently to suggest that the interview was over.

McCormick rose and extended his hand. 'Thanks. You've given me a pretty complete picture.'

'Not at all,' Walter said, shaking hands. 'You'd be surprised what I didn't tell you.'

The front of 9 Worthington Street, a new white-painted neo-colonial house of medium size, separated from its nearest neighbours by the width of an empty house lot on either side, was dark, but light was shining through the drawn blind of a window next to a side entrance on the right. McCormick pressed the side entrance bell, heard the sound of a chair being pushed back inside the house and waited for the door to open. Soon it did open but only a few inches. She had it on the burglar chain. A deep, possibly feminine voice asked thickly, 'What do you want?'

'I was a friend of Millicent's. I just happened to be driving by when I remembered her brother and step-mother lived around here,' he improvised. The door began to close slowly. He found himself wishing it would close all the way. But she was only releasing the chain. She swayed in the dark entrance, a stocky figure clutching a wrap to her neck. He gave his name.

'Mi-les—the soldier. Weren't you the man she was living with?'

'We lived with each other.'

She invited him in. He followed her through an inner door into a large, newly equipped kitchen where the air was faintly redolent of old wood smoke, charred timbers and new plaster and watched her sit down heavily at a table covered with blistered white paint. She was strongly built, with thick ankles and wrists, but the puffy, subliminally bruised look of the flesh on her arms and face, and the filmy eyes, betrayed the habitual female drinker. Her only astounding feature was her hair—white, wiry and streaming outward from her scalp in all directions to form a Medusa halo. On the table in front of her was a heavily scored racing form and a half-empty quart of ale. Under her chair was stored a case containing eight more unopened quarts.

She looked at him side-long out of little piggy eyes. He pitied the local make-up artist and wig-maker who would have to prepare her for her next triumphant appearance at the Parker House. But at least her teeth were good, if in fact they were hers. The old bawd.

'I'm sorry for Millicent,' she muttered. 'I was always sorry for her. But we were an impossible combination she and I.'

'Two women under the same roof . . . trouble,' the librarian murmured. 'An old Chinese proverb. Also extant in Algonquin, Finno-Ugrian and all the western tongues. Certainly there's no harm in people who don't get along keeping a certain distance between them. My own mother chooses to live in Florida. And we don't even have the excuse of hating each other. I mean we half get along, sort of,' he finished in a rage of qualification.

'What is all this about harm? You look pretty harmless to me, young man.'

'Don't bet on it. I'm vicious when aroused.'

She grinned lewdly. 'Sit down then, soldier boy. You can have some of my ale but I have nothing stronger in the house.' He sat down opposite her with alacrity. She lifted a quart bottle from her cache and slid it across the table along with an opener. Evidently there were to be no glasses.

She was still grinning. 'Tell me, Mr McCormick, am I very much like your mother?'

'You are her exact anti-type.'

'You like that?'

While drinking off about an imperial half-pint the librarian considered. Licking foam from his lips he said, 'On Freud's view I should and I shouldn't. The old

ambivalence. Anyway I like this conversation. So far.'
'You're very exact. *Vous êtes écossais, n'est-ce pas?*
The conscientious Scot.'
'American-*Irlandais*, actually. And please don't say it's
the *même chose*.'
'Ah, so exacting. I like exacting men.'
The way she said it and the loll of her head conjured
up a preposterous vision of a moustachioed hussar, booted
and spurred but otherwise unencumbered with garments,
flourishing a whip over something soft and squealing
chained to a silken bed. Throw me a life-buoy Kraft, I'm
ebbing. 'That's not the same thing either,' he said firmly.
She leaned forward, stabbing two thick fingers in his
direction. 'Millicent told you I'm vicious and have no
conscience. I think she didn't tell you how a very wicked
man practised on me with black magic and vile spells
until he killed my conscience.'
If there had been a flute at hand he would have asked
her to say it again and blown an obligato accompaniment
in six flats. But he was not prepared to hear her reminiscences about the Indiana satanist. Steer her off that. Why?
St Francis or Prince Myshkin—or any of the Nip-Inn
regulars—would have listened. Oozily, the latter boozily,
oozing compassion. In former times listening rapt in
Pilchard Clinic to the afflicted yachtsman-poet while they
both waited for the Hour to strike. Superb technical
details about reaching to windward near Boston Light,
mixed with sad psychotic stuff about a wizard lighthouse
keeper on the Reef of Norman's Woe who operated a
black beam that was poisoning his blood. Onset of stam-
mer, mental storm furrowing the tanned brow. Then the
strangulated voice: 'Christ! What are patterns for?'
Again and again. Impossible to look away from that vor-
tex. A difference. He afflicted, trying. She afflicting, lolling
at beery ease. Her uncovering story a cover-up story. Important to be sure. He was sure. Although somewhat
under the influence of drink she didn't convince as some-
154

one under a spell. French Margarite was a woman possibly pretty once, with a roving eye and a swift leg under her. She had made the most of her immoral opportunities in her day and now was come nearly to the end of them. To business.

'Milly said almost nothing about you, but she did let me know at the end that she had a brother she was fond of.'

'My son Gerard, her half-brother only. What do you want to do with him, librarian? Read him a book?'

Ignore sudden hostility and it may suddenly go away. 'Maybe I could take him out once in a while. To the zoo or a Red Sox game. I have the idea that Millicent used to take him around a bit.'

She produced a look that was simultaneously calculating and suggestive in a near-prurient way. 'And would you have in mind taking him out and keeping him with you overnight?'

'Nothing like that,' he said drily. 'On a Saturday when the weather was sunny we might spend a few hours looking at things. I grew up without a father myself and I think I'd have enjoyed a few excursions with an adult man—even with a librarian. Sort of pre-Boy Scouts.'

'These scout masters—sometimes they are very naughty, isn't that so?' Discouraged, he remained silent, thinking that if she persisted in this line he would have to give the project up. She drank from her bottle, ran a knuckle along her mouth and said, 'I think you *are* harmless. You liked Millicent and now you want to do something for her little brother. And why not? Gerard certainly needs something, that's a fact. I expect you're lonely these days—like me.'

'Not really,' he said quickly. 'Nowadays my life seems to open out in all directions. I'm constantly surprised.'

'Be that as it may—*quoi qu'il en soit*—what an extraordinary expression!—you'll have to decide between you if you can get along. I'll call him down from his room if he hasn't fallen asleep yet.'

The librarian sat in new, acute embarrassment while she slip-slopped down the hall next to the kitchen and called up to her son. What was it the little maid, Penny, had shrieked in *Gone with the Wind*? 'I don' know nothin' 'bout babies, Miz Scahlett!' Or words to that effect. At least the kid oughtn't to be staggered at the sight of a strange man in his mother's kitchen.

Gerard seemed very thin for his build. His mouth and nose were like Millicent's but his black straight hair and sallow Alpine complexion were perhaps from the mother's side. Smiling largely, she plumped herself down and set him on her lap. His bare feet almost touched the floor and the bones of his ankles jutted sharply beneath his pyjama bottoms. 'What do you think of my little Belsen beauty?' she asked almost gleefully.

'Hello, Gerard,' McCormick said.

The child did not respond to the greeting. His glance roved the room, taking in everything except the guest and finally fixing on his mother's ale bottle. 'Give me a drink of ale, Mum,' he said.

She lifted the bottle and tilted it into his mouth like a weaning cup. After he had taken a couple of swallows she pulled it away. 'He's very wicked, don't you think, Mr McCormick? At his age to want ale? He smokes. He eats mayonnaise and sugar by the tablespoon and he won't eat salads and vegetables.'

'A hard case,' McCormick remarked, catching Gerard's eye for the first time.

The boy's remote smile seemed to indicate that he had been through this routine with his mother's night callers before. His teeth were in a shocking state with black decay showing along both gum lines and between all the front teeth. If things worked out something must be done in the dental department. Perhaps a swift detour to Forsythe Infirmary in the course of a wander through the Fenway museums or on the way to the ball park. Gerard with gleaming teeth, his frame filled out, smartly dressed

156

for a modest cash outlay at Filene's Basement. The boy looked bright if strange. Pilchard or the Judge Baker Clinic could be enlisted for psychiatric refurbishing. What then? A hardship scholarship to Shady Hill followed by Harvard on the McCormick Scholarship and the now-compulsory European tour. Infinite horizons. 'Uncle Myles, sir, I've been thinking of medical school.' 'Sure son, with your *summa* degree it's a push-over. What'll it be: Zürich, Padua or Physicians & Surgeons in Dublin? Your sister would have been proud of you.' What about Margarite? Maybe she'd disappear south of the border with a ginzo-speaking coffee planter. Or let herself be persuaded to surrender her interest in her son for drinking money after she ran through the real estate. McCormick felt wildly excited and struggled not to show it.

She put her son back on his feet and said, 'Mr McCormick wants to make your acquaintance, Gerard. Show him the house or take him upstairs. I need to be alone while I finish handicapping tomorrow's races. By the way, Mr Librarian, have you any tips?'

'Not my sport, I'm afraid.' Her eye wandering towards a cabinet under the sink. Probably her store of hard stuff. Blandly he exited after the boy.

Gerard was pointing at a room off the hall on the left. 'The new dining-room.' He looked in and saw it was empty.

'Your mother hasn't gotten the new furniture yet?'

'She bought it but it hasn't come.'

Mounting some stairs behind Gerard he asked him if he liked school and got no answer. On the second floor he saw where the new construction joined the older part of the house and said, 'Did the fire frighten you?'

Gerard stopped and turned around. 'I screamed and screamed. Some girls said it's chicken to scream. Do you think so?'

'No. You were smart to scream. What happened then?'

'I jumped out the window in the snow. Those girls said

it was brave to do that without a parachute. The girls around here are dumb. A parachute wouldn't open.'

McCormick swallowed hard. 'I guess you were smart to jump. You might have gotten smoke poisoning even if you didn't get burnt. Was there a lot of smoke?'

Gerard, who seemed to be pondering something, did not answer the question. He said, 'I want to talk some more about screaming.'

'What about it?'

He took a big breath. 'My house is sometimes very noisy. In the kitchen mostly. It wakes me up and I scream.'

'You mean you call out for your mother.'

'No no no. When the noise is very loud I scream that loud. When it's not so loud I don't scream so loud. So nobody hears me. I like it that way.'

McCormick thought about it. 'I can see that. When you make your own noise, other people's noises can't bother you. It's cozier that way. But of course when you're in real trouble you want to scream loud. You know all about that.'

'I do,' Gerard agreed. 'Can you tell me a story about screaming for help? I bet you can.'

'Certainly I can. Listen, Gerard. Many years ago I was having fun swimming off a dock in front of a beautiful hotel on a big lake in Italy. The place was called Malcesine. This German lady swam far out and then in again and the water was very cold and very deep right up to the dock. And she got a leg cramp about five yards from the ladder. In feet how much is five yards?'

'Fifteen.'

'Right. You're a smart kid. Now there were lots of people lying on the dock in their bathing suits and this lady looked at them and she was too shy to call out about her trouble.'

'She thought they didn't like her?'

'No. She was simply too polite to make a disturbance.

158

She was ashamed to be in trouble! Can you imagine it? And listen to this. Those people on the dock were watching her closely and they all knew from her face that something terrible was happening. And not one of them jumped in or even asked her if she was all right. Because they were afraid of making a disturbance too. So she started going down, quietly, in the deep water, only a man was swimming by and he caught her and dragged her to the ladder. *Then* lots of people jumped up and helped him lift her up, because she had fainted.'

'You have to cry or faint or something before anybody helps you.'

McCormick sighed. 'It shouldn't be that way but it often is. Anyway, people always come when you yell.'

'Not everybody,' Gerard said with an inscrutable smile. 'I know somebody who would never come. If Armand was on that dock he'd put his foot on the lady's head and push her down.'

'Who's Armand?'

'He's my half-brother, Professor Darling's son. He's all grown up because he's twenty-one. Armand doesn't live here any more.'

The librarian received this information with a certain amount of scepticism. Milly had never gotten around to mentioning an Armand. Still, she hadn't gotten around to mentioning Gerard either, until pretty late in the day. And Gerard, for the moment, seemed real enough standing there with his thumbs hooked into the waist of his pyjama pants and his shoulder blades projecting through his undershirt like vestigial wing bones. 'Tell me about him,' he suggested warily.

'His room's down there.' The boy pointed down the older corridor to a closed door at the end. 'And my room's here.' He walked half-way down the corridor and stood against a closed door on the right. 'For a long time he played a mean trick on me. He pretended I wasn't there.'

159

It was a new twist. A fantasy brother who refused to believe in the existence of the real brother. 'You mean he wouldn't talk to you.'

'He walked on me.'

'What! I don't get it, Gerard. What did your brother do?'

'Well, he would come out of that room and walk along this hall, and if I came out of this room or if I was out in the hall fooling around he would walk through me. Just as if I wasn't visible. I would try and go back in my room. Sometimes I ran down to the kitchen. Once I fell down and he walked right over me. It didn't hurt but it made me feel queer.'

McCormick didn't believe him. 'Why would this Armand do such a thing?' he asked.

'He caught me looking at some things in his room. Do you want to see those things?'

'Yes indeed.'

They went into the room at the end of the corridor and Gerard switched on the light. He vanished into a deep closet and re-emerged carrying a large flag furled around a standard and a painting in a home-made frame. The picture had been executed in oils. The colours were harsh, the modelling inept. It showed a male figure clad in Wehrmacht uniform and wearing S.S. insignia complete with swastika armband goosestepping into a flaming sunset or sunrise, one arm raised rather woodenly in the Nazi salute. The flag, unfurled, revealed a large white circle on a field of red and within the circle a large black swastika.

McCormick sat down heavily on the stripped bed and drew his hand across his eyes.

Gerard said, 'He was mostly mad about me reading his diary. He took that away with him on his motorcycle.'

'Oh,' the librarian said faintly.

'It was just poems—about car accidents and people called Hebes and Kikes—stuff like that.'

160

'You know, Gerard, I don't think I want to hear any more about Armand right now.'

The child was looking at him intently. 'Why did you visit me?' he asked.

'I was Millicent's friend. She asked me to look you up and say hello.'

'Milly's dead now.'

'Yes. She was a nice girl—your good sister.'

'My good half-sister,' Gerard amended. 'I have to tell you about Milly and Armand. Let me. I told her he walked on me. She yelled at him. She said, "Get out of my father's house, Armand. Get out or I'll put you behind bars." And you know what he said?'

'No. What?'

'He said "Nigger-fucker".'

McCormick felt bad. He was afraid he might cry. That would not be a good idea just now. 'Did he go away then?'

'No. But after a while my mother told him to go and he went. To the land of Dixie.'

'Down South.'

'Yes. Sewannee. He would sing about those places. He has a nice voice. And a little moustache.'

McCormick got up then and returned the National Socialist memorabilia to the closet. He said, 'Your sister and I had a lot of fun together—just kicking around when we were off work. I thought maybe you'd like to come out with me some Saturday morning when the weather was good. We could go for a drive or climb the Blue Hills or anything we wanted to. How does that sound?'

Gerard looked troubled. 'I don't like to go away from this place much. Didn't my sister tell you?'

McCormick was taken aback. On reflection he discarded the idea that the boy didn't trust him. When you thought about it, Gerard's agoraphobia was natural, even predictable. He felt safer here harbouring in the ruins of middle-class respectability than out there where an Armand might be lurking with a Lüger or an invisibility ray, where a good half-sister like Millicent got done to death by cancer. Power, and therefore a wretched kind of security, lay with the bawdy, beat-up mother. She had survived, and it was on her say-so that the Hitler youth had cleared off to make a dark career in the sunny South-land. Where had all the fathers gone? Silently he cursed the whole idle, whinging, perpetually receding vague lot of them.

'Your mother thinks it might be a good thing if you got off with me once in a while. What do you say we try it once anyway—not right away but a few weeks from now? If you don't like it much we'll forget about it.' He hoped he had kept the wheedling note out of his voice.

Gerard Rogers yawned nervously and bent down to pick at his bare feet. He said, 'All right. Not now but a few weeks from now.'

13 ✇

May came. He had three balls in the air, he decided, with no obscene intention. They just might turn out to be indian clubs—heavy skull-bashing ones. First, and always, Eithne. He believed he was in love with her and wanted to marry her. Second, Gerard. He wanted to rescue him from horrors. Third, Panayot Petkov's position as Head of the Rare Books Room. He wanted it.

At or near apogee, these objects whirled midway between the dazzle of overhead lights and the stage apron, and the task was to coax them down and into nimble hands without committing a stumble. Followed? A nifty bow to torrents of self-applause, a quick trot out of stage door, the apotheosis of a vast, fortunate future. Possibly something less. Because when you came down to it vaudeville was dead.

He had gone over there to Pinkney Street one evening after dawdling the streets of Beacon Hill trying without much success to contrive the perfect excuse for turning up on her doorstep so soon after the movie excursion of the night before. Maybe she'd like to come out for a drink or a meal, or simply a stroll through lilac-fragrant night air in the Public Gardens. And maybe, sadly, she wouldn't. Eithne was at home but dressed to go out in a green ball gown of lustrous silken stuff with her hair done up by professional hands into fluent dark waves and ripples. Standing before her mirror making delicate pats and passes at the waves on top and at the back she explained that the occasion was the annual formal dinner dance of a local Planners' Association. Her white neck and shoulders seemed to flower from a green living sheath and he was stricken with recognition that a very large part of her life—the people she knew, the places she went—was led well outside his knowledge and control.

Her telephone rang. Masking the intentions of a spy under the manner of a faithful friend he leaped to answer it. Could Mrs Gallagher accept a personal call from Mr and Mrs Gallagher in Philadelphia? She could indeed and did. Was there anything in particular? No, nothing in particular—just that they'd been sitting around talking about her and wondering how she was getting along in funny old Boston. The apartment? The job? Was she having any fun? And, by the way, Jack had.dropped in, was there now in fact. Somehow when Jack visited their thoughts and talk had a way of centering on Eithne. Ha Ha! And wouldn't she like to have a chat with Jack before they rang off?

When Mrs Gallagher's ear-daunting tones were replaced by a low masculine murmuring that was never intelligible to the casual sitter-by, McCormick's ears, and eyes, went out on stalks. Eithne smiled, blushed, glanced sideways, tapped her foot and then looked into a blind corner.

Yes. Yes. No. Oh nothing like that, Jack. Of course she would write again soon. Busy? Yes, pretty busy. She liked it yes—pretty well. About New York at the end of the month—she'd still have to see. Things had a way of coming up. She would write. Yes indeed she liked his letters! By the way, how wonderful the latest promotion. Where he found time to lecture as well at Temple Law in the evenings was a mystery. Torts was an odd word. She must look it up. Yes, right away. Tomorrow. All right.

164

maybe even later this very evening. No he mustn't say that, although she didn't mind in the least his thinking it. No never. Always. And would he put Daddy Gallagher on now to say hello and good night? Good night.

When her cab came McCormick saw her into it downstairs and walked slowly home. Halfway to Phillips he saw with perfect clarity that Jack, a corporation lawyer from her husband's old University of Pennsylvania crowd, who had pursued her with dog-like devotion for several years, was not the real problem—no matter how many rendezvous in New York he proposed or how vigorously the mother-in-law continued to thrust him into her path. Eithne was beautiful, clever and humane, and the world was full of Jacks and super-Jacks looking for a woman with those qualities. Until now she had withheld herself, grieving over her dead lover and burying herself in work that was, whatever functional autonomy it had acquired over the years, a tribute to Jimmy G.'s shaping influence on her. Yet it was inconceivable that she should continue withholding herself forever, or even for very much longer. There for him the great danger and, equally, a great opportunity lay.

Going on with the rumination, carefully, it seemed to work like this. She thought him feckless and aimless, and, therefore, no threat to her present equilibrium. Where she burned incense to an idol in a little locked room he didn't enter or seem to want to. During the past few weeks they had been to bed together several times, always in his apartment and never in hers. In her lovemaking she was friendly, playful and altogether remote with respect to her deeper feelings. Each time afterwards he had wanted to knock his head on the floor worshipfully before her, or at least tell her how lucky he counted himself. Instead he had played it cool, friendly and frolicsome, suspecting that at the first hint of anything more serious she would begin to feel like a thief again and soon send him packing. The trouble was, Eithne was a serious person. Sooner or later she would fall in with a nice man of aim, ambition and accomplishment and realize it was time to come out of that little room, lock it up for good and throw away the key. Once that happened she would not look back. Or maybe she would look back for a few moments and say, 'Thanks, Myles, for helping me through a dreary time with your aimless little chats and walks, your feck-less little love-making. Goodbye now and take care of yourself. Men like you, dear, should never marry. Like father like son.'

The librarian gasped and sank to the curb of West Cedar Street with his back up against the cool flutings of an iron lamp post. He could not settle for that. He wanted her. Even if he couldn't make her completely happy again he wanted her. Without Eithne the life he had led up to now made no sense. With her it made the perfect sense of having led up to her. Without her the future wasn't worth sticking around for. He had known too many people, especially in Ireland and the trans-Mississippi mid-West, who went on living just to see what would happen next; more accurately, just to see what would fail to happen next. Thanks a lot but no thanks.

And so, over the next few days, he evolved a plan. She liked him now for his undemanding aimlessness and reserved her deeper admiration for men of constructive ambition and humane aim, men like Jimmy G. Very well then. He would arrange it so she came to realize, appar-ently all on her own, that he, Myles McCormick, was just the kind of man, deep down, that she admired, and that the air of fecklessness, even paltriness, he wore was a mere superficial aspect. Seeing this she might just take it on herself to reveal to him his own deeper potentialities and in the process find she had fallen for him. Wheels within wheels.

He got up from the curb and walked on. The Gerard project would serve to dramatize his humane purposes, and an active campaign for the Rare Books Headship was going to have to make do to suggest his underlying drive for recognition in the world of ambitious men. Unfortunately, she knew the library well enough to know it didn't lie in that world. Nevertheless, she had seen at first hand what a mess the Rare Books department was in and she might imagine he was responding to a Toynbeean 'challenge' rather than volunteering to preside over the decline of the West, culture-wise. At the very least it was a permanent job with a fat salary and largely undefined duties, and whoever went into that chair was going to look big when measured against the man about to creep out of it.

The great thing was to keep a light bantering tone while involving her attention in the details of both enterprises. He had already struck that precise note in describing Gerard's plight, mainly from shock and to keep her from thinking that Milly's peculiar legacy meant all that much to him. She had been shocked too and had shown it. She kept calling Margarite a middle-class delinquent and kept wanting to know when he was going back down there and take little Gerard out for the day. It would be soon. On a perfect May Saturday he planned to entrap Eithne into coming out with them both, to the woods, or the mountains or the water. Under bright skies and after eating and drinking up a luxuriant box lunch prepared by Slymyles, she would warm to the kid and then remember, with a little touch of tachycardia, a small enchantment of the heart, that it was high time she resumed thinking about a family of her own. Gerard would wander off along some shore or path and he would pour out to her his love along with the information that prospects for the Headship were looking well indeed.

Yet were they looking well indeed? Were they even visible? It was time to get working on that, especially since Dr Petkov had recently begun to pull a slow fade from even his minimal responsibilities, only showing up a couple of days each week and then tarrying just long enough to snarl at the Chester A. Arthur portrait and scatter his voluminous notes and drafts for the official biography all over the glassed-in enclosure.

McCormick commenced his canvass by speaking to Sarge Kearsarge, the First Assistant of Rare Books and his own immediate boss. According to library lore she had loved Dr Petkov all her life and might even have spent an illicit weekend with him at the New Ocean House in Swampscott some twenty-five years earlier. Clearly she would take a direct personal interest in the question of the succession. Miss Kearsarge was all for Assistant McCormick, as it turned out. Not only had she found his biographical notes on heretofore neglected members of the Hartford Wits literary circle, which had appeared in the spring issue of the *Bulletin*, extremely suggestive, but also she positively dreaded what a new Head recruited from outside the library was going to think of them all. If only Helen White hadn't taken French leave like that—although to judge from the state of her desk she hadn't been doing a blessed thing for several weeks before quitting. And what was Personnel doing about filling the vacancy, even though you had to admit that girls with Helen's knowledge of Old Romance tongues (and with other points in her favour too, McCormick mused) didn't grow on trees? As for their not giving the Doctor another young assistant so he could finish the biography before retiring, or at least get it in shape to go on with at home after retiring, why she called it sheer treachery, that's what she called it. So often nowadays she felt like quitting herself, but at her age what other library would take her?

Miss Kearsarge was sure the doctor would favour the McCormick candidacy, but she was also quite sure that the present was no time to approach him about it when he was so distracted and saddened by his treatment at the hands of the Director, Pillsbury Pinkham. As for what else one might do, she really didn't know. She supposed he would have to wait with his fingers crossed until fall

168

and pray they didn't advertise the vacancy in the professional journals.

McCormick promptly relayed this discouraging appraisal of possibilities to the Chief of Cat. & Class. 'For an intelligent woman Dorothy Kearsarge is an utter fool,' Roberta said. 'Her only way of getting by is to let people step all over her. That's been the trouble with this institution for years. Too many doormats and boot-scrapers, and mostly female ones.'

'Be my campaign manager,' McCormick urged. 'I want that job so badly I can taste it. Tell me what to do.'

Her bleak gaze swept the long room like a beam from a battered, indomitable lighthouse. 'In the first place stay away from Dr Petkov. His endorsement would be the kiss of death.'

'I'd figured that.'

She was silent a moment, considering. 'Here's how it shapes up,' she then began in a voice pitched just low enough to prevent any of her staff from picking up juicy grist for the library gossip mill. 'Points in your favour. You're about the right age and you're well enough educated by our standards. And you're masculine. Traditionally that appointment goes to a man and there's a terrific shortage of men in library work these days. Most important, you're already working up here. You've got your foot in the door.'

'Hot dog! What about points against?'

She grinned and he braced himself. 'Only this. It's a very fine position in its way. If this were any other large library in the country there'd be some absolutely first-class people after it. Now don't get sore but you'd never strike a real librarian as someone with a real calling for library work. However, here that isn't even to your disadvantage.'

'I guess I strike you all as exiled royalty,' he said peevishly. 'Do you realize I've done eighty-eight main cards on your wretched collection of Ukrainian chants in my

169

spare time? And what do you mean it isn't to my disadvantage?'

'Shh. I mean the job is entirely at that man Pinkham's disposal. And he can't tell a librarian from an orthodontist. Do you know he expects me to rename my department the Inventory Control Division B? But don't get me started on him. Anyway, most of the men on the present board of trustees are as ignorant as he is. I predict they'll rubber stamp any candidate he puts up.'

'So if I'm going to get anywhere I'll have to storm the Director's Room.'

'Exactly. And the sooner the better. Try to see him this week before he sneaks off on another speaking tour. Meantime I can go on talking you up a moderate amount to the other department chiefs. Most of them don't know you and that's in your favour too. Because when you're well known and well liked by five influential people in the B.F.L. five others will hate you just to keep things evened up and slowed down. In any case the endorsement of the heads of main departments won't count for much with that silver-haired idiot on the fourth floor.'

There was an opening in the murk up ahead and daylight shone through it. Exercising suavity and guile he would storm the Director's Room on the fourth floor. 'You're the best, Roberta Colley,' he said enthusiastically. 'If you'd gone into public life you'd have been another Madame Perkins.'

'Flattery will get you nowhere,' she said astringently, and sent him back to the Vari-type keyboard to sweat out more *Kafizma Blazhen Muzh* cards in pidgin Ukrainian until five o'clock.

14 ⌀

Thinking it over later and recalling several junctures at which the interview had veered towards disaster, McCormick tentatively concluded that it had been successful in the bitch goddess, or perhaps more accurately in the bastard god, sense. Pillsbury Pinkham had begun by prosing about theirs being a service industry and how you never knew where executive talent was apt to surface in the pyramid. He also had a good deal to say, probably in oblique reference to Dr Petkov's fancy business cards, about the need to put team loyalty ahead of personal ambition without any sacrifice of self-starting initiative. Then he withdrew behind his long teak desk, which was constructed in the modern drawerless manner and was quite bare except for an intercom box, three telephones, a pile of illustrated brochures and a brown folder, put on an immense pair of black-rimmed glasses, opened the folder and said, 'Before we talk turkey about your future in the library let's check out the personal data file from Personnel. Their records are very inadequate but we're about to reorganize that department.'

McCormick sank deeper into the cushions of a large couch placed at right angles to the front of the desk, inspected his well-polished, newly half-soled shell cordovan shoes for previously unremarked deposits of courtyard pigeon plop and said, 'I'll be glad to fill in any gaps.'

'Let's see. You interrupted your university studies to go in the army. Which way did you go? Europe or the Pacific?'

'Well actually I only went to North Carolina. It was a small Army Medical Corps field hospital undergoing basic training as a unit in the foothills of the Smoky Mountains. They call it the Piedmont down there. Certain bugs developed and before they were straightened out the war ended. Both wars, that is.'

Pinkham's boyishly unlined face looked patriotically pained. 'Bugs? What kind of bugs?'

'Well. The commanding officer, Dr Koski, was very enthusiastic about vocational aptitude tests. He kept on giving the men batteries of these tests and getting conflicting results. So he would just keep moving us around from job to job and asking Headquarters Command for more training time. After a while they took away all his physicians. About the time I got transferred for discharge there was a rumour going around that they were going to court-martial him on a charge of crypto-pacifism. I guess with the war ended they let it go. Personally, I thought he was a very nice man. After the doctors left he used to handle Sick Call himself and he was always very kind. For instance, he had a theory that malingering was a form of mental illness that could only be cured by giving the man extended home leave. I used to clerk for him and make out the furlough orders.'

'Good God! He sounds like a nut or a subversive. Of course in those days vocational aptitude tests were still in the pre-scientific stage. So after the army you finished up at Harvard and went to do graduate work in Classics at a place called Trinity College, Dublin. But you didn't get an advanced degree there. Why not?'

'That's sort of hard to explain too. You see I went there on the G.I. Bill of Rights and there was a mix-up back in the States about the monthly checks. Anyway, none came for the first six months or so and then they all came in a bunch. After I'd paid my debts and gotten my Liddell & Scott Greek dictionary out of pawn I didn't have any more money and another Trinity bill was due. So the Registrar advised me to disenroll myself and come to classes as an auditor. But when I disenrolled myself no more G.I. Bill checks came. So I had to get a job and this made it difficult to come to classes regularly. It was sort of a vicious circle.'

'What about this job you had in Dublin? There's nothing here on the form about it.'

McCormick gestured vaguely. 'It hardly seemed worth putting down. A man named Dunphy had a small nationalist newspaper called the *Crumlin Clarion*. He hired me to write book reviews and to correct the English of his editorials. The paper was mostly editorials.'

Pinkham shook his head and looked avuncular. 'I'm afraid you're wrong about that, Mr McCormick. Experience as a journalist in a foreign country is definitely worth mentioning. Don't hide your light under a bushel. Now fill me in on this nationalist approach. It wasn't Red or anything like that, was it?'

'Not at all.' McCormick hesitated. 'You understand I only did book reviews?'

'You said that.'

'Well, let me see. He wanted a military expedition to the North to liberate the six Unionist counties. He wanted the Republican government to cancel its subsidies to all secondary and primary schools that wouldn't limit their athletic programmes to games approved by the Gaelic Athletic Association—you know, hurling and Gaelic football for the boys, camogie and step-dancing for the girls. Also, he wanted the government to confiscate all land owned by English nationals and give it to Irish-speaking farmers from the Gaeltacht. And a few other things like that. When he started an anti-semitic series of editorials, I resigned the job and went to France.'

The Director's facial muscles seemed to be stiffening

173

beneath their camouflage coat of executive tan. Was it distaste or merely an effort to suppress a rising yawn? McCormick put himself under stern orders not to panic.

'This Dunphy fella' sounds like a nut too,' Pinkham said sourly. 'What sort of salary did he pay you?'

'He didn't actually pay me a salary. He gave me a free bed and breakfast in his house in Crumlin and sometimes he handed me a couple of pounds when he wasn't broke himself. Also, I used to sell the review copies down along the Dublin quays.'

After that there was nothing to do except to get on to the years in France and England as quickly as possible. Here things went much better. Pinkham professed to see the point of spending two years teaching English in provincial French lycées as a way of picking up a lot of French and the further point of spending a year and a half teaching French in a London business college as a way of capitalizing on the lonely dismal months in Autun and Toulouse. But the sun really began to shine when they came to the two and a half years he had spent as a textbook publisher's representative in the Middle West. Interrupting the flow of personal data the Director remarked that he had several squash partners in the publishing game who were convinced nowadays that the best men for the editorial staff were those who had proved themselves by successful selling in the field. They didn't want a bunch of long-haired, down-at-heel reading addicts, they wanted men who could read a balance sheet and then turn around and estimate at a glance whether a new manuscript had what it takes as an item of merchandise in a highly competitive business characterized by sky-rocketing costs and diminishing profit margins per unit of sales.

McCormick thought he saw his opportunity and took it without a backward glance at grieving conscience. 'I agree with them,' he lied. 'Furthermore, I think the same attitude could pay big dividends in the library field.'

174

'You're darn right!' the Director said, pulling excitedly at one of his big fleshy earlobes. 'People come into library work because they want to *read*! That's got to be stopped. The professional library schools have accomplished miracles recently in upgrading standards, but you still get the little guy with stains on his necktie who goes off in a corner with a book and snarls at the public when he should be saying "At your service, sir." As I said only a few weeks past at the Mid-Atlantic A.L.A. convention, the library of the future will consist of book technicians and book promoters. Library management will speak the language of business management and share the same objectives: to raise the Gross National Product and strengthen our Free Enterprise system. We don't want any more goofy little guys hiding in corners while the customer hunts in vain for mislaid copies of *U.S. News and World Report* and the *Kiplinger Newsletter*. We don't want any more bums coming in out of the rain to study terrorist literature in well heated well lighted Reading Rooms. We must never forget that Karl Marx got his start in the British Museum Reading Room. I'd like to see that fact engraved on every Library School diploma.'

The trouble with Pisser Pinkham, McCormick reflected, was that the man didn't know when he was already home and dry. Because if old Karl had had to rely on the services of the B.F.L. Reading Room as they now stood he would have succumbed to senile dementia long before acquiring even a smattering of the learning upon which he had erected an ideology. Don't rock the boat, P. P.

The Director was looking at him keenly. 'And yet,' he said emphatically, standing up and resting his knuckles on his desk, 'and yet,'

'And yet what? Mr Pinkham.'

'And yet when I mentally review your record— Harvard, graduate study and book reviewing in Dublin, school teaching in France and London, book promotion in the Midwest, followed by your very successful work here for Miss Colley and apparently up in Rare Books as well—something is missing.'

What was missing? Did Pinkham know about the six months he had spent hustling bitter and mild at the Bull & Mouth public house in Holborn after getting fired from the business college for always coming to classes late? That tool, Watson-Smith from East 11, had turned him in to old Smathers. And just because Watson-Smith had overheard him putting in glottal stops and cockney elisions in conversation class one day and had thought he was mocking his French accent. He hadn't been mocking him at all. The typist girls needed to know how their French would sound to a Frenchman if their pronunciations were ever going to improve. At ease! Pinkham couldn't possibly know.

'What's missing?' he queried cautiously.

'Inevitability! Aim! Pattern! Focus! Strictly speaking, what does your career up to now amount to? Just one damned thing after another as the fella' said. Suppose I turned your personal data file over to our management consultant team and asked them to extrapolate a prediction of what you'll be doing five years from now? Would they ever predict you for Head of Rare Books? Not a chance. They might give you some points for all-roundedness but they certainly wouldn't give you a point for consolidation of career gains and aim achievement. I doubt they'd want to predict anything at all about your future.'

Who wanted them to predict his future? They should leave that to gypsies, ju-ju priests and tea-leaf readers, people who had, after all, pursued the work for centuries and had acquired along the way a certain amount of skill, discretion and humility. He looked down at the deep-pile, wall-to-wall beige carpet and smouldered inwardly.

Pinkham chuckled.

Funny guy. You mother you.

'Come on, McCormick,' the Director said softly. 'That slot in Rare Books has to be filled by someone. Come on and talk me into it. Somehow I feel we talk the same language.'

It was a crux. The man was inviting him to join him in his nightmare of executive nomenclature. He must try to do it—for Eithne and for Tiny Tim down in Walpole. It shouldn't be any more difficult than diving headfirst and open mouthed into a barrel of rotten eggs.

'Of course we talk the same language,' he said forcefully, 'even if our intonations are a little different.' Whatever that meant. 'Consider, Mr Pinkham, only a few years ago you were the vice-president of a tire company. What management consultant firm would have projected you then for the Directorship of the B.F.L.? Yet here you are and thank God! Do you know what you are as a library man? You're what the personnel boys call nowadays a late bloomer. Do you know what I am? The same. We're both born librarians—new style—only we weren't born knowing it. So we both kicked around until we knew the score. And then we found our way into this library where practically nobody appointed before you came knows the score.'

'Keep it up, McCormick. Don't fail yourself now,' Pinkham chanted with a wide smile.

McCormick rose from the couch and paced forwards with his left hand grasping his coat lapel and his right forearm riding the top of his rump behind. 'When you came here you found a certain amount of chaos—the good old-fashioned chaos of the good old-fashioned library —and you resolved to build an order, an organization. You are building the organization step by step. An organization to process books and an organization to promote books. What is the present state of Rare Books within the larger organizational picture? It's a pocket of chaos

177

and a pocket of resistance. Now I know, Mr Pinkham, that new books and the newer library services—film strips, micro-printing, a computerized reference service and automated book shelving systems—are of greater moment to you than those old books upstairs with which I happen to be associated. Nevertheless, I believe you also realize that there is no way, barring a fire on the fifth floor, of getting rid of those old books. Nor can you ever succeed in sealing off that department—that festering pocket of chaos—from the rest of the library.'

'Does Dr Petkov claim I've been trying to seal him off? He should have his head examined!'

'Never mind what Dr Petkov says,' McCormick resumed with a graceful flickering sweep of his forward hand. 'Let's assume—let's pretend!—that he's a distinguished scholar of the old school and has had his day. What you now need is a man who can put the old books in order and bring the Room into line with your major organizational objectives. I seriously believe I'm that man. Give me just six months as acting Head, with no strings attached, and I'll improve the technical services a thousand-fold. I'll win back four times over the special reading public who used to avail themselves of our public facilities. Much more important, I can show you right now how one part of our work in Rare Books, under my direction, can be re-shaped to strengthen the library's image and your image as well, locally, nationally and internationally.'

Pillsbury Pinkham came around the end of his desk, sauntered across the carpet and laid himself full-length on the long couch. He crossed his ankles, trailed one hand to the floor and said, almost drowsily, 'Quite a lot of money goes with that job. A man could live very well. Now skip the technical stuff. I've got assistants who can check that out. I want to hear about the image.'

The fish was in the net and the gaff was at hand: his long-meditated scheme for jazzing up the *Bulletin*. Years

178

hence he would confess to the man, over brandy snifters in the Hotel Bellevue bar or coming off the squash courts, that he had reminded him lying there for all the world of— Of what? Of a basking shark.

He spoke to the Director about the B.F.L. quarterly *Bulletin* as seductively and winsomely as he knew how. It was expensive to produce although handsomely endowed. The meagre subscription list and constantly declining number of requests for article offprints showed that its current standing in the scholarly world was abysmally low. It was, however, a going concern in an inflationary era when costs of launching a new periodical were prohibitive. What then should be done about the *Bulletin*? Now he would tell him.

At moderate initial cost, soon to be recouped from advertising revenue and a rapidly expanding circulation, it should be completely redesigned, renamed the B.F.L. *Review* and issued monthly in glossy magazine format. The *Review* would publish articles of broad interest on the arts, politics, culture. It would contain deep think pieces on, say, new trends in corporate management and the defense establishment. From time to time they would run a column from congenial correspondents abroad in the major cities of Europe. There would be an ample section of book and record reviews emphasizing publications of current interest and each issue would include deft and witty graphic illustrations, which could be prepared at trifling cost by some of their own people in the Graphic Arts Department. Finally, each and every month some eight pages or so, averaging three closely printed columns per page would be set aside for a feature entitled 'From the Director's Desk'. Here Mr Pinkham would be able to describe his current activities, his plans for the B.F.L. and for the library field generally, reprint his speeches, reminisce, comment and inform. It would be a feature comparable to 'The Easy Chair' in *Harper's* or 'The Conning Tower' in *Newsweek*.

179

As Rare Books Head and *Review* editor he, McCormick, would undertake the workaday editorial tasks, including the lining up of a distinguished roster of free-lance writers, arranging for newstand distribution, foreign sales, etc. Otherwise he would keep out of sight, leaving the Director full say and free play in issuing his opinions and policies. As the magazine made its way forward, swiftly finding its inevitable place somewhere between the old *Dial* and the present *Atlantic*, the library's image and the image of its management would go forward also—locally, nationally and internationally—into a bright new era.

McCormick fell silent and wiped the sweat from his forehead with an unsteady hand. He had shot his bolt. Pinkham uncrossed his ankles and sat up looking thoughtful. Then he looked at his watch and said in a voice of utter sincerity, 'Mr McCormick, this has been one of the most rewarding discussions it's ever been my privilege to hold with a member of my staff.'

'About the job,' McCormick quavered.

'Give me two weeks. The southern people seem to want to hear me again on the theme of library service modernization in the light of technological change in a free society. When I land in Baton Rouge tomorrow evening it'll be my thirty-ninth set-down of the current year.'

'Maybe I could do something further on this project while you're away,' McCormick said. 'Like getting up some figures on costs for this type of magazine. On my own time of course.'

'You can do something. I want you to file a memo with my secretary, Miss Jennings. Go all out in describing your plans for improving the Rare Books services and for the *Review* but don't exceed two pages double-spaced. Then come and see me again in two weeks.' The Director extended his hand and said, 'Don't hesitate to address me as P. P. Roger?'

'Roger Ack-Ack, P. P.,' McCormick said.

15 ᴑ

He found Gerard in the kitchen of the house on 9 Worthington Street sweeping up broken bottles and glassware with short, inexpert strokes of a corn broom. Some of the linoleum tiles in the new floor had risen up. The broom kept snagging the lifted edges of the tiles and sending debris under them.

'Let me finish that. The workmen who laid this floor didn't do a good job. Your mother should make them come back and do it right.'

The boy leaned against the sink with his hands in his pockets. McCormick swept up several dustpan loads of breakage and deposited them in a bin. 'I guess last night was one of the noisy nights,' he said.

'Yes. My mother had the Daily Double. She's asleep now.'

'Why don't we just let her sleep? I already spoke to her on the phone yesterday about this trip. There'll be one other person going with us.'

'Oh, that's all right,' the boy said politely, shifting his eyes from one part of the floor to another while he picked up a red sweater from the kitchen counter and tied it around his waist by the arms. 'She won't wake up till night-time, not even if you went up and yelled in her ear.'

It was about ten-thirty when they reached Pinkney

Street. Eithne had already come down and was sitting on the front steps of her apartment house. She wore a green head-scarf, a milky grey jersey pullover above a white blouse, a khaki cotton skirt, white socks and sneakers. McCormick got out of the car, pulled her to her feet and said, 'You should sit out more often. It picks up the whole neighbourhood.'

She sent swift looks in the direction of the Rambler and said, 'I don't want to pick up the whole neighbourhood.'

'Nervous?'

'No. Are you?'

'Sure. On the way up here from Walpole I found myself babbling. He didn't say anything at all—just watched the road. Maybe it'll snow,' he added, staring up through the fat new leaves of a small sycamore tree into the warm, cloudless sky.

They went to the car. Eithne put her head in the open window and said, 'Hello there, Gerard.' There was no answer. As McCormick got in behind the wheel he saw that Gerard had climbed over into the back seat and was now sitting huddled up in a corner fiddling with the dangling sleeves of his sweater. He said, 'This is Eithne Gallagher, a friend of mine, Gerard. You can ride up front and watch the road if you want to.'

Eithne had started to get into the front. She began to get out again but stopped when Gerard said, 'I don't want to watch the road.'

Near Soldier's Field, as the librarian turned the car into the approach road of the river bridge which made the connection to Route Two and points north, he decided that the excursion atmosphere left something to be desired. Part of the trouble was that the boy's silent broody presence was making normal conversation with Eithne impossible. And then she wasn't exactly sparkling herself. He said, 'As we were going past those Harvard Houses back there I remembered I used to know a student
182

in Adams House who had a very curious concept which he called the concept of the castrated conversation.'

'Oh?' Eithne said.

'Yes. It went something like this. Several people who didn't know each other very well might end up eating together at the same table in the dining-room. So one might say to the others—you know, mumbling it through a mouthful of pulped parsnips—"I understand that all the best lacrosse players come from Baltimore, Maryland". And it would go on like that.'

'I understand all the best lacrosse players come from Baltimore,' Eithne said.

'So I asked for it. Now, Gerard, we can do better than that, can't we? Tell me what you think of this car. It may not be as shiny as Armand's motor-cycle, and the radio's broken, but the wheels turn around. What more can you ask?'

From his corner Gerard said primly, 'My mother said you stole this car from Millicent. She said my sister wanted to give it to me but you took it when she died.'

It was now the librarian's turn to act prim. 'I'm afraid your mother's a little mixed up. She can have it if she wants it but you can't have it till you're old enough to drive it.'

Eithne muttered, 'Jesus.'

Suddenly furious with her, McCormick was about to ask why she didn't contribute more to the conversation if she thought he was doing poorly, but before he could open his mouth Gerard said loudly, 'I heard what she said. She swore.'

'So what if she swore. Everybody does one time or another.'

Eithne turned around and said, 'I guess you don't like me, Gerard. Well, I'm sorry about that.'

'I don't know you and I don't want to.'

There was a long weighted silence. Eithne was looking out the side window. He took one hand off the wheel and

183

reached to pat her knee. At that moment a trailer truck, racing to get up speed for the hard climb up Belmont Hill, roared past and then swerved into the right-hand lane with all the insouciance of a Volkswagen. During the next few instants, while he braked, hissed in panic, cursed, and watched the truck's massive tailgate approach within inches of the Rambler's radiator ornament, he could undertake no missions of personal diplomacy. As soon as the road had cleared again Eithne said tensely, 'This isn't going to work. There are bus stops along here. You'd better let me off and I'll go back.'

The suggestion had to be ignored. 'We're all pretty nervous because of my driving. Let's lift our thoughts and look ahead. Pretty soon I'll switch off this highway and go along the back road through the beautiful village of Lincoln. We'll go past the Gropius Residence and that will interest Mrs Gallagher very much because it's a famous feature of modern architecture. Then we come to this little road and proceed up it to a lake. At one end of the lake there's a beach, a bath-house, some diving boards and some ice-cream joints. At the other end there's a train embankment where trains go by about twice a year. And there's woods and paths on both sides. Beautiful! Beautiful Lake Walden, known to the whole world as Walden Pond.'

'Walpole has ponds. What's so special about this pond?' Gerard wanted to know.

For the first time the boy's voice held a definite, if cold and distant, note of curiosity. He was rising to the bait like a cautious little lake perch. 'Why this is the most famous pond in America and maybe in the world. Henry David Thoreau built a cabin and planted some beans there and lived alone in the bee-loud glade. He was a man from Concord who believed most people live lives of quiet desperation. He also said that men go down the road of life carrying a big house and a lot of furniture and real estate on their backs.'

184

'Well I don't live a life of quiet desperation and people can't carry houses and stuff no matter how strong they are,' Gerard said. 'He sounds like a liar.'

'Oh no. He was a poet. He put down his experiences in a great book called *Walden*, after the pond. I bet Eithne has read that book.'

'Sorry, Professor, but I never could get into it. All that jazz at the beginning about how many cents he spent on nails and boards. It just didn't grab me when we were supposed to read it in college.'

'You should give it another try,' McCormick said seriously. 'The best part comes near the end when he stands on the railroad embankment watching the early spring mud ooze down and he sees all the organic forms of nature there in the mud. Wild!'

'It sounds to me as if he were forcing it quite a bit— unless it was very unusual mud. But now I remember what I don't like about Thoreau. That funny business about going to jail.'

'What do you mean? He went to jail for his principles, didn't he?'

'Sure. And he came out the next morning because Emerson paid his taxes. Don't tell me it wasn't a put-up job.'

'God!' McCormick exclaimed. 'You're more Irish than I thought you were.'

'And while we're on the subject,' she continued, 'I don't think much of Emerson either. All that U.S. Chamber of Commerce crap about self-reliance. And look at what was happening in this part of the country while Emerson and his crowd went around being self-reliant. Young girls used as chattel slaves in the mills of Lawrence, Bradford and Lowell. Slumlords sucking the blood of the immigrants in Boston—right under Emerson's transcendental nose. Railroad cartels.'

'O.K. Down with self-reliance,' he said wearily. 'But it's a nice pond anyway. You'll see.'

'If he went to jail, this Thoreau must have been a crook,' Gerard offered.

McCormick sighed, 'You're fighting me. Both of you are fighting me.'

Eithne turned and smiled sweetly into the back seat. 'You see, Gerard,' she lilted. 'You and I do have something in common after all.' . . .

The parking lot above the Metropolitan District Commission beach and bath-houses was empty. The beach itself was occupied by a lone, elderly, one-legged man who seemed to be hunting after something he had lost in the mud-coloured sand; for he constantly eased himself from place to place, supporting his weight on his down-thrust hands and the tip of his foot, and he did not look up when they passed him. The man had rolled his extra trouser leg above the stump, which ended in puckered folds of flesh at the knee joint.

They went along the right bank of the pond, following a faint trail through the thin woods. Gerard dawdled behind. McCormick shifted the burden of the cardboard carton containing the lunch from his right shoulder to his left hip and said, 'He'll probably warm up to us after a while.'

'You think so,' Eithne responded, in a peculiar drawling tone which he had never heard her use before.

'Certainly. When I saw him down in Walpole, he was much more welcoming, in a weird sort of way. His horrible experiences have made him afraid of being outside— you know, a touch of the old agoraphobia.' He glanced back along the trail and added, 'Perhaps I should have started this project off by taking him to a movie.'

'Or a dentist. His teeth are completely ruined. The kid's a wreck.'

They came to a small inlet of the lake, a hundred yards or so from the railway embankment, where the trees stood back from the shore and the water was shallow and clear. It was the way McCormick remembered it from

186

twenty years before including the cairn-like pile of granite building stones situated between water and woods which one could pretend on this occasion marked the site of Henry David's strenuous hut. Eithne gathered up a few rusty cans from the stone pile and threw them into the woods. 'It seems your Thoreau was quite an ale drinker in his day,' she commented.

Gerard came up at last. 'You can poke around while I'm laying out the lunch,' the librarian said. 'If you want to go wading go ahead, but keep an eye out for broken glass and don't go up on the tracks.'

The boy continued around the other side of the inlet, found a long stick and used it to pry into the water and to lash the eel grass growing in the shallows. McCormick took a bottle of Tavel Rosé, a six-pack of beer, and several bottles of soft drink out of the picnic carton and sank them into the chill waters of the lake.

'I'll fix the food,' Eithne offered. 'What have we got?'

'Broiled chicken busts, potato salad and cole slaw, rye bread, pickles. And there's a head of lettuce and a jar of mayonnaise. Anybody who feels like dessert can walk back to the Walden Breezes and have an ice cream.'

Sitting on the ground with her legs drawn up under her and her skirt wrapped around her knees, she quickly divided the food and put the portions on paper plates. He had forgotten paper napkins. She said lightly, 'And here is the food to save a part of a day I had rued.'

McCormick flinched and said, 'I appreciate your coming out here with us, Eithne—after all Gerard's not your problem—but really you shouldn't call him a wreck.'

'His teeth are certainly wrecked. He needs a complete new set—upper and lower. And what, really, do you imagine you can do for him? Whatever you are, you're not a dentist.'

He took a small corkscrew out of his pocket, sat down

on the ground, and began to open and close its collapsible handle. 'I told you what horrors the mother and brother are, didn't I?'

'Yes. Family breakdown. But every community has agencies to deal with that sort of problem.'

'Agencies,' he repeated scornfully. 'You and that planner's mentality of yours. Some old battleaxe down in Walpole wants to stick him in a children's home. That's what you get when you start horsing around with agencies.'

'Rubbish,' she said calmly. 'First of all there are homes and homes—as you call them. The worst wouldn't leave his teeth like that and the best could do much more for him than an occasional picnic or movie with a man he hardly knows and doesn't seem to trust is going to do for him.'

'You sound like you don't trust me either.'

'Don't be silly. Your motives don't come into it.'

Not sure of what did come into it he asked, 'What could —or should—I have done?'

She stretched out on the ground, leaning on her elbow. 'Let's begin with what you did do. You read a note from Milly, talked to a tavern keeper and visited heartbreak house once. And here we are. And there *he* is.' On the far side of the inlet Gerard stood motionless, looking away towards the railway embankment. He looked lost. 'Now what might you have done?' She went on to indicate that he could have gone to the local Family Service Bureau and found out whether they had a line on the domestic *moeurs* of Margarite and Armand. He could have contacted Gerard's school principal and teachers. The family must have had some friends in town—at least before the Margarite take over. These people might have been located and the situation talked over. Then there was the family doctor. And the Masons. Because hadn't something been said about Milly's father being a Mason?

'So now I know,' he said morosely. 'But why didn't you

do the Citizen's Advice Bureau routine for my benefit—
for his benefit let me remind you—before this?'

'I have my own projects, let me remind you, so maybe
I didn't have time for yours. Besides, I was curious. I
wanted to see what you were up to.'

'Up to?' This hollowly.

'Whether you were serious or just having an adventure. *Are* you serious? You can still do all the things I've
mentioned.'

Her tone and the trend of her remarks suggested he
wasn't up to much. He stood up and murmured, 'Just having a paltry, meaningless, idiotic adventure.'

'I didn't say that,' she said quickly. 'I was only specu-
lating.'

He called Gerard to the sylvan collation, discovered the
package of paper cups in the cardboard carton, removed
the wine and a bottle of soft drink from the lake and
opened them. The boy pushed his food around on his plate
with marked distaste. Watching him suck at his pop
bottle the librarian decided, without self-reproach, that
at least for the time being he loathed him. Eithne ate and
drank with much more gusto. Still, wasn't there something rather steely in her manner this day? Wasn't there
something about the bend of her neck over the viands, in
her efficient management of plastic fork and spoon almost
school-marmish? What would Julia Ward Mack think
of her? That she was too clever, accomplished, hard-
working, healthy, wholesome, decisive, in a word too
good, for the heir apparent of the Bartholemew—Myles I
—Joseph barren legacy? Indubitably. And so the old man
had cleared off and could you blame him? Without knowing any of the details he blamed him.

But then Eithne sent her plate skimming towards the
barren Thoreauvian rocks, pulled off her head-scarf and
her pullover, shook out her hair, lay back on the scanty
new grass with her breasts lifting heavenwards and her
skirt halfway up her fine full thighs, and said languorously,

189

'How lovely to be out in the sun again.' Julia Ward Mack could go peddle her papers.

And what about a convenient delivery route for Gerard? 'I notice you didn't eat much, Jerry,' he said suavely. 'Here's half a dollar that says you aren't man enough to walk back to the Walden Breezes and shout yourself to a large chocolate walnut sundae with whipped cream and a maraschino cherry on top.'

The boy's eyes shifted covetously from Eithne's legs to the coin and back again. 'I might get lost,' he complained.

'Not a chance. You can see where you're going from here. Just stick by the shore and we'll keep an eye on you all the way there and back.' That is if they had nothing better to do.

At last Gerard accepted the money and walked off. McCormick put the picnic gear, used and unused, back in the carton, poured out two more cups of Rosé wine and walked on his knees to where Eithne lay with closed eyes under the pouring sun. He bent down over her and kissed her eyelids, then the outer corners of her eyes where lines of care and character had formed over the years of her twenties. When she opened her eyes and brought up her hand as a sun shield he sat back on his heels and put a cup of wine in her loosely curled hand. He stroked her hair, which was hot from the sun and seemed to release a scent of cleanness into the warm spring air like newly baked bread. She was a shining loaf in nature's kitchen. Lightly, lightly he remarked, 'Let's forget about the kid for a while, darling. There's a couple of things I wanted to tell you.'

She turned her head and contemplated him with slumbrous eyes. 'Tell me what you want to tell me, Myles dear,' she said softly. Her voice was full of buried treasure.

'Well first about the library.' Ever so gently he placed his hand between the warm inner slopes of her lower thighs. Ever so gently she drew her legs together, trapping

190

the hand where it warmly lay. Ever so whimsically, yet with hints of serious purpose glinting through the anecdotage, he described the opening in Rare Books, his scheme to transform the B.F.L. *Bulletin*, the favourable interview with Pinkham, the kind of aureate future lying in store for the successful candidate in the competition.

Eithne sat up, shook back her hair and drank of her wine. Watching her carefully, the librarian asked her lightly what she thought of it all.

She looked at the ground. 'It beats me,' she said after a while.

His heart dove into his colon. 'What beats you?'

'It beats me why you don't do what you want to do. Why you don't do *something*.'

'And you don't think this job would be doing something? Maybe I haven't emphasized the challenge—'

'Stop it!' She stared angrily. 'I've seen you at work in the library. I've seen you hiding out there. You seem to forget that.'

'Hiding out!' he said hotly. 'I like that. You've never seen me cataloguing those half-assed Russian music books for Miss Colley. . . . Directing the Rare Books Room is an important job. In fact it's much more important in the long run than flattening the West End with bulldozers and hustling a bunch of poor old tenement dwellers out of town. I like that.'

'Of course it's an important job. And it has *nothing* to do with you. You know nothing about it and you care nothing about it. You know nothing about editing a magazine and you care nothing about it. That Pinkham must be crazy to listen to you. I feel like calling him up and—'

'Eithne!'

'Don't you understand anything? Don't you know anything about yourself, Myles? At your age haven't you even got a clue? And for God's sakes get up off your knees and stop goggling like that.'

McCormick sprang to his feet and strode rapidly around

191

the clearing. He rushed to the rock-pile and kicked it. Selecting a large piece of rough hewn granite from the top he ran with it to the shore and slung it two-handed into the water. At the splash a large greyish bird rose from the upper branches of a tree close by and went flapping off over the lake in the direction of Waltham. It left behind it in the glittering air several derisive cries.

He ran back to where she sat watching him and said, 'You're impossible. You know that, don't you?'

'No I'm not,' she said coolly. 'You're impossible.'

'How can a nothing be impossible?' How could it fail to be? he reflected. Morbid tears threatened at the thought that in her book, in her school-marmish mark book, there was a string of zeros beside his name. Fight those. 'That career stuff was only supposed to be a vamp,' he said thinly. 'I brought you out here to tell you I loved you.'

She put her hands over her ears. 'Please. I don't want to hear it.'

'Of course not. Or that you were everything I thought I wanted. All five foot eight and a hundred and thirty-three pounds of you, poignant memories and marginal guilt complex concerning a dead husband included.'

'Don't be nasty, Myles. You might get more than you bargained for.'

'I'll try not to be nasty. Just laughable. Laughable old McCormick and his joke career plans. Go ahead and laugh. I don't give a damn.'

She put her hands over her eyes. 'My God, what am I doing here? And what have I been doing? It's like sleepwalking. I'm going to be thirty in less than a month.'

'Don't worry, you'll make out. The thirties are the prime of life. That is, for people who are up to anything, people with a clue.' He turned his back on her and surveyed the picnic scene. It was paltry, it had always been paltry, and Thoreau, that paltry self-reliant, self-

192

employed, self-wallowing Yankee shit, could keep the rest of the beer and wine, the used paper plates, the half chewed chicken breasts. For all he cared, Thoreau and Emerson and Alcott and the rest of that thin-shanked whey-faced crowd could let down a celestial hook, snag the goodies and have themselves a party up there in that gas bag they called the Oversoul. For all he cared!

He made for the path and stopped at the edge of the clearing. She was still sitting with her hands over her eyes. 'I'm going after the kid. We'll meet you at the car,' he snapped and limped rapidly up the trail feeling a soreness in his foot where he had kicked the stones.

Gerard wasn't in The Breezes, nor was he visible anywhere along the beach or the road. Crossing the parking lot for about the third time, McCormick saw Eithne approaching and cried, 'The end of a perfect outing. He's got himself lost.'

'Have you looked in the car?'

'You can see he isn't there—unless he's down between the seats. And that's an idea.'

Gerard was in the car, lying between the seats in a reek of tobacco fumes, clutching a half-smoked cigar and a half-empty package of cigarettes, his eyes closed, his brow beaded with moisture, his complexion sallow to an extreme. McCormick pulled at the boy's feet and grated, 'All right. Penrod. Get up out of there. The party's over.'

Eithne, looking in from the other side, cried, 'Stop that. Can't you see he's sick? Don't bully him.' She drew Gerard out tenderly and carried him a little distance away and set him on his feet with her arm around his shoulders and a hand holding his forehead. Soon he bent forward and vomited. She found a handkerchief in her skirt pocket and wiped his face and mouth with it.

All the way home she rode in back holding Gerard up against her. Glancing from time to time in the rear vision mirror McCormick saw her run her hand through the child's hair and twice saw her kiss his damp temple. Once in the mirror he saw Gerard regarding him with a stare of perfect non-recognition as he lolled with the back of his head on Eithne's bosom, but at no time did the eyes of the librarian and the eyes of Mrs Gallagher meet.

16 ⌒

On Sunday McCormick awoke late and spent a long time looking up at the ceiling. He would not think about events and personalities of the previous day. Instead he would think about going into the army.

After girding up his loins in 1944 at the Fort Devens Reception Center he had ungirded them almost immediately when assigned to the little Army Field Hospital undergoing Basic and Intermediate training in the Smoky Mountains of North Carolina. The war was drawing to an end in the opinion of many. Following a few feints at training under simulated battle conditions the hospital had been stripped of its doctors, who were posted to large station hospitals for work with the returning wounded. While Dr Koski locked himself in his office and wrote papers on vocational testing, with particular attention to a statistical concept known as the chi-square, the men lapsed into somnolence. He had spent nearly nine months typing and retyping army orders, learning pidgin Russian out of Bondar's *Commercial Grammar*, drinking orangeade at the NCO club and practising the top line of a set of Mozart's flute quartets in the Orderly Room. At the end of the day he often hiked a mile or so through the woods to Hickory Mountain College, a progressive-educational sandpile where the music faculty gave excellent chamber music concerts and where every co-ed had a private study-boudoir to which she alone possessed a key.

It was in one of those cosy cubicles that he had made love for the last three months or so to the New Jersey girl whose surname appeared on the label of one out of every seventeen cloth coats manufactured in America. She had been, and remained, the ugliest girl he had ever seen up close: with a sprung bottom, spidery limbs, dropsical breasts, wrinkled knees, flat feet, a bad complexion and an offensive odour: a kind of female 4-F. Bad tempered to boot, she had assumed he was after her money and had accused him of chasing other heiresses in the ill-spelt letters she sent for about six months after his return to college.

The affair had seemed to fit the tranced, Rip Van Winkle-ish mood of those months of idleness spent among worn, fertile and depopulated mountains. What *had* old Rip been up to during his twenty years of poor man's divorce? It was inevitable and human that he should have claimed to have slept away the whole time of absence; but it was much more likely that he had been indulging an intense *nostalgie de la boue,* embracing troll wives and female warlocks in the hills while wifie drew her survivor's pension at the village post office, way down in the valley the valley so low.

Something of the trance effect had persisted when he returned to Harvard and moved into Kirkland House on funds provided by the G.I. Bill. The school was full of wised-up vets eager to get somewhere fast. For modest fees he had helped a few of them on their way by taking an occasional language exam for one, writing an occasional English A paper for another. In the late afternoons he had inveigled a series of University Hall typists down to his room and become knowledgeable about pantie girdles and the taste of pancake makeup. The idea was to disarm these deeply suspicious girls by turning on the local accent and reminiscences but the proportion of sneak

196

novena-addicts among them had remained high. He had certainly done less well than the Shaker Heights Don Juan across the entry who adjusted his climaxes to a scarred Kostelanetz transcription of the *Liebestod*. Of them all he remembered best the girl from the Record Room: her false fingernails, the suspiciously slack, post-partum look of her thin stomach, her asking for money on the way out.

Add in Penelope Dicey in her shaggy sweater of re-used wool. Add in gaunt Claudine in Toulouse, her freckles and her stainless steel false teeth. How foolish to have thought that the past was past, that one could change one's luck or destiny as easily as socks. Add in Milly, their half-life together, her dismal death. Add in Helen White. . . . No. She was not in that class. His class. Class will come to attention. There will be no giggling and wriggling and weeping if you please. No teasing of hair or teacher. There will be no tears please. Please.

He got out of bed, limped into the next room, and picked up the mail from the couch where he had dropped it upon coming in from the previous evening's movie marathon up and down Washington Street. He opened the letter with the U.N. frank first.

Deer old Myles,

Felicitate me! I have fallen in love with a Williams man named B. J. Kincaid and weer getting married just as soon as poor Evan finalizes the divorce. Billy invents things and will be joining one of those genius firms along Route 128 in a few months. And boy! Is he inventive in certain essential departments!

Anyway, as you see I'll be back in the Boston area before long. I do hope to see you again. I mean strictly on the up-and-up. I've told Billy a certain amount about you. You both would like each other. (Myles honey, stop making me blush!)

What about you and that Eithne? I trust my hunches in these matters and she *is* lovely.

Anyway, I hope you are happy, Myles deer, because I am very happy.

xoxoxo
Ur frend,
Doo-ee

P.S. Say hello to those kreeps in Rar Buks.

xoxo
D

PPS. I'm getting vague on the old Dewey-dismal *sprache*, but am I sharp on current useages from the continent! You should hear what gets said, and *doesn't* get translated, at some of our closed door sessions on the East River.

XO—Helen

Closed doors. They seemed to be swinging shut all up and down the line. How abject to pretend that this particular one had ever been ajar. To him. Yet how easy and how satisfying so to pretend. Getting really old was grey, self-exculpating lies about pastlastlost chances . . . Helen sounded happy. He wished her well. And with a keen pang he envied her. She had gotten her ass in a dusty Boston bag, had bolted, had been rescued by a jovial inventive Kincaid. Girls made the better adventurers, because if a man didn't see them through, their superior characters and animal faith did. Thus Julia Mack: after the blind economic staggers of the Depression and the War fetching up on Florida's golden littoral. Not much in the animal faith department there though. Hers was a depressing and characteristic triumph of character. You shouldn't try so hard not to love your mother, Sidney once had said in a non-non-directive moment. That's enough out of you, my fool.

She had written to him. That was the other en-

198

velope, bulky, and addressed in a giant's hand as usual.

Dear Myles,
   Today is my birthday. Thanks for remembering it.
Ha! Next week is Memorial Day. I don't feel old but I
do feel bored with things and people, except for the
swimming. You will scoff and say I'm losing my wits
when I tell you I have been thinking about the past,
but that's just what I've been doing. People change, even
at 74.
   I have been going through old papers I've kept
around for years—old letters, photos, cancelled house
deeds, cancelled insurance policies, etc. I have even
come across some of your stuff. Boy Scouts Merit Badge
certificates, a try you made at writing a song with flute
'obligato': 'show me no more where Jove bestows
When June is past the blushing rose'— Do you remember? Are you blushing?
   I note that you received a Merit Badge for Pathfind-
ing. I think that's very funny, don't you? And I came
across a copy of a letter I wrote to the Freshman Dean
just before you entered college. In the summer he sent
out a form letter asking the parents to tell him anything
about the boy which would make his adjustment to
college life easier. I enclose my reply with this letter.
Maybe it will interest you—

   It did interest him, for in those days she had professed
to see little difference between his going to Harvard and
his getting a job in the Charlestown Navy Yard, except
that the latter would make more of a contribution to the
war effort; and she had certainly never mentioned at the
time that she was filing intelligence reports with the Harvard authorities. He fished in the long envelope and drew
out a single sheet of onion skin.

212 Walden St.

Cambridge, Mass.

July 19, 1943

Dean Delmar Leighton
Harvard University
Cambridge, Mass.

Dear Sir:

I am glad to be able to answer a letter from you about my son, Myles.

His health is practically perfect. He seldom has even a cold. If he has any defects in his character it would be laziness and forgetfulness. He dislikes and ignores competition.

He has some persistence. He decided some years ago he was going to Harvard, and he has made it.

He likes music and with no help outside himself, has acquired an extensive knowledge of it for his age and opportunities.

I am sorry to say he doesn't want to make a lot of money. His idea is to enjoy Culture.

Sincerely yours,

McCormick began to laugh then stopped. A sullen anger suffused him. Where did she get off anyway? By what imperial right . . . ? As a piece of epistolary art it insisted on being compared with the sort of messages certain savage-waggish autocrats like Ivan the Terrible and Peter the Great had enjoyed sending out: 'Bearer believes this letter contains an order for his promotion to Captaincy in Imperial Guard. He is to be taken out by a firing squad of Streltsi and summarily executed. Haw! Haw! Haw!' The librarian reread his mother's ancient letter to the Dean with shaking hand.

On further consideration he decided he liked it. The widow-at-graze in the rickety three-decker facing the clay pits of North Cambridge had addressed the ivied Yankee men of mind and money without knuckling her forelock or her son's, and without maundering on about allergies, night sweats, and banal boyish triumphs at sport or at book. The writing was incisive and she had gone to the trouble of hunting up a typewriter—probably the one in the shabby office of the W.P.A.—Lanham Act Federal Nursery for Working Mothers Project in the basement of the Cambridge City Hall—and had also bothered to make this carbon copy as a memento. *Nihil Obstat. Imprimatur.* Miles Macormacus Archepiscopus. Laus Deo. And as for her pungent sketch of his character at age seventeen, doubtless it would repay reflection but at some later time, say, about 1988.

He sprawled on the couch and hunted in his mother's main letter for the point at which he had interrupted his reading of it.

. . . and maybe it will not. It's now some years since I've had any real idea of what interested you and what you wished to do with your life apart from going to that psychiatrist and hanging around the library and living in Mortal Sin with poor departed Millicent. Of course this past year you've been at me for information about your father but his life, when you come down to it, doesn't and never did have much to do with yours.

Nevertheless, my son Myles, you have kept at me and at me about him in your brief, uninformative monthly letters. If what I'm going to tell you now about how your daddy left us distresses you, remember! you have only yourself to blame. And you are not to reopen this subject in any future letters or when I come up to New England this summer. I will speak now and forever after hold my peace—

The huge words in Palmer cursive blurred before the librarian's eyes. He sprang up and took several turns around the living-room before coming back and picking up the letter again. He had asked for it and now he was going to get it. If only she hadn't used the words 'daddy' and 'us'. For a husband, a 'he', to desert a wife, a 'me', was bad; for a grand old dad to desert an 'us' was somehow ever so much worse. As a matter of fact it more or less put the stars out and broke the universal axis. But hold on. He, Myles II, hadn't even been born? Or *had* he been?. . .

I'm sure I told you he went back to his job at United Fruit after the war. Well it didn't work out. I mean he soon saw he was being passed over for promotion and he got restless when he saw young men he had broken in put over him. He would keep after me about making a change, but I said 'Change to what?' and 'A bird in the hand is worth two in the bush.' He couldn't do anything with his hands except type.

In the midst of his discouragement I gave him an idea. I said, Get out of office work and into work where you're making something, even if you have to take less money. Look at my father. He began with nothing but a cart going around collecting carcasses from the slaughter houses and he ended up with a tidy little rendering business.

It struck him, as I intended it should. I remember him staring at me and saying, So you think I should get in business for myself? And just how am I supposed to manage that?

There were ways. I had nine hundred dollars which was my share of my late father's house in Somerville. When your father knew something about starting a business he could have that to start it with.

Well, we looked around with the idea of getting him into some kind of production work where he could see how things are made and go on from there. Soon he landed a job as assistant supervisor in an East Cam-

202

bridge paper mill owned by some first cousins twice removed of mine named Scanlon. So he made the break from big business and started in.

He didn't like the paper business much at first—he couldn't stand the smell of the chemicals they mixed with the wood pulp—but he was learning how a small 'primary producer' organized a labor force, made and marketed a product. And they, the Scanlon brothers Paddy and Matt, liked *him*. Most people liked Joe. They were just ordinary working men from Brick Bottom who'd built a business and they appreciated somebody with nice manners and a careful dresser who could meet customers when he wasn't on the floor looking after the actual production of the paper.

They raised him twice, until he was making eighty-five dollars a week, and then in 1926 they gave him a special assignment to go out to the West Coast, up north in the lumber country near Seattle, and investigate the possibility of Scanlon Bros. opening a second mill in that area.

He set out in early June, 1926, and before I got his first letter I found out you (!) were coming. Then his first letter did come and it was full of excitement about an idea he had for getting into business out there on the West Coast.

He had found prospects for a new paper mill only so-so. On the other hand, he had found that the whole Northwest Coast was virgin territory as far as the manufacture of soap products was concerned, and he had met a man starting a soap factory who wanted him to come into it as a limited partner. This man, whose name was Diller, was willing to let Joe in on the ground floor for a cash payment of under a thousand dollars and a scheme of payments out of Joe's share of the net profits for the first three or four years. He said he wanted a younger man with a combination of business and production experience like your father's. Otherwise he wouldn't dream of letting anybody in on the profits for such a small investment.

Am I boring you, son Myles, with this stuff about the real world which you always have pretended doesn't interest you? Well you just pay attention.

I thought it over for a couple of days and the proposition sounded right to me. I was sure that was the way they did things out West, with quickness and dispatch instead of hemming and hawing in the time honored New England way. I knew something about soap. Because where do you suppose my father found buyers for the fats he rendered? It all ended up in soap products.

I wrote Joe, advising him to make a cautious investigation of Diller's bank credit and standing in the community. If these were all right I advised Joe he should buy in fast with my money. The prospect of moving west and starting a new life in Washington State didn't daunt me at all. It would be an adventure.

Soon he wired me a reply as follows: DILLER'S CREDIT AND NAME EXCELLENT WILL PROCEED IF YOU SEND MONEY JOE I still have that telegram. I sent him the money.

To make a long story short, from the day I sent the money until this day I never saw or heard from my legally wedded husband, Joseph Anthony McCormick, again. Don't think I didn't make inquiries, and the Scanlon brothers too. We did repeatedly and neither the police, nor his hotel, nor the bank which cashed the Transfer of Funds were able to trace him.

You want to know what happened to him. So did I in the old days. Maybe that man Diller bilked him and fled to Canada and Joe was simply too ashamed ever to come back and face me. Maybe he was set upon and robbed and killed and his remains disposed of by a gang of those tough Seattle longshoremen. Maybe he fell into the clutches of a designing woman. Maybe he went walking on the beach after cashing the draft and was carried away by a wave while he was dreaming of a golden future for us all. The coastal waters of the Pacific Northwest are said to be very dangerous.

At one time I got the idea fixed in my mind that he might have sneaked back to Boston and be living somewhere around the city under an assumed name. I would see men on the street who resembled him from the back and I would pass them and give them a long look.

When I first moved to St. Petersburg there was a man living alone in a trailer in Lot # 102 who looked to me a lot like the way Joe might look after a certain amount of aging. I amused myself by pretending it was Joe— not that I would ever have let on I knew him even if he had turned out to be Joe; for I believe in the wisdom of that law which says your spouse is dead for all practical purposes after an absence of seven years. But anyway I danced with him one night in the Rec Hall and of course he wasn't anything like Joe.

If it matters to you now you ought to know that your father never did learn that you were coming. The letter containing the good news was, as I recall, the first returned to me from the West marked Address Unknown.

Your loving mother,
Julia Ward McCormick

17 ◌

The front of the Boston Free Library looked east across a small square and consisted of five neo-classic orders executed in granite one above the other. The main entry was wide, tall and canopied in bronze, with sculpted bronze outer doors which were never closed before midnight. On most days and in all weathers a wispy old man with double cataracts stood beside the entrance wearing over his clothing a magazine bag on which appeared the faded legend AWAKE! He had mastered the tedious art of dozing standing up and was never seen to proffer copies of *The Watchtower* to passersby.

Along the entire length of the front, to right and left of the entrance, ran a stone ledge which jutted out at a height of about two and a half feet above the pavement. Adults used it to sit on, children to run along, and pigeons as a landing strip and to stain. In warm sunny weather an elderly, powerfully built woman with a dark gypsy complexion and abundant, white, unkempt hair spent much time sitting on this ledge, falling asleep in the glare of the sun, and waking up and moving to a new location along the wall whenever the progress of the day caused a shadow to fall across her. She habitually appeared at mid-morning, wearing on her back a U.S. Army infantry pack crammed to overflowing with old picture magazines, *Look, Life, Pic* and *Quick.* After sitting down on the ledge she would take several magazines from her pack and
206

place them on her lap. Then she would turn her face up to the sun and fall asleep. As her sleep became more profound she would slump to one side and gradually straighten her legs, causing the magazines to slide down onto the pavement in a slow cascade.

Inside the main entrance, beyond a small dark foyer, was situated a much larger entrance hall faced in fossil-infused yellow travertine from which the great central double staircase, also of travertine, mounted to the main Reading Room and Public Catalogue on the second floor. At the bottom of the stairs, to left and right, were large empty niches, both of the dimensions to hold a life-size statue of a standing man or woman. In the right hand niche there often sat hunched up, with her face buried in her hands, a lanky woman of about forty dressed in shabby black clothes.

Arriving shortly after nine o'clock at the main entrance of the library on a sunny morning in late May, then entering and moving up the grand staircase towards the Director's Room on the fourth floor, Myles McCormick noted with gloomy satisfaction that all three of these sentries were in their wonted places. There had been days in the past when he had amused himself by attributing to them various fanciful literary, or allegorical, significations; for instance, the woman in the niche appearing as a rematerialization of the pathetic and sinister Miss Jessel, or serving in the emblematic style of the earlier seventeenth century to remind regular users of the library that an occupational hazard of a career of hard scholarship was melancholia. On this day each figure, unmoved and unmoving, signified nothing but his own, and their own, fathomless private inertia and numbness of being. And if he was not at all sure what the words 'fathomless private inertia and numbness of being' meant, they still, he insisted to himself, rang true.

In Pinkham's outer office his chunky secretary, Miss Jennings, sat at her glossy desk opening mail.

'I called Friday for an appointment this morning with Mr Pinkham.'

'Righty-o, Mr McCormick,' said Miss Jennings. 'However, the Director can't be here. Mr Rankin is covering his appointments this morning.'

'Really.' He found difficulty in going on. He felt inert and numb.

Miss Jennings tore at the tapes and staples of a book container with fingers and paper knife and didn't say anything.

'Mr Rankin?'

'Wynston Rankin. W y n s t o n. He's the Director's *special* administrative aide. Hasn't been here long but he's on top of everything.' She fiddled with the paper knife and looked arch. 'Pink calls him Red Rankin. I like to call him the Southern Rhodesian.'

Startling. Sinister. The phrase evoked a bandoliered white settler in sweatstained khaki shirt and *lederhosen* pistol whipping a moaning 'Bantu' into a prison compound somewhere near the Rand. Not exactly reassuring. 'Why do you call him that?'

She smiled and looked self-complaisant. 'He's from Albemarle, South Carolina and he once won a Rhodes Scholarship. Family responsibilities kept him from going to Oxford and he went into library work instead. Mr Pinkham picked him up on one of his recent trips south. You went to Oxford or something like it, didn't you, Mr. McCormick?'

'No never,' he said quickly. 'Since we both missed the scene we have a common bond. Anyway, he sounds pretty competent.'

'Brilliant! Already he's taken a load of responsibility for the reorganization plan off the boss's shoulders.'

That figured. Maybe though there was something to be gained from this morning's unlooked for development. Suppose he and this Rankin should hit it off, see eye to eye, get down to cases? Between them they might lift

208

the entire library off 'Pink''s well-tailored shoulders behind his back. Stick him up as a figure head, keep him
waffling along on the convention circuit, while they got
the B.F.L. back on its feet as an institution of learning.
What price inertia now? Eithne Gallagher, you'll see . . .
She would never see because she had stopped looking.

'He's about my age?'

The casual once-over. 'Younger I should say. His hair
is a nice deep red. No grey.'

McCormick smiled winsomely and patted his carefully
combed hair. 'Preemie grey.'

'Is that what you call it?'

'Yes. For the last twenty years or so.'

Mr Rankin was seated behind the Director's desk when
McCormick entered the inner office, and he stood up and
came around front to shake hands. He was tall and walked
with a bounce and wore a dark three-piece suit with a
jumbo-sized Phi Beta key chained to the vest. Probably
from the triple Zeta chapter of the Lucius Vardaman Bilbo
College of the Great Pine Barrens, now presided over by
G. S. (known to intimates as 'Specs') Bird, McCormick
thought snidely while gathering a first impression. The
administrative aide had flaring ears, a broad flat face,
small orange eyes, and a rufous complexion which went
with thick, reddish-brown hair, and he winked once during the medium-firm handshake and once again after
reseating himself behind the desk.

McCormick sat on the couch. There were good white
southerners and they often moved to the north, he told
himself. 'Mr Pinkham told me to come back in two weeks
for his decision on the opening in Rare Books after Dr
Petkov's retirement. I guess you must know that.'

Mr Rankin winked. Evidently it was a nervous tic.
'Yes. The Director spoke to me of your interest in that
position.'

'Frankly, I think it's gotten beyond the being-interested

stage. Do I get it or don't I?' There were risks in hewing to a line of bluntness but at least it was a line.

'Ah appreciate—ah respect—your directness. Mr Pinkham empowahs me to give you the cold dope on this situation. During the past two weeks, evah since you brought it up, we've given a lot of thought to this question of replacing the Rare Books Head. And we've decided it's only fair and professional to open it up to *all* qualified candidates. That means, among othah things, advertising the vacancy in the professional journals and in *Publishers Weekly*.' Here he winked.

'Does that mean I've been eliminated?' McCormick grated. Of course it did.

'Bah no means. Only to be fair, we expect that many hahly qualified'—this word he pronounced 'quohleefahd' —'candidates will come forward when word gets out.'

'After talking to him I thought Mr Pinkham was sold—' McCormick stopped and flushed, and Mr Rankin angled a tender wink towards a corner of the ceiling. Hang in there. 'What about organizational loyalty—continuity? I mean, things are in pretty rough shape up there on the fifth floor. Miss Kearsarge—the First Assistant—why *she* feels she just couldn't face a new man coming in from outside.' If he had a point to make why did it keep breaking up into bits of gibberish? But there was still the point about the magazine.

'Miss Keahsarge will have the chance to present her views at the propah time. And you will have the chance to present your excellent quohleefeecations for the position —at the propah time.' Here he winked and added smiling, 'Of course you'll have to countah the argument that a new broom sweeps clean, while an old broom sometimes merely bristles.'

'On the other hand, a Rare Books Collection isn't a floor,' McCormick countered coldly. And this was the man he'd thought he might get in cahoots with to filch the library from that jackass Pinkham. Could it be possible that sweet Helen White had spent a substantial part of her nonage in the same state that had produced Rankin? Fuckin crackah raidneck hawg! Cool it.

Touching the tips of his fingers lightly together, Mr Rankin confined his immediate response to looking quizzical.

'What about my proposal for the magazine? The B.F.L. *Review*? I know the Director likes that idea. Surely he wants me to go ahead with that, never mind who gets the Rare Books post.'

'This brings up another important point,' the special administrative aide said smoothly. 'We believe your scheme is very fahn, though a mite too ambitious during the present stage of the Redevelopment Programme. So we have modified it. We will suggest to the Trustees that the *Bulletin* should suspend publication after the summah issue.'

'No more magazine at all? Some modification!'

'Yes there will be a magazine. It will come out monthly on glossy paper and it will be called *Library*. *Library* will contain Mr Pinkham's regular feature, along the lahns of your very helpful suggestion. It will also feature photo-essays on new activities in the various departments, and some human interest stories on some of our more distinguished staff members.'

Here McCormick felt a keen pang of boredom and Mr Rankin winked.

'We will build up our circulation by distributing *Library* free to top people in the library and publishing fields. Also, a copy will be sent to everyone on the mailing list of the F.B.F.L.—the Friends organization—and to a group of senior citizens who meet monthly at the library, called, Ah believe, the Nevah Too Late Club. Although the Friends organization has been in decline recently, we hope to get it moving again.'

'I wanted a real magazine and you and the Director have *modified* it into a public relations house organ,' he

211

said tightly. 'A back-scratching operation, a snow-job.'

Mr Rankin shot out a serpent glance but remained calm. '*Library* will certainly be a real magazine. As a matter of fact Ah am planning it along the lahns of the very newest trends in the institutional periodical field.'

'*You* are planning it? I thought you were Mr Pinkham's right-hand man and I was the man for the magazine.'

Red Rankin made a large lump out of his freckled hands and contemplated it. 'Mr Pinkham did not discuss with me the possibility of you editing the magazine.' He looked up with a modest air and continued, 'Actually, Pink has asked me to look after the magazine in an editorial capacity for the first year or so, and I've agreed to take it on in addition to my othah activities. Much as I might like to have you with me, our operations will be too circumscribed to permit making propah use of a man with your hah quohleefeecations. Besides, as you were quick to see, *Library* will be pretty clearly a P.R. operation, and Ah gathah you wouldn't like that.'

'In sum,' McCormick said angrily, 'I haven't got a chance in hell to become Petkov's successor, and the Director doesn't want me near the so-called magazine. I wonder now why I bothered to come here two weeks ago and offer certain constructive suggestions. Does he always reward initiative this way? You should know. Miss Jennings says you're on top of everything around here.'

Mr Rankin, unruffled, smiled and winked. 'Don't be ruffled, Mr McCormick. The Director and I have taken up the mattah of a suitable reward for the initiative and loyalty you've shown by coming forward. And Ah do think we've just the proposition for you.'

'That so?' This with deep suspicion and a tight throat. 'I'd sho'—sure—like to hear that proposition.'

'You're acquainted with Miss Humpahdinck?'

'Of course. She's attached to our department.'

'She is finally retiring as keepah of the Treasure Room this coming July. The position is two increments higher in the salary schedule than the one you now hold, it's permanent, and you would be your own boss.'

McCormick suddenly stood up. 'You can't be serious.' His voice had a tremor in it.

Mr Rankin held up his hand. 'Heah me out. Granted Miss Humpahdinck hasn't made the most of the opportunities there, we feel that a man with your ideas and strong educational background could do a lot with it. We would be prepared to—'

'The Treasure Room? My God. Somebody must have put you up to it. Whatever did I ever do to you or to the Director, Mr Rankin? At least where I am now I have work—of sorts. I can move around. Breathe. See people. But the Treasure Room! Why— Why it's a mausoleum— a living entombment. You're asking me to become an attendant in a burial mound. It's like sentencing me to solitary confinement for the rest of my working life.'

Mr Rankin stood up and said stiffly, 'Ah'm sorry you choose—'

McCormick interrupted. 'It's where you put people you want to hide away. Like Engleberta Humperdinck, the poor old thing. Old people. Batty people. Nobody ever comes there. And there's nothing in there, except those filthy old exhibition cases with those filthy old Increase Mather sermon collections in them. Do you know how Miss Humperdinck spends her days in that room? She sleeps! The rest of the time she studies palmistry diagrams in astrology magazines. I know, because I've gone in to spell her when she's had to come out to go to the bathroom. We used to joke about buying her a policeman's friend for her hundredth birthday.'

Red Rankin frowned. 'You're not talking to any purpose now, Mr McCormick. For one thing you haven't been eliminated yet as a candidate for Dr Petkov's position.'

'Don't hand me that. You want me in the Treasure Room. Fantastic! Why?'

He shrugged, winked and sat down again. 'Have it your own way then. Pink and I took another look at your rathah *peculiah* employment history. Also, we evaluated *and* substantially discounted certain rumours about you that have been running around the library—'

'Rumours?? Which you ha! *substantially* discounted? Would the Director like to know some of the rumours about him and his reorganization plans that run around this library? I suppose the Director's been getting poison pen letters about me from that creep Rooney in Public Cataloguing. Or is it phantom phone calls? "McCormick's a whore master, a red atheist, and he eats lamb stew for lunch in Sharaff's restaurant on Fridays." Well here's an accurate rumour for you. I'm going to go out and find Rooney and break him in two!'

'I've never heard of this man Rooney,' said Mr Rankin a shade too insistently. 'If you believe he's making trouble for you, you can take it up with Personnel. I'm sorry—'

McCormick shot away to the door, 'I'm sorry Pinkham didn't have the guts to conduct this little talk himself instead of shoving it onto you,' he said over his shoulder and walked out.

'How do you like Red Rankin, our special administrative aide?' fluted Miss Jennings from across the anteroom.

'Your rusty hatchet man, you mean,' McCormick yelped.

He would go downstairs and find Rooney loafing in Public Catalogue and say to him, 'Rooney, the next time you're in church chewing the altar rail and praying for the late Senator McCarthy, and cursing those Jewish cardinals who heaved the Feeney cult out of the church, I want you to say a little prayer for me and my coloured mistresses.' Then he would take away the sharp little key that the catalogue clerks used to remove the rods from the card cases and would slash all the buttons off

214

Rooney's shirt with it. Then he would break him up and stamp him out.

He would do nothing of the sort. He would go back up to the Room and try to decide what to do.

By the time he reached Rare Books McCormick was grimacing so broadly that near-sighted Miss Kearsarge, on duty at the front desk, smiled back and gaily waved, and the entranced Miss Meachum emerged from catalepsy just long enough to produce a sharp disapproving sniff through her dusty-crusty nose hairs. He went down the room to his Coxe Collection work area, picked up the hand vacuum cleaner, and carried it into the South Stack, closing the heavy door behind him.

Here the silence was like heavy surf. Almost you could wade in it, dive under it, drown in it, but it was really too insistent and palpable as a setting for connected thought. He remembered a miserable late winter and early spring when he was nine, his mother out of work, and they had been reduced to living on E.R.A. canned beef stew in a borrowed summer cottage next to the sea at Winthrop, while his mother took the ferry up to Boston every morning it ran and hunted for a job. They had had no heat, except for a small kerosene stove which they carried from room to room, and at Easter time a spring tide had flooded the kitchen more than a foot deep. He remembered it as a time of constant Northeast storm, of huge waves that battered at and flashed over the sea wall, twisted the stout pipe railing on top of the sea wall, plucked gulls out of the air and smashed them against the side of a stone bungalow with boarded up windows which stood nearest the ocean of all the cottages along that raging shore. . . .

He found an outlet under a slit window, plugged in the vacuum cleaner and flipped the switch. The motor whirred and hissed, the air intake made throaty sounds, it became possible to think to some purpose.

He was finished at the library. They were through with

215

him and he was through with them. And the most nauseating part was having to admit that when they had suggested the Treasure Room they were only offering him what he had come looking for at the library in the first place—a solitary room to sit in while he thought about his 'neurosis' and boned up on psychiatry and psychoanalysis in the standard works and periodicals. But that was nearly two years ago. What about all the months in Roberta Colley's department cataloguing the Hebrew, Greek, Irish and Slavic books, learning how to use the Vari-typer, making a semblance of order out of the chaos of Ivan Gorukhov's vast compilation of Russian liturgical chants? This was not shameful. Then the move up to Rare Books and the Coxe Collection. This *was* shameful. In three months he had done nothing to justify the promotion. If the pamphlets on the English religious wars of the seventeenth century had been a shambles locked up in Alcove H, they were now doubly a shambles thrown about on the temporary shelves in his work area and shrouded under the dust cloths of half a dozen book carts. With that project he had made less than a beginning.

Even Pinkham, no doubt with some help from that foul ball Rankin, had sifted him and seen through his pretentions and deceptions. And if Pinkham could do that, what must Eithne have seen? He groaned aloud. He would never see her again, grasp her strong white arms, kiss the corners of her eyes. He had hounded her with his fakery about being ambitious, with his gross, ill-timed and angry declaration of love, just as he had hounded Milly's half-brother, Gerard, with his fake benevolence. Eithne had seen that too and had loathed him for it on the day of the picnic.

She would never speak to him again.

And hadn't he been hounding his mother all year long with insolent demands that she break her stoical silence about her former relations with her husband and the circumstances of his disappearance? He might have had some right if he had been a good son, but he had been, and was, a bad son. For one thing he had never really forgiven Julia Ward Mack her bad luck in mislaying her husband and his father, or for the consequent poverty and monotony of their life together in a series of Depression-haunted rented flats. In face of her natural disposition to be ambitious, energetic, and patriotic to the point of fierceness, he had disclaimed from infancy onwards any interest in specific careers or worldly success; had drifted through school and college 'enjoying Culture' in her terms and lounging against walls in his; as a draftee had requested the uncombative service of the Medical Corps while she, clad in a fatigue suit of coarse blue dungaree, had drilled and dug fortifications on Boston Common as a private soldier in General Eleanora Sears's Massachusetts Women's Volunteer Corps for the duration of the emergency.

The last straw had been his return from the Midwest, after the collapse of the textbook salesman's job, and his announcement that he intended to spend several years in the Boston area getting psychiatric treatment in a public clinic. For it was then that she had scratched together a down payment on the lot in the Florida old person's colony with its shabby trailer *in situ*, taken her name off the active substitute list of retired public school teachers, and gone south—but only after stating that she refused to stay in the same area as an only son who professed madness as a fashionable pose and mask for constitutional indolence.

McCormick was filled with wincing remorse. For having failed everyone. For having merely gotten through time instead of living. He had taken the breathing body of time and butchered it slowly. Taken the carcass of time and rendered it into slime. Time's butcher, time's knacker. And why had he done that?

Never mind. At this late date explanations were merely

excuses. Actual faces and places were down in that slime, befouled by it. He had put them there.

He switched off the vacuum cleaner and the silence of the South Stack came beating back. The air was full of its spray.

18 ◦

'Take it.'
  'No.'
  'Take it!'
  'No!'
  'Take it!!'
  'No!!'
It was ridiculous. There was a limey joke, involving a
lecherous and sadistic vicar, a terrified young girl and
a whip, that went like that. 'Please Prentiss,' he hissed.
'Take the cheque and let me get ready.'
  'I won't cash it.'
  'Take it anyway.'
Prentiss Beal picked up the cheque from the table and
put it in his pants pocket. He said anxiously, 'You've
got a gaunt look around the eyes, Myles. For God's sake,
don't bolt. You don't realize it but you've been under
strain. Ever since Millicent got sick.'
McCormick pushed past the landlord and went into
the bedroom. He found some sun glasses in the upper
drawer of the dresser and put them on. When he returned
to the living-room the landlord had taken the cheque out
again and was prodding it from place to place on the
saw-horse table with a skinny forefinger.
  'I don't *want* two months' rent in advance. I hate it
when old tenants decide to disappear. It's uncivilized.'

'I'm not bolting or disappearing, can't you realize? Off and on I've been wanting to take this trip for years. Now put the cheque back in your pocket.'

The telephone was ringing. McCormick went to answer it.

'Is this Myles McCormick?'

'Yes. Is it Miss Colley—Roberta? I suppose you know all about the fiasco. I should have called you though.'

'I do want to hear from you what happened.'

He described to her briefly the progress of the interview in the Director's office on Monday.

'Disgusting,' Roberta said. 'And using that man Rankin to do his dirty work for him makes it doubly disgusting.'

'But predictable? I mean, me being me. Be honest, Roberta. It was a pretty weird idea all along, wasn't it?'

'You mean, they being they. It was never a ridiculous idea. Only you should remember that you never had better than an outside chance. You simply can't let it bother you too much.'

'I have nobody but myself to blame. Nobody.'

The Chief of Cat. & Class. sighed. 'That's the trouble with living alone. Really, at times like this one ought to be married.'

'Let's you and me get married. For you I'd even go through with a church ceremony. No high nuptial mass though. A scoffer has to draw the line somewhere.'

'Not me. I'm not the marrying kind.'

How characteristic of her not to simper, or prose about age differences, or bridle at the very idea of a bridal. He said feelingly, 'I've never dared to tell you how nice you are, Roberta Colley. Now that I'm going away I can risk it.'

'Never mind that. I guessed you might want to get away and that's really why I called. Where are you going?'

'I'm flying to Ireland later today.'

'That's all right then. A trip will do you good. I was

220

afraid you'd try to join the navy or the Foreign Legion. You never know—at least I never know—what men are apt to do.'

'There isn't any more Foreign Legion. I think it died off like the G.A.R.'

'Well, thank heavens it did. Now listen. When you come back I want you to resume working full time in my department. You may think you dished yourself at the B.F.L. by blowing up at your interview with that repulsive conniver Wynston Rankin, but you haven't. Pinkham knows I know he sold you down the river, and he's far too concerned over the department chiefs' resistance to his asinine reorganization plan to risk a blow-up with me over you. I'll ask Personnel to fix you up with an unpaid leave of absence, and you can come back when the spirit moves you or when your money's all gone.'

He felt close to tears. 'Roberta, you're just being charitable. You don't want me. I'm not a good cataloguer. A good cataloguer would have finished with the Gorukhov liturgical music collection weeks ago.'

'Stop denigrating yourself. You may not be a great cataloguer, like Alice Dwyer, but you're as good a cataloguer as I'm apt to get my hooks into nowadays, what with the rest of my gang getting older and crazier every day and with Mr Coakley gone back to the monastery. So try and have a nice time and don't brood too much. I've been to Ireland and you have to admit it's a perfect country for brooding in—all that damp weather and all that soft wet green ground.'

'I may not come back at all.' He hated himself for trying to wring further compassion from her.

'Then that will be that. But come back.'

'I'm grateful, Roberta. I'm truly grateful.'

She rang off. Prentiss Beal immediately said, 'I won't cash your cheque. And what do you mean you may not come back?'

McCormick stuck out his hand. 'Time to say goodbye, Prentiss. My taxi's coming in a few minutes. I stuck Milly's Rambler in dead storage at the Bowdoin Square garage. Her bicycle's in the back. I've got a feeling that the step-mother wants to claim it. If she comes by here tell her the keys are under the front seat covers. All she has to do to get the car out is pay the charges.'

Prentiss had avoided the hand and now was pointing at various pieces of furniture. 'What shall I do with your stuff if you aren't back within two months?'

'Keep what you want, give the rest to the St Vincent de Paul, fumigate, and re-rent.' He forced his hand upon the landlord and indian wrestled him to the door and out. Before leaping downward from the landing Prentiss said hopelessly, 'Without wanting to seem nosey, I wish I knew what you had in mind disappearing off to Ireland like this.'

'Go ahead and seem nosey,' McCormick suggested, slowly closing the door, 'it doesn't bother me at all.'

Alone, the ex-librarian changed quickly into an olive drab wash-and-wear suit laid out on the couch and checked his pockets for money, traveller's cheques, and the passport which he had kept renewed for all the recent years of staying put. What had he in mind then? 'We must hang together or we shall hang separately'— B. Franklin. 'Fine art is the only teacher except torture'— G. B. Shaw. 'The normal alone can overcome the abnormal'—Author Unknown or forgotten.

He had been a great memorizer back in the days when he was too poor to buy books and so often alone that his main access to civilized conversation was through imaginary dialogues with himself. 'Tell me, sir, do you have any considered views on pairing off?' 'On jerking off, did you say?' 'Quite the contrary, on PAIRING OFF.'

'Why yes, as it happens, I do. *Of all the forms offered to us by life it is the one demanding a couple to realize it fully which is the most imperative. Pairing off is the*

222

fate of mankind. And if two beings, thrown together, mutually attracted, resist the necessity, fail in understanding, and voluntarily stop short of the—the embrace, in the noblest meaning of the word, then they are committing a sin against life, the call of which is simple. Perhaps sacred."

He had heaved a sigh over that one, over the stammering Conradian-Major Hoople (umpf kaff) dash, sitting in the British Museum Reading Room on a cold evening, with one elbow resting in *Chance* and the other in *Civilization and its Discontents* ('the conflict between civilization and sexuality is caused by the circumstance that sexual love is a relation between two people, in which a third can only be superfluous or disturbing'). And then had gone home across the wintry Atlantic to search for Miss, Mrs or Mistress Right.

Now if you wanted a good durable phrase, a message winging across the gulf of years and generations from one mislaid individual to another, you couldn't go wrong with 'Address Unknown'. A message, make no mistake, that a man might usefully devote a lifetime to keeping in circulation.

While inspecting the contents of his large, canvas-and-leather Boston bag, he saw himself in a bad light and wished he was a person he did not have to see at all. Self-divorce was impossible but maybe some kind of Captain Boycott device could be applied in the appropriate country, Ireland. To become silent, flavourless and opaque to one's self, putting consciousness into Coventry for a while, closing down the foundry of the mind, turning a deaf ear to the clangour and the hammering, carrying into effect an austere, hard-nosed Kohler-of-Kohler sort of self-lockout. Could it be done? No. Because no one enjoyed such absolute self-ownership, could practice successfully such drastic arts of self-management.

He returned to the bedroom, burrowed among old split sheets and torn blankets in the bottom drawer of

223

the dresser, and withdrew the sealed metal canister containing Millicent Rogers' ashes. He shook it next to his ear. No muffled cries, not even a sifting. If she persisted, it was as mere genie-vapour and alchemical fried air. He put the urn at the bottom of his bag, beneath a layer of rolled socks, and left the apartment to await the arrival of the taxicab in front of the house.

At Logan Airport, as the taxi came opposite the Eastern Airlines sign, a tall gangling man with hair the colour of wet cement, wearing an old-fashioned summer suit of puffy striped seersucker and very large, wrap-around dark glasses, limped into the roadway frantically waving a knotty black walking stick. The driver braked, put his head out the window and said, 'Get out of my way. This passenger's going on to the International Departure Lounge.'

'That's all right, driver. I think I know the man. I'd just as soon walk the rest of the way anyway, and if you let him in here, you'll be sure of a return fare back to town.'

The driver pushed down the meter flag, and McCormick paid him while the man with the cane came to the door, fumbled with the door handle and climbed in. 'Good God! You Myles!' he ejaculated.

'No other. But what happened to you? Were you run over?'

Frank Meat, for it was he, said, 'No accident. Not on your life. Do you remember Parkhurst?'

'Sure. Your trusty coloured aide-de-camp. You brought him the night of Milly's wake. Seems like decades ago.'

'His title was adjutant. Not an aide-de-camp at all, you silly ass!' Meat squealed indignantly. 'He turned on me and beat me up. Look.'

He carefully removed his glasses. McCormick gasped. There were dark, lacerated bruises around both eyes and extending to his temples. Massive swelling had eliminated

224

the optical cavities for the time being, giving him a King Bullfrog or Toad of Toad Hall look. 'Jesus! He really put the boot in, didn't he? You shouldn't let him get away with it.'

Meat slipped the glasses back on with wincing deliberateness. 'He isn't going to get away with it. I've just been seeing to that down in Washington. Some day I'll tell you all about it.'

'Why would he do that? I thought he was your trusted batman, though now I remember, someone that night implied he was dangerous.'

'Too bad you didn't mention it at the time—instead of restricting yourself to insulting my patriotism.' This with bitter sarcasm. 'We think now that Parkhurst is an agent for Black Nationalism. He was counter-infiltrating us.'

'Infiltrating a bunch of Canadian army veterans? It doesn't sound sane.'

'We weren't Canadian army veterans. That was just a front.'

'Indeed.' Conversations with Frank Meat always came to this, McCormick reflected—to idiocy, incoherence and inconsequence. The old rumour in Dublin had it that Frank had been a spy during the Second World War. He pitied whichever side the man had given his service and allegiance to. He climbed heavily from the vehicle. As he prepared to walk away Meat rapped on the door panel with the head of his stick.

'Where are you off to, Myles?'

'The old sod. If I run into any of your former crowd of Ascendancy buffs around the Trinity pubs, shall I fill them in on your patriotic endeavours?'

'Never mind that. What are you doing in Ireland? I thought you had a steady job.'

Several cars, which had accumulated behind the standing taxi, were blowing their horns. McCormick brought his face close to the window and looked sly. 'If you don't

225

blow the whistle on me, I'll tell you why I'm going to Ireland. As it happens Frank, I'm a Muzzy myself. And some of the guys down at headquarters thought I should get over there and do some recruiting among the Black Irish. Hyah! Hyah! Hyah!'

'Facetious swine! You know who you are Myles?'

'No. Who?'

'It's been said that you can get the Irishman out of the bog but not the bog out of the Irishman. That's you.'

On this note the taxi drove off towards an exit road and McCormick, after a moment of irresolution, carried his bag into the Eastern Airlines section of the terminal and started looking for a bar. It was still a full hour before the check-in deadline and he was not anxious to join the happy gadabout international set with their golf equipment and exotic luggage stickers until it became absolutely necessary. Down here, just in case anybody came looking for him—in case the Mayor and the city greeter shot out from town along with a platoon of Ancient & Honorables and the Harvard-Radcliffe chorus under G. Wallace Woodworth singing, 'For He's a Jolly Good Fellow', 'Home on the Range', 'We Were Only Only Fooling', and 'Come Back Paddy Reilly to Ballyjamesduff' —they wouldn't be able to find him.

The cocktail lounge was behind the snack bar and was dim and empty except for the bartender and a massive balding man in shirt sleeves drinking beer down at one end of the counter. His buttocks overflowed the stool. McCormick ordered a daiquiri and studied himself darkly in the blue-tinted bar mirror. The square jaws were going mushy, the 'whimsical' blue eyes were doubtless becoming rheumy behind their protective shades, and the prematurely grey hair really had lost its claim to prematurity now that he would never see thirty-five again. What about the big outstanding, confidence-inspiring ears? They stood out all right. Staunchly.

226

Handles for an amphora or jug. Close by, a jet plane coming in reversed power explosively, then whined its way beyond earshot. The ex-librarian nuzzled the dregs of his drink and considered whether he wanted to depart from his native scene drunk.

His shoulder was gripped and a friendly voice said, 'Have another.' He swung around, pushing his glasses up into his hair. It was Louis Doxiades, Angelina's uncle, looking natty in a lustrous suit of gunmetal Italian silk, black straw hat and ice-cream shoes. A foulard neck scarf took up much of the space between his rich, clean-toothed smile and his white shimmery shirt front.

The bartender hovered near. 'Uncle Lou, the student of society,' McCormick said. 'What brings you here?'

'Drink up, Myles, and have another.'

'All right. A daiquiri.' Lou ordered beer for himself. The bartender served them and went away to cut up fruit.

Lou raised his beaded glass. 'What are we drinking to? Good fortune about to come winging in? A few days on the town in New York with a tall beautiful brunette?'

'Fantasy again,' McCormick said bleakly. 'I threw up my job and I'm hotfooting it to Ireland on the late afternoon Aer Lingus flight. Me and all the other failed immigrants. What about you?'

'Athens. Except I don't have a booking so I'm standing by all over. What about the Irish plane? Heavily booked?'

'I doubt it unless there's a diocesan pilgrimage going and they usually get charter deals. Come on my flight. Irish planes never crash—they're kept aloft by the power of prayer. We could try the reservations desk after we finish this drink. But it's a roundabout way of getting to Athens for a man in a hurry.'

'I'm in a hurry and not in a hurry. You *were* going alone, weren't you?' Lou added rather pointedly.

'Quite quite alone.' McCormick gazed straight ahead

227

into the bar mirror. The bulky man at the end of the counter was watching them.

Lou Doxiades moved a little closer. He smiled brilliantly but he spoke with urgency. 'Myles, don't look at the big shitbum who's watching us in the mirror, just shake your head if you noticed him. . . Good. Now nod and look amused if you think I'm a trustworthy person.' Feeling the hairs on the back of his neck erect themselves McCormick managed a sick smile, pushed down his dark glasses to cover his eyes, and nodded.

'So far so good. Now I'll explain. That individual over there thinks he has business with me—nasty business. With a little help I can settle his business in about seven action-packed minutes. But you have to trust me. Me. Angelina's Uncle Louis Doxiades.'

'Of course I trust you. He looks awfully big and tough though. Why don't I slip out and get a cop?'

Lou broke into loud chortles, wiped his eyes, took a sip from his beer, smacked the bar with his hand, and said tensely, 'This isn't cop business. Now heads together while you show me something out of your billfold.'

McCormick picked through his wallet with fingers suddenly grown larger than bananas and as boneless. He found a snapshot of Julia Mack and Milly sitting together on the scorching sands of Crane's Beach. 'Millicent —the girl whose wake you came to—and my mother,' he said softly.

'A nice composition but a little too much front light— so here it is. Next to the telephones across from the snack bar there's a Men's Room with an out-of-service sign on the door. It opens. Go down the line of crappers to the fifth booth, where the coin lock's been taken off so the door swings free, in and out. In a couple of minutes I'll arrive with the big man. We'll walk down in front of the booth. You'll be hidden in there, sitting down with your feet up out of sight. When you hear me say, "Be reasonable, Leo," I want you to shove that door with
228

your feet just as hard as you can. I'll manage everything else. Got it?'

'Fifth booth, feet up. . . . But what if somebody sees me going in? What if that monster pulls a gun—or a knife?'

'Relax. Nobody ever sees anything and nobody's going to get hurt. Trust my judgement in these matters. This could even be fun. Now double up as if I was fracturing you with my jokes and then a fast casual farewell.'

After walking resolutely into the Men's Room and down to the fifth booth, McCormick had moments of severe panic when he saw that his Boston bag would be visible on the floor to anyone entering the area in a suspicious and watchful mood. It was a little too large to rest securely on the top of the water chamber, but when he lowered the seat and sat down, bracing his feet on the left and right door posts, he was able to hold the bag in place with the back of his head. The position was not uncomfortable for the time being. However, if there *were* any shooting, it was a rotten, compromising position and place to die in. Supposing torpedo Leo left him and Lou tumbled about in booth # 5, with blood and brains spilled all over? The *Midtown Journal* headline writer would have a field day: GANGLAND FLUSH TWO QUEER BIRDS IN AIRPORT JAKES. And so, leeringly, forth. Had his life pointed towards this obscene juncture all along? It was too ridiculous. He thought of Marat in his bath, then forced himself to read slowly through the plaintive messages and anatomical diagrams covering the walls of the booth. On the door someone had pasted a printed legend: A MAN NEVER STANDS SO TALL AS WHEN HE STOOPS TO   A BOY. The third to last word had been written over with so many improper suggestions that only a greasy grey smudge remained. Wasn't that the Big Brother motto? So ends a big brother, stooping into a hail of bullets. Was it 'help'? HELP!

There were voices, Lou's and a high-pitched raspy one.

229

Lou was saying soothingly, 'By your leave, Leo, just a word.'

The other one said, 'Don't play with me, Louis, don't clown. Albert says he's sick of you clowning around. He says bring him.'

'I like the tie. White on white. Tasteful. But the big Windsor knots are out since ten years ago, Leo.'

'Get away from that door before I break you in two, you fucker you, Louis Doxiades!' There was a cruel hysterical edge in the eunuchoid voice. McCormick's braced legs began to tremble violently. He heard footsteps approaching. He closed his eyes, clasped his hands behind his head and drew his knees up to his chest. On the other side of the door the big man was saying, 'O.K. the word. Let's have it.'

'Let me collect my thoughts,' Lou said. 'Oh yes. You shouldn't do this foul work for Albie, Leo. Albie is a foul person, a soggy, half-smoked cheap cigar. He's a man made out of sick turds, a grease ball.'

There was the sound of a blow. McCormick stopped breathing.

'Be reasonable, Leo.'

He kicked out with both feet, felt the door strike hard against something massive yet yielding, then grabbed his valise and came out swinging it like a sandbag. Louis Doxiades had Albert's man, Leo, facing into the wall opposite with his right arm twisted up behind his back. Leo was having trouble with his breathing. Whenever he reached back with his free hand Lou used both hands to put a tighter twist in the arm he held captive. Lou's mouth was bloody at the corner.

'He hurt you! Let's kill the bugger,' McCormick howled, rushing to and fro and waving his Boston bag in the air. Actually he would be satisfied to set him up again against the door of the booth and take several more pile driver kicks at him. And *that*, Pillsbury Pinkham! And *that* all enemies and thwarters!

230

Suddenly he ran out of adrenalin and felt abashed and frightened. How could two medium-sized men prevent this man mountain from turning on them and launching a few kicks of his own just as soon as he got his breath back?

'Shh Myles, and cool down,' warned Lou. 'We don't have much time.' Using leverage on the arm, he swung his gasping prisoner round and shoved him into # 5. The big man went thumping down in a sitting position, his legs extended towards the back of the booth, his face hanging over the front edge of the toilet seat.

McCormick crowded forward, anxious to help. Grey-faced, Leo looked over his shoulder and whined, 'For Christ's sake, Louis, keep that nut in the sun glasses off of me.'

'I'm doing that, Leo, but no false moves,' Lou said sternly. 'He tends to go off like a firecracker.' In a moment Angelina's uncle rushed out carrying an enormous trouser belt, flung himself under the door of the next booth, squirmed beneath the side partition, and used the belt to tie Leo's ankles together in such a position that he would have to uproot the base of the toilet bowl in order to begin freeing his legs.

Leo was sitting as fatly and tamely as a ewe undergoing shearing. 'You know I wasn't really gonna hurt you, Louis,' he said almost petulantly.

Lou carefully brushed the knees of his finely creased Italian silk trousers, re-entered # 5 and swiftly removed Leo's wide white tie. 'That's right, you wouldn't hurt a fly—No Myles! Get back! This isn't a garrotting situation!' he cried with a quick backward leer, then tied Leo's wrists together, raised the seat, and passed a loop through the centre of the seat ring before making the final tight knots. After that he straightened up and stepped back to look attentively at his handiwork. Leo sat plumb up against the toilet in the position of a very drunk or very tired man waiting to vomit.

'That's all we have in mind for you this time, little Leo,' Lou said briskly. 'Consider yourself lucky.'

'My feet hurt. Can't you loosen the belt, Louis?'

'Of course not. Now I wonder what made him so brave?' He crouched and put his hands in Leo's side trouser pockets, drawing out a chunk of metal which he flung into the toilet bowl with an exclamation of disgust. 'Brass knuckles! Wait'll Calliope hears about this. She'll knuckle you, you dumb Greek!'

'Oh shit, Lou. You wouldn't tell Cally.'

'Who's Calliope?'

'His unlucky wife—sort of a third cousin of mine once removed. I used to be married to her myself.' Lou bent down behind his remote relation by marriage and mismarriage and said coldly, 'My friend from Chicago and I are going now. You sit tight for a while, Leo, and maybe I won't say anything to Cally. One word of advice: keep away from Korones' place the next few days—until my friend from Chicago carries out his mission and leaves town. Meanwhile, watch your local papers for some startling developments.'

'You're clowning again, Louis. Always the clown,' Leo said sulkily.

'Don't bet on it.' He straightened up, closed the booth door and said snappily as he made for the exit, 'Let's go, killer.'

Once outside they made a run for the International Departure Section. The girl at the Irish Airlines desk reported available space on the afternoon flight. While Lou got his bags from a locker and bought his ticket, McCormick stood around grinding his teeth and listening for the wail of police sirens. A little later, as the big plane went trundling out to the flying runway, and girls in green were distributing pieces of hard candy, and a sweet voice over the intercom explained that the plane was named St Laurence O'Toole and would arrive at Dublin around five A.M. after a brief stop at Shannon,

232

McCormick turned from the window and said, 'Maybe we're going to make it after all. No cops in sight and no hoods.'

Lou popped a soft-centre cherry drop into his slightly swollen mouth and put the wrapper in the armrest ashtray. 'Sure we're going to get off. Now ask me some questions and I'll tell you no lies.'

'Was that big creep Leo really going to beat you up with a knuckle duster?'

'Never. He was after a fifty buck shakedown. But it's a bad precedent handing money to a clown like that. So thanks a lot, Myles, I'll pay you back.'

'Who's this greaseball Albert? What's that all about?'

'It's simple. You might call it a jurisdictional labour dispute with petty gangster overtones. I run a small dignified operation bringing in waiters from Athens to work around town. I do the leg work rounding them up and fixing them up with visas. They sign into my union local when they get here, and they're all experienced men so there's no sweat and no sweating. Albert Korones has set up what we call a paper local and he wants to steal my waiters. First he tried to buy me into his racket and now he's trying to muscle me out of my legitimate work. But he's a born loser.'

'It sounds pretty Greek to me.'

'In this town waiters' work tends to be a Greek thing.'

'So at last I know what you do. What do you do when you're not working?'

Louis Doxiades closed his eyes and sank back into the tweed upholstery. The plane began its hurtling run for take-off. McCormick plucked at his seat belt fastening. Lou said, 'I kid around. I dig things.' He sat forward and opened his eyes. 'What do you say when we get to Dublin we rent a car and take a little tour? You could show me some castles. That is, unless you're tied up.'

There was a slight bump as the wheels left the ground. 'I don't have any immediate plans. I'll be glad to show

you around, if we make it across the Atlantic,'
McCormick said uneasily. 'With your interests you'll
probably never get to Greece.'

'Greece can wait. What about manor houses?'

'Galore.'

'Pedigrees and peerages?'

'There's a coat of arms on every cottage door.'

'My Lord Bishops?'

'About every tenth male is a bishop. They come in
two varieties, with gaiters and without.'

Louis Doxiades looked pleased. 'When you live in a
big fast country like America,' he said, 'it's great to
have a small slow country like Greece or Ireland in re-
serve. But tell me, Myles, whatever went wrong between
you and that queen, Mrs Gallagher? I don't want to be
nosey but Angie and I really had you and her figured
for a honeymoon trip by now.'

'I'm sorry,' McCormick muttered. 'Suddenly I'm exhausted. I think I'm going to have to go to sleep now.'

'Sure. Get some rest,' Lou said solicitously. 'I'll call
you when they start passing out the steaks and the Irish
coffee.'

19 ∽

The tinker made a secret sign from the head of the lane. The deserted street ran slightly uphill, they were not observed. He crossed over to him quickly. Thick tufts of reddish hair sprouted from his cheekbones, his brown homespun suit was filthy, and his broken shoes were tied around with strips of rag.

'I found him.'

'Show me,' he said gruffly.

'Come on then.'

They went along the lane, between dilapidated cottages, some roofless and abandoned, some with moss growing on the thin, mouldering thatch, and out of the village on an empty dirt track that led over rolling bogland. The itinerants could not be trusted, they were inveterate prevaricators, he must check him every inch of the way.

They were passing between walls made of piled white stones. Light shining above the low distant horizon through the chinks between the bleached stones gave the walls the appearance of fine lace. Ahead lay a crossroads with a grassy verge. The caravan was parked there with its shafts supported on a boulder. A Connemara pony and an ass grazed to one side; two small children sat under the caravan wrapped up in plaid rugs and watched with glittering eyes; there was a crackling wood fire.

The tinker's wife knelt on the ground before the fire washing her hair in a pot. She had taken off her blouse and the straps of her petticoat had slipped down from her plump white shoulders. Her heavy, water-darkened hair made an arc into the water and she did not look up.

'There'll be the key,' he said, pointing at his wife. The key was down under her petticoat at the end of a string tied around her neck.

'Get it from her,' he said impatiently.

'She won't give it me. You must get it yourself,' the tinker said.

He put his hand down between her warm dangling breasts and drew out the key string. She sat back on her heels and turned her face up to make it easier for him to lift the string over her head. Her face was a weathered red and covered with freckles. It was raining.

'Over there,' the tinker said. He pointed up the right arm of the crossroads towards a high hemispherical mound covered with glistening white quartz pebbles.

'Why it looks exactly like the tumulus at New Grange!'

'Is that what you call it?' the tinker said mockingly. 'We call it "the witch's tit".'

They mounted the massive retaining wall that ringed the mound and passed beyond the inner ring of pillar stones. He unlocked and opened the iron gate and reached in and flipped the light switch. 'You wait out here,' he commanded. He did not trust the tinker to squeeze through the long unlighted tunnel and enter the chambered cairn with him.

When he crawled through into the great underground chamber he found that the electricity was not working. He cursed the tinker for his treachery. But enough daylight filtered down through the round hole in the high, funnel-shaped roof to render dimly visible the three recessed sacrificial cells with their basin-shaped floors.

A man lay face down in one of the cells. He ran to

236

him and knelt, anxiously plucking at his coat sleeve. 'Daddy, Daddy, wake up!' he shouted. 'I got here at last.' But there was blood on his hand, the body was sodden with blood, there was blood everywhere.

He turned the body over on its back. The sacrificial victim had been ripped open with a savage stone axe from the base of the throat to the groin. He began to sob violently. 'No no no. They weren't supposed to do that. Not until June 21st when the sun would come through the ceiling hole at exactly the right angle. They should have waited.'

He gazed at the blood-bedabbled face with a wild desolating tenderness. He had seen that unconvinced expression somewhere before. Suddenly the eyes flew open, fixing him with a cool professional gaze. 'Tell me, Mr McCormick,' Dr Sidney Beispiel queried, 'why it is that you always expect other people to wait until you've completed your arrangements?'

McCormick woke up halfway out of bed next to an open window through which the light came and went. A blackbird on a nearby bough was observing him through its bright yellow eye ring. When he moved, it retracted its bright yellow legs and flew away.

'Jesus!' he muttered, shoving himself back onto the bed, 'Jesus!' After a considerable interval, during which he opened and closed his eyes several times over, he said, 'Get out of my dreams, Sidney.'

Where then? The other bed in the room was empty and had been slept in, and somewhere in the building Ray Charles was singing 'I can't stop loving you' over the radio. The wireless. The wallpaper was of a flocked fabric dyed a deep burgundy. That fixed it. He had woken in Concannon's Guest House (Class C), in the town of Innishannon, on the Bandon River, in Co. Cork, and New-grange Tumulus, thank God, was over a hundred miles away in County Meath. What could have set off so appalling a dream? Maybe the glimpse of that shaggy graveyard in the village yesterday at dusk, as they walked up after arranging to get the slow leak fixed.

He sat up, putting his legs over the side of the bed. His brains were musty-fusty, his teeth scummed, the stomach queer, the tongue dry. All that brandy after dinner. They had sat up very late in the tiny bar down-stairs, drinking large ones and slipping complimentary Tia Marias to the barmaid, Miss O'Brien, in honour of Lou's departure today for London and Athens. Lou had slipped her a few feels as well and she hadn't seemed to mind at all, until Concannon himself came in and started putting out the lights. Then McCormick had called Concannon a 'gombeen man'. After that relations were strained, and they had all gone to bed, but not before he had made the landlord a sincere apology.

Louis Doxiades was alone in the dining-room, lingering over the remains of a big breakfast, eating brown bread, drinking coffee and reading *The Cork Echo*. He looked fresh. He was wearing his heavy-knit Aran sweater and his wellington boots.

'Top of the morning, Myles. I'll ring for young Patrick.' A boy in a white jacket and corduroy pants came in from the kitchen. McCormick ordered a large pot of coffee and some brown bread and butter. 'Why the boots, Lou? You're not by any chance planning to shovel some manure this morning?'

He looked affectionately at his black rubber knee boots. 'It's my last chance to wear them before shoving off. In Greece wellingtons are not worn.'

'What day is it anyway?'

He looked into his newspaper. 'June Sixth. Do you know a local poet named Callinan? They've got some-thing he wrote on the editorial page. Very patriotic. I'll read you—'

'No, please don't. I've got a head. What about Concannon?'

'He's been around. No hard feelings. He said the gentleman had drink taken.'

'He did not lie.' Actually, he was feeling much better. The weak coffee dissolved the oral crud and the brown bread had already smothered all but the most nimble death's-head moths in his stomach. 'June Sixth. That makes eight days. What a slave driver you are! You must have booted us through every village in the Republic except Knockcrockery and Hackballs Cross.'

'We never did get to North Donegal,' Lou said thoughtfully.

'All those castles. All those high crosses. The plinths and the megaliths and the ring forts. You should be a tour guide. I'd hate to tangle with you in Greece.'

'I dig the antique. In Greece though, I never get a chance to look around. I'm usually too busy signing up waiters and chasing tail.'

From the standpoint of tail the trip had been chaste enough, although Lou had managed a few tender conversational passages with country postmistresses when they had stopped to let him send off one of his mysterious business telegrams. 'What I can't understand is why we should end up here in Innishannon after all your expertise with the guide books. No antiquities, no castles. It's not even listed.'

'How could I know Concannon's taste in wallpaper when I made the reservation back in Dublin? When you travel you need a definite place you're going to get to by a certain date. In case anybody's trying to reach you.'

'I haven't noticed any accumulated mail,' he said rather peevishly.

'But you never know, do you?'

'That's true. So when do you take off for Dublin?'

'What about you?'

'I thought I'd hang around the district for a few days more. After all this is my ancestral county.' He

239

added, wincing slightly, 'on the paternal side, that is.'

'I remember you told me. I figure I should get to see you kiss the sacred soil before I go.'

'When I woke up this morning I thought I'd been eating it.'

Lou maintained he was in no great hurry to leave so they agreed to take a walk along the river bank and into the village before he collected the Renault from the British Petroleum service station and checked out. But first McCormick went upstairs and brought down the little green airline bag in which they had carried bottles of beer and lumps of heavy soda bread for refreshment between meals throughout the trip.

They stood on a ramshackle wooden boat dock in front of the inn and watched the river turn light and dark under the changing sky as it ran straight towards the village, swerved left around a handsome, salmon-coloured Georgian house and passed out of sight. For a town without antiquities it did all right in the ruin line, McCormick reflected, counting three abandoned nineteenth-century churches and a fire-scarred roofless manor house lining a high ridge to the north of the Cork-Bantry highway.

'Hey Myles, look at the fish. There must be a million of them in there.'

All at once the river was full of large brown fish with pale bellies, slipping over and under each other, milling about, moving in no consistent direction, breaking the surface with their fins and tails in a thousand different places.

'What do you suppose they're doing?' he asked vacantly.

'They're just horsing around,' Lou said and began to laugh. He jumped off the dock onto the bank, found some pebbles and began flipping them into the water. 'What a country! Where I come from if you find a fish in a river it's a national event. As a matter of fact there are no rivers where I come from.'

He waded a little way out in his wellington boots and put his hands down in the water, screaming with laughter. 'I can feel them,' he shouted. 'Come on fishes, come to Papa, you mothers!'

'Well at least the rivers aren't depopulated,' McCormick said. He jumped onto the bank. Lou had his face practically in the water. 'Come on, Doxiades,' he said severely. 'Let's go before they bite your nose and fingers off.'

In the village they stopped at a pub in the main street and drank a bottle apiece of Phoenix beer. Lou wanted to linger for a while and play a game where two or more contestants flipped rubber rings onto numbered hooks on a board screwed into the wall, but McCormick insisted they visit the graveyard.

'Where is it?' Lou asked doubtfully. 'I don't feature cemeteries much. Antiquities yes, bones no.'

'If we cross the road and go down one of those lanes leading towards the river we'll find it,' McCormick said. 'It's got a big beat-up belfry tower sticking up in it. I saw the main gate from up the block when we came away from the service station yesterday.'

But the iron gate was locked and there were no other openings in the high wall surrounding the graveyard on three sides. It stood apart from the nearest houses in its own lane in a level river meadow where the grass grew knee deep.

'A great place for a murder,' Lou remarked. 'I guess we're licked, huh? Unless we try an amphibious assault from the river side.'

'I want to get over that wall,' McCormick said urgently. 'Hoist me up.'

'What's your hurry? When you're dead it's for a long time.'

He put his shoulder to the rough stone wall and

McCormick climbed on him and then onto the top. He reached down and Lou passed up the little green bag. Next, using all his strength, he began to draw Lou up. 'You're dead weight,' he said, breathing heavily. 'Find a toehold for leverage and I'll jerk you up.'

The toehold for leverage and the sudden jerk coincided. Lou came swarming over the wall in a rush and they both went crashing down into the graveyard together. He fell on bedded dry weeds and rattled down a little bank under broad dank green leaves. He stood up and found himself in a wilderness of burdocks and overgrown grass. Some of the burdock plants were six feet high, and the spaces between the thick fleshy stalks were crammed with dead weeds.

'Louis! Where are you? Are you hurt?' Lou looked out from among the leaves of some extraordinarily well grown burdocks. 'This isn't a cemetery, it's a tropical forest. Man-eating plants.'

McCormick parted the leaves in various directions. 'I guess the Irish aren't too big on Perpetual Care.'

'But man do they make free with the fertilizers!' He fought clear of an entanglement of shrubbery and came forward rubbing his elbow. 'Kidding aside though, how long do we have to hang in here? I almost fell in a tomb. Some joker left the lid off.'

All around them, sheltering among the giant weeds, lay large stone tombs, some lidless, others with lids that had cracked, fallen in, or slipped partially open when the bases tilted down into the dank soft earth. 'It looks like some giant Irish ghouls came in here with a bun on and threw their weight around,' Lou said shakily.

'It does indeed. Maybe they were riding giant Irish elks like the one we saw in the Trinity museum. Let's go take a look at that tower, anyway.'

Leading the way, McCormick pushed through the burdock plantation, narrowly avoiding some yawning holes in the earth which were only partially filled with a debris of fragmented stone and weed, until he struck into a vague path. Here the growing burdocks were fewer and were interspersed with thistles, the graves smaller and, to judge from the fact that a few inscriptions on the weathered stones were still visible, not so old. But there was the same general air of devastation, with grave markers fallen on their faces, stone crosses tilted and skewed, and innumerable generations of grey and brown dead weed still rooted in the earth around and on the mounds.

The ground rose slightly as they approached the tower. It was clutched by a great spread of ivy that grew from a single massive stalk whose gnarled roots entered the ground beside an arch let into the base. As they came close, the path widened and cleared and the monuments on either side had legible inscriptions.

'There must have been a church here once,' McCormick said. 'We're walking where the centre aisle used to be— right through the congregation, only they're all dead. The belfry must have been directly behind the sanctuary.'

'You don't say. And what about those moaning sounds? Would that be Dracula waking up and smelling fresh blood?'

'Forget it. He's tucked up in bed in Transylvania. He could never make a score in this country. Too many crosses and too much holy water. What you're hearing is doves up in the tower.'

They came in under the arch. The ground was partly covered by a floor of old dark bricks and the way up to the bell loft had been cemented in. There were some discoloured marble commemorative tablets fastened to one of the walls.

'So here's your tower, so what?' Lou said. 'It's not even prehistoric. What do you want to do now?'

'Hang around for a bit.'

'Not me. I think I'll go see about the car.'

'Go ahead. You can get over the wall by yourself where it's banked up.'

Before going Lou looked at one of the tablets. '1768-1830. REVEREND T. R. O'HANLON, M.A. T.C.D. KNOWN AS THE O'HANLON,' he read. 'Now there's an ancestor for you to commune with.'

'These aren't my ancestors. This is a Protestant cemetery.'

Lou began to retrace the way they had come. 'Why don't you come now?' he suggested, looking back. 'We can hoist a few in the pub and flip those rubber rings.'

'I'll meet you there in half an hour.'

'O.K. But if you hear me scream in the next couple of minutes you'll know one of those Things in the big tombs over by the wall reached out and got me.'

'Remember,' McCormick said, 'if it's wearing gaiters it's a Church of Ireland bishop.'

'Sure, I know. The Ascendancy. All right, boys, whatever you do, don't ascend on me now.'

20 ❀

He went back under the arch and through it to the other side of the tower. Here he found two large tombs standing side by side. They were of recent brickwork crudely mortared and lacked inscriptions of any sort. Just beyond them the giant burdock plantation thrust up again, perhaps continuing on this side all the way to the river bank. Was the cemetery still used then? Did it still accommodate the occasional C. of I. dogsbody—new decay put down in the middle of old decay, under this spectacular dilapidation and burgeoning of weed? Apparently. And why not? Certainly you couldn't fault the Irish, Catholic and Protestant alike, for what they knew about the first and worst of the four last things—croaking. The whole island, serene and shabby, beautiful and devastated, fertile and semi-deserted, was one big moist necropolis. They were still digging skeletons from the time of the Famine out of ditches, bogs and gravel pits, some arranged in family groups from grandfather to baby, the less resigned with bits of grass sticking out of their jaws. The ancient abandoned potato drills on remote mountainsides looked like mass graves, and a hitch-hiker they'd picked up near Corafin, in Clare, had pointed out five towns which had utterly vanished from the surface of the earth after 1850, although he claimed you could still see the pattern of the streets and surrounding farm fields from a low-flying aeroplane.

So why had he come to Ireland? Merely to luxuriate in decay? No. He had come because he had some burial work to get done, and when you wanted something done properly you went where the people really knew the business.

The sun gleamed whitely through rips and slits in the blue-black, constantly metamorphosing cover of low-lying clouds, from which occasional spurts of rain came down. Rooks in the tall trees out in the lane were conducting a sleepy, whining sort of conversation. They sounded as if they were counting their grievances but didn't expect things to change much. There was a large hole going down in the earth at the base of one of the brick tombs, made by some sort of large burrowing animal whose intentions would not bear looking into.

Drop the whole last decade down there. Shove in the ageing, tiresome tone-deaf person with his project for playing life by ear that had turned more than ten green years of early adulthood into a rerun of the Great Hunger mixed-metaphorically speaking. Bury his projects along with his metaphors: the one with Dr Beispiel called How to Stand Still by Playing the Zany; the one with Eithne called How to Insult a Widowed Professional Woman; the one with Millicent called Terminal Carelessness; the one at the library called Fraudulent Career Gains, (Personnel I.B.M. card code acronym FREEG); the one with Gerard called Big Stoop Strikes Out; the one with Joseph McCormick called Digging for Pops in the Gravel Pit of the Past, or, Taking a Tumble in the Tumulus of Time.

He had put enough rubbish down there to suffocate King Rat or whatever it was that had done the tunnelling. And now to complete the business.

He went back through the arch and along the main path, and in among the giant weeds and up the bank to the wall. He stood on tiptoe, reaching to the top of the wall, and took down the green airline bag. Unzipping it, he removed the canister containing Millicent's ashes. He
246

found an old marble tomb with a slipped lid a few feet back in the burdocks and tried to take exact note of its position relative to the wall and some tombs near it. Then he knelt, thrust the canister under the lid as far as his arm would reach, and let it drop. For a sickening moment he believed that there was something in there which would tear open his hand and forearm to the bone with poisoned teeth, but his trembling and revolted flesh emerged unscathed. He stood up and thought, 'Goodbye, Milly dear. I've put you here, even though you really aren't anywhere. Someday I'll come back and get you. That'll be our own private judgement day—just between you and me and the lamp post.'

Suddenly he was swamped by a feeling of wild, desolating tenderness for her, and he wished that he had held onto her, gotten in bed with her to warm her, somehow gotten through to her on that evening in New England General Hospital as her life lapsed, been with her then like a husband, or at least a lover, or even a brother. Why hadn't he kissed her, even though she was too far gone to know he was there? If only he had kissed her. If only.

There was a watchful stillness in the graveyard. He turned around to face the wall. Eithne Gallagher was sitting on it. She wore a black Aran sweater and a green tweed skirt. With many a ray serene. My tum tum tuve. My own true love. My dark Rosaleen. He knuckled at his eyes. She was a vision. He was going to be with her in the vision and leave the world. He put his hands up and she reached down, pulling him up. 'You creep,' she wailed. 'Come up out of there.'

They were together on top of the wall. He put his face in her hair and kissed her wet cheeks and felt her heart heaving under his hand. Then she shoved herself away and dried her eyes quickly on her sleeve. 'Don't take anything for granted. It was just the shock. Jet fatigue. And getting here. And then seeing you kneeling there by that tomb. You looked as if you were in process of burying yourself.'

'Eithne! I thought you'd never speak to me again!' He shook himself out of his daze. 'How did you get here?'

'Your friend Lou kept at me with telegrams. "Come dance with us in Ireland. Myles is your man. He loves you. Innishannon by the fifth. Concannon's. Louis Doxiades, P.P." What's P.P.?'

'It means parish priest. One of his little jokes.'

'So anyway I got to Dublin and rented a car and started down here, but a man in a filling station gave me wrong directions so I ended up yesterday way west, by an island called Innishboffin. When I saw my mistake I had to drive all night to get here. I thought you were gone and then I saw Lou going into a bar-room with a girl up in the main street. He seems to have gone native.'

'He's my favourite native of the human race,' McCormick said with conviction.

He moved closer to her and circled her waist with his arm. She let the arm stay. 'I do love you, Eithne. And you must care something about me. Otherwise you wouldn't have come all the way over here.'

'Don't be so sure. I finished my main report for the Redevelopment Project. Then I had a big fight with my boss. He didn't like me saying that the West End Scheme was lousy unless you happened to be a highway engineer or someone who could afford a fancy apartment with a view of the river. I also said they ought to start next time with a few ideas about people instead of with a battalion of demolition experts. Anyway, I figured I needed a vacation after that. I thought why should those two have all the fun? So I came over.' She closed her eyes and leaned her head on his shoulder. 'I must have dodged a thousand sheep on the road last night. I'm tired.'

Feeling his arms full of warm treasure he kissed her eyelids and then her mouth. After a time he said, 'I really thought you were through with me. Then there was this
248

big blowup at the library. I ran away to Ireland just to get my bearings. It was an accident that Lou came along—a miraculous accident.'

She stretched out on the top of the wall with her head in his lap. Mr and Mrs Humpty McDumpty. The cloud cover had thinned, letting more of the pale sunlight through, and there was no more rain. 'I know all about the library,' she said yawning. 'I went to see the woman you work for in the Catalogue Room.'

'Roberta. What did she tell you?'

'She said you were a mixture of introvert and extrovert, but O.K. And she said you really ought to be married. I expect she was hinting.'

He bent over her. 'Please marry me, Eithne. We belong with each other. We really do. Please.'

She sat up and looked across the graveyard for a long time with her shoulders hunched and her left hand, wearing its broad gold wedding band, curled under her chin. 'Doesn't this remind you of anything?'

He tried to see what she was looking at. 'No. We never did go sit on a cemetery wall before.'

'Remember the first time we met.'

'Sure. It was up in Rare Books, and I was closing up.'

'You were locking the alcoves. I said, "What do you keep in those things? Bodies?"'

'Yes! And I said—'

'Never mind what you said then. What do you say now?'

He looked at her intently. 'I see what you mean. Well, appearances notwithstanding, I'm not just a tomb haunter. From now on I'm going to let the dead bury the dead. Let the decayed bury the decade. Me for the nineteen sixties. Me for you.'

'Today's my birthday, Myles. I'm thirty.'

'Happy birthday, Eithne darling, I mean that.' He took her ring hand in his own right hand. 'Look. We can go anywhere and do anything we want. The next ten years

249

can be our great redevelopment decade. When you come down to it, we've both been trailing around with bodies tied to our necks.'

'So you're not so deadset against Planning any more?' She was faintly smiling.

'I love Planning. After all, the New Deal kept my ma and me from starving through most of the Depression. That good free Graham flour and powdered milk and E.R.A. canned beef stew. Those big blue cheques from the W.P.A. And I love a lady Planner. Just show me a slum and I'll destroy it.'

'You'll what?'

'Just in a manner of speaking. Actually, I'll do it on the Gallagher Plan. We start with some ideas about people. We look at old maps. We get all the people together and find out what they need. We respect the human thing.'

'We're looking at a slum.'

'This graveyard. You're not kidding. Of course there's a lot of powerful growth going on in there too. Take those burdock plants. Wild! I suppose that's Ireland— a slum with growth potential.'

'That's everywhere and everybody. A lot of worn-out things tangled up with a lot of growing things. That's what makes my work interesting—even when it doesn't work out. It makes *life* interesting.'

He kissed her. 'You make my life interesting, Eithne. I PLAN to marry you. What do you say? Don't say, "Let's wait and see whether you've changed." Say yes.'

She kissed him. 'I like you the way you are. Mostly anyway. That's why I got so sore when you pretended you were executive material at the library. I say yes, let's get married and *then* we'll see.'

Behind them someone began making owl noises. Louis Doxiades stood outside the wall. Knee deep in lush meadow grass, he seemed to be gnawing his thumb knuckles. Observed, he stopped hooting and said, 'Oh you

250

Irish. I heard the last part of that. You were talking like a couple of diplomats fixing up a non-aggression pact.'

McCormick pointed down at him. 'Louis Doxiades, the old panderer himself, Uncle Eros,' he said. 'He thinks we should moan at each other through a chink in the wall, like Pyramus and Thisbe.'

McCormick jumped down from the wall and tripped him into the grass. Eithne climbed down. 'Now we'll have a dance,' McCormick said, 'and then we'll go back up the river and let Lou play some more with his fishies.'

'Then we'll find a terrific restaurant and have a four-hour lunch,' Eithne said. 'With lobster and champagne. Because it's my birthday and my engagement day and I haven't had any breakfast.'

'I must go,' Lou said. 'The car's out in the lane. I'm driving a certain Miss O'Brien up to Dublin. It seems she has an appointment to do the town with sombody she met. I'll take a raincheck on the banquet for when we're all back in Boston.'

'I hate to see you go,' McCormick said seriously. 'We haven't settled accounts for what we spent on the trip. It seems to me I owe you some money. And what about the telegrams? You've got a lot of payment coming there.'

Lou shook his head. 'Didn't I say I'd pay you back for helping me fix that big haemorrhoid, Leo, at Logan? We're even now.'

Standing together, they watched him sprint through the meadow and wave back before disappearing around the end of the cemetery wall. 'We'll never be even,' McCormick said. 'Not ever.'

They lay down in the grass. She had nothing on under her thick sweater except a bra which unlatched front and centre. 'Myles,' she murmured after a while, 'I haven't eaten anything for about twenty hours. When you do that it makes me hungry.'

251

He sat up. 'We'll go and eat the big set lunch at Concannon's. Then you'll sign the register as Mrs McCormick and go upstairs and take a nap. Then I'll join you and we'll make love. After that we'll hack around the district for a few days, and then we'll take a slow boat back from Cobh to the U.S. Maybe we can get the Captain to marry us. How's that sound?'

'That sounds all right for a start,' Eithne said.